THE ENI
THE ENDLESS REFRAIN
THE ENDLESS REFRAIN

ALSO BY DAVID ROWELL

The Train of Small Mercies

*Wherever the Sound Takes You: Heroics and
Heartbreak in Music Making*

THE ENDLESS REFRAIN

MEMORY, NOSTALGIA, AND THE THREAT TO NEW MUSIC

DAVID ROWELL

MELVILLE HOUSE BROOKLYN • LONDON

The Endless Refrain
Memory, Nostalgia, and the Threat to New Music

First published in 2024 by Melville House
Copyright © 2024 by David Rowell
All rights reserved
First Melville House Printing: August 2024

An earlier, briefer version of "OK Computer? On the Road With the Dead"
was originally published in *The Washington Post Magazine*.
Lyrics from "Overlord" reprinted with permission from Wendy Dio.

Melville House Publishing
46 John Street
Brooklyn, NY 11201

and

Melville House UK
Suite 2000
16/18 Woodford Road
London E7 0HA

mhpbooks.com
@melvillehouse

ISBN: 978-1-68589-139-8
ISBN: 978-1-68589-140-4 (eBook)

Library of Congress Control Number: 2024940619

Designed by Beste M. Doğan

Printed in the United States of America
10 9 8 7 6 5 4 3 2 1

A catalog record for this book is available from the Library of Congress

For Kim, No. I on the charts

The relationship you have to a song can change over time. You can outgrow it, or it could come back to haunt you, come back stronger in a different way. A song could be like a nephew or a sister, or a mother-in-law.

—BOB DYLAN

CONTENTS

OPENING ACT

THE SONGS REMAIN THE SAME

D o we even *want* new music anymore?

OK, that might be rushing in a little too quickly. I opted for a "Hey Jude" approach, starting with the chorus from the opening note instead of easing in with more intricate fanfare, à la the Who's "Baba O'Riley." But there it is, a naked first sentence with no mystery but plenty of urgency, because, music lovers everywhere, the matter is urgent.

It's hardly the first time I've posed the question. I once spent a week following one of my closest friends, Bob Funck, who had managed to line up a string of performances at cafés and bars in the Northeast despite no one knowing who Bob was. Bob, who like me is from North Carolina, had landed a gig at a place called Andy's Old Port Pub in Portland, Maine— it was his first time in New England—and he was playing all original music. He might have fared better, though, if he had recited nature-inspired haiku, because so few people were listening or giving him any kind of chance. Just to stretch out his set for the three hours he was booked, Bob threw in a cover of Tom Petty's "You Don't Know How It Feels." I happened to be the only one in the establishment jotting notes about the irony of that as a selection—Bob hadn't chosen it for that reason—but as soon as he began, the scant crowd reacted as if Tom Petty himself had stepped through the door. Because here was the rapture: hearing a song that they already knew.

When Bob brought it to a close and went back to his own songs, the small group of men and women there for dinner or drinks went right back to their practiced indifference, seemingly unaware that they'd been sucked into a hole in the space-time continuum for nearly four minutes. In trying to capture that moment there at the bar I wrote for the first time, "Do we even want new music anymore?" Later that night, at the hotel, I dashed off a few paragraphs riffing on that idea, and the next morning I went back to writing about Bob's lonely crusade to play his music for a world that couldn't hear it because, well, they didn't *already* know it.

Ever since, I haven't been able to shake that question. I've asked the question of friends, people I didn't know at all, and also some famous musicians who could have been offended but weren't despite the fact that they recognized their answers might have revealed some uncomfortable truths. I asked it of people who had a role in the music business and of people who made a living writing about music. Sometimes I asked it in my dreams.

I asked it of a woman at the Quail Creek Country Club in Naples, Florida, after watching a Tom Petty/Stevie Nicks tribute act. Janet Seidl had spent most of the evening dancing in a state of admirably unselfconscious joy—sometimes entirely by herself—in front of the stage, and now that the show was over she wanted to know why I had been scribbling in a notebook. I explained that I was writing a book about this central question, but this time, instead of posing the question like I had a million times before, I just said, "What I'm writing about and arguing in this book is that we don't really want to hear new music anymore," to which she quickly said, "Correct. I would fully agree with you on that." And then her friend Jill Nilsen, standing next to her, added, "For a certain age group," and I quickly said yes, she was right about that—I wasn't talking about teenagers or people in their early twenties. But pretty much everyone older than that.

A note on narration: When I interviewed music critic Ben Ratliff to get his thoughts on all this, one of the first things he asked me was, "Well, who is *we*?" I had to laugh at that because when I speak about these matters, I tend to speak as if I was standing in for all of humanity. Ben admitted he could be guilty of that himself in his writing. "I think that by 'we,' I mean a generalized 'I'," he said. That sounded right to me. I was talking about myself, no question, but I'd also convinced myself that the issues went well beyond what *I* thought.

Here's a disclaimer that's as important as Ringo's drumming on "Come Together." I am largely focusing on the hold rock and pop music from the past has on us. I am not including country music because while country has become an increasingly pop product—often the only difference being that the country tunes include two bars of pedal-steel guitar—the country charts aren't the same as rock and pop charts. And if I were to write about country, then how could I leave out Polka, Memphis Blues, Zydeco, Bouncy Techno, Ranchera, Pirate Metal, Noisegrind, Ragga Jungle, Sufi Rock, Dark Cabaret, Anti-folk, Cold Wave (but not Dark Wave; Dark Wave, I owe you nothing and disavow you completely), Psychobilly, Diva House, Nintendocore, Mathcore, Easycore, Sadcore, Happy Hardcore, or any music associated, directly or indirectly, with the Earth's inner core?

This book is the equivalent of a triple album featuring one studio record and two live recordings. Think of the first third as me hunkered in the studio for months, trying to fully conceive of and get down the opus in my head. Some featured musicians make appearances. The compositions are all mine and I'm playing most of the instruments, but these guests come in and lay down their parts beautifully, which makes it all so much better. Then, for the last two parts of the book, I hit the road as I further explore these ideas, for reasons that will be clear when we get there, at a Journey tribute band's sound checks, in their dressing rooms, and in the crowds of their various performances—to capture the manifestation of this obsession with music from our past. From there we go from analog to digital: on the trail of music holograms and the various ways we are not just hanging on to beloved songs, but the dead creators themselves.

Ultimately, this is a book about music and *feeling*. I'm not ruminating on the findings of scientific studies focused on the brain's relationship to new music as we age, so there are exactly as many long passages about neural pathways becoming more fixed over time as there are digressions into the little nesting-bowl helmets Devo wear in their "Whip It" video.

It's also not data-driven, though there is data in these pages. Instead, this is a book about the landscape all around us as I see and hear it, and how a particular era of music has so fully permeated that landscape that it's become a kind of reverse gentrification—the old music isn't going anywhere, and the new music is in search of permanent residence. It's about the music from our past, our present, and future. It's also about the still-mysterious and inspiriting way a person or group of people we've never met and will never know once created something that lasts three to four minutes and, then and forever more, the emotional attachment we formed with it became as important to us as any memory, being, or entity in the world.

SIDE ONE

ALL THINGS MUST PASS . . . BUT WHEN?

HOW OLD MUSIC BECAME NEW AGAIN

Men at Work released their first album in 1981. It was a smash by any commercial standard. There were three hits from the album, with "Who Can It Be Now?" and "Down Under" both reaching the U.S.'s *Billboard* Hot 100 top spot. Wait, what was a vegemite sandwich? No matter. Men at Work were everywhere—dropping by the MTV studios, charming us with their zany Australian antics, their Australian accents, their . . . Australianness. After extensive touring, they released their follow-up album, *Cargo*, two years later. As with so many sophomore efforts, the album felt short of the sales of the first, but it still sold millions. The singles didn't hit quite as big this time, but both "Overkill" and "It's a Mistake," a middling piece of mid-tempo, reggae-inflected pop, cracked the top ten of *Billboard*'s Hot 100 chart.

Staying true to their name, two years later they released their third offering. Can't easily remember the title? Well, as third albums go, it's not quite thought of in the same vein as other famous third albums—Radiohead's *OK Computer* or The Clash's *London Calling*, say. By the time *Two Hearts* came out, there were real problems at work. Three of the band's five members had left the band. The only two original members left set out on tour to promote the album, backed by musicians-for-hire. Before the end of the tour, only the singer, Colin Hay, remained. The next year Men at Work officially broke up, and there was never another studio album.

And yet, all these decades later, to go by the number of times I hear "Down Under" and "Who Can It Be Now?" and "It's a Mistake" when I'm in the drugstore, or the grocery store, or at the rental car office, or at FedEx or Baskin-Robbins or the dentist's office or the athletic store, the bank or a department store or Jiffy Lube or Great Clips or Ace Hardware or the taxidermist, it would be only natural to conclude that Men at Work was the most important band of the twentieth century. What else could explain the omnipresence of those songs?

Had they proven timeless not because they were great, but timeless for reasons that had nothing to do with music?

I'm not at all saying Men at Work was a terrible band. I had their first album, and I liked it. They had a handful of catchy songs, but the point I'm making is, nothing about their career justifies how much we hear them today. They arrived in the '80s, and for reasons explored in these pages, that alone feels like the biggest explanation for their presence today. What we hear these days is not even about the music itself anymore—the Clash's music vs. Men at Work. It's that we're more nostalgic for Men at Work than we are for the Clash, and that's what troubles me. (While they're a much newer band, I'll just point out that we've never been nostalgic for Radiohead, and that distresses me even more.)

In 2024, we've arrived at the point in which the few hits of Men at Work and a remarkably select number of songs within the scope of the history of recorded rock and pop music—a great many of them from the '80s—are playing right now in all forms of commercial dwellings across this once great musical land of ours. On the airwaves they are hawking everything from Geico insurance (Homeowner: "We do have a Ratt problem," which cuts away to Ratt playing in the basement), to

TurboTax (Spandau Ballet's "This Much is True") to Yoplait (Boston's "More Than a Feeling") to Fiber One (the Scorpions' "Rock Like You a Hurricane"). Hey Scorpions, come clean: The impetus behind "Rock You Like a Hurricane" was *always* about the importance of fiber, right?

Somehow we got so content with the music we know from long ago that we became dangerously well-gorged on it. And at such a state we decided—however consciously or unconsciously—that we just didn't need any new music.

We've arrived at this lamentable juncture due to two powerful forces—one deeply commercial, the other deeply human: repetition and nostalgia. With the arrival of MTV, the Video Age was here, and with it came consequences that still play out today. As MTV became more mainstream, Top 40 radio and MTV fed each other incessantly. If a song was a hit, it had a video in constant rotation. And if it was a popular video, the song seemed like it was on the airwaves nonstop. Sometimes the video was insipid; sometimes the song itself was terrible. Often it was both, but that hardly mattered. On *Billboard*'s biggest Hot 100 hits in 1984, you have to go to the No. 47 spot to find a song that didn't have an official music video for it: Peabo Bryson's "If Ever You're in My Arms Again."

From the beginning, music had always been an important part of television, from *The Lawrence Welk Show*, in which Welk, with his heavy accent amid a haze of bubbles, led his orchestra through a broad range of standards or songs of the day, to *American Bandstand* and *Soul Train*, but TV had never functioned so much like a radio before the dominance of MTV. With TV's first twenty-four-hour music channel, we got stuck in a new kind loop of musical periodicity, but we weren't complaining. None of us had never seen anything like MTV—songs with accompanying films! Had we really settled for all that bowling coverage on ABC and *Baretta* in the years before?

The commercial consequences of MTV's popularity were astronomical. When MTV debuted in 1981, record sales were at 3.9 billion. Ten years later, that figure had doubled. MTV was as defining a cultural element to the decade as the British Invasion was to the '60s or the advent of disco was to the '70s, but there was a kind of curse in that, which would take some decades to see clearly. Despite all the new music made after the height of MTV, it turned out we still couldn't get enough of those songs from the MTV era, no matter how good or bad they were. And there were more bad songs from the '80s than there are known species of birds.

But these songs have survived like the Great Pyramids thanks to the deepest layers of fervent nostalgia for the era that birthed them. We have always been a nostalgic nation, and every generation claims the great art of their time as the best, the most important, but this is different. We're currently in the grips of a nostalgia like nothing any of us have known. This state of longing has had an enormous set of repercussions for listeners—and also for the artists who came after these songs and whose music had its own virtues and vitality but failed to shape the culture as it might have because by that point we were already starting to tune out.

Nostalgia, writes Mike Edison in *Sympathy for the Drummer: Why Charlie Watts Matters*, "is one of those rare things that can swing between the pathological and the pathetic (why can't things be like they used to be, back in the good old days), or be a bonding force, the celebration of a shared experience that brings us all together." In that passage he was lamenting how a Rolling Stones concert could be an homage to the band's past, which he said made him a little sad. I'm a little sad, too, but not because of the Stones, although I was disappointed that they carried on after Watts died, since Keith Richards had been on record that the band couldn't exist without their stalwart heart. "No Charlie, no Stones," he'd said. An easier declaration to make when your drummer is still alive, apparently.

As the years have clicked on, we've increasingly listened to new music with all the openness of the crowd at the Newport Folk Festival in 1965, when Bob Dylan trotted out his Fender Stratocaster and attendees reacted with booing and screaming and generally committing to dying right there on their blankets because of such a villainous act of musical double-crossing.

I know the enterprise of new music—the writing, performing, recording, the marketing of it, the indie label's tweets from a PR rep who could get axed if she's not effectively getting the word out about the latest album—is a part of daily life for many thousands. And sure, the Ed Sheerans and the Pinks of the world continue to put out new albums, and the

Recording Academy keeps handing out Grammys. But as a general trend in this century, music sales have been plummeting. By the early 2000s, the music industry, as it had existed for so many decades, was in full collapse, with revenue losses in the billions and the CD quickly becoming our generation's 8-track cassette as iTunes and digital sales took over. By the end of 2023, the idea of downloading a whole album or even a single song felt about as current as Tony Orlando and Dawn; digital sales of albums were down again, having dropped 9 percent by the end of 2023. Sales of physical forms of music, however—led by our renewed love of vinyl—were up almost 9 percent, according to Luminate, an entertainment data company. While streaming was everything now, there is a very long string of indicators capturing our collective waning interest in the music being made today.

In 2021 viewership of the Grammys broadcast, which exists to celebrate excellence in new music, had dropped more than 50 percent from the previous year to a new low. In 2023, it jumped up 30 percent over the previous year, but in the same year MTV's *Video Music Awards*, once the must-see spectacle in music of the year, saw a jump in viewership and still managed to rope in fewer than a million viewers. More than seven times that viewership sat down for the third Republican debate two months later—and that was *without* Trump.

Let me clear: I don't believe music means less to us now— far from it. Between the compulsion for our listening devices and the number of songs streamed across the planet and the onslaught of music biopics perpetually showing up at movie theaters, it feels like we've never had a greater appetite for music or had it play a bigger role in our daily existence. It's just that we can't stop looking to the past for our musical gratification.

Our relationship with the other arts isn't nearly this in flux. We go to museums to see new exhibits—the latest mixed-media works from artists in Iceland or South Korea, photo galleries centered on our dying earth, avant-garde films that make us rethink the visual beauty of 1970s-era teen drunk-driving educational movies. We head out, if unenthusiastically, to see the latest installment of the grade-C superhero trilogy at the cineplex ("Dude, he completely loses his powers in this one"), and we eagerly embrace addiction to the latest TV shows on Netflix and HBO and Hulu. We devour the latest thrillers by our favorite authors and talk ad nauseam about new podcasts we've discovered.

Of course, there has always been a tendency to keep finding new ways to rhapsodize over the old masters, whether it's a new performance of *Swan Lake* in the ballet world or a new film treatment or Broadway production of *West Side Story*, or yet another exhibit of Picasso's *Blue Period*. But in music we remain content to recycle through all the albums we've been listening to our whole lives, to gobble up the latest deluxe editions of music we already own—with poorly recorded original demos! Versions of songs deemed not good enough to release! False starts!

Part of this whole phenomena is that the old songs find us as we much as we find them. You don't go to your favorite deli only to wander upon a staging of *Our Town* by the cheese section, but there you will surely hear the song that was playing in the food court when Melanie Newton told you, "I just want to go back to being friends." And thus that song, be it "I'm Not in Love" by 10cc or "The Safety Dance" by Men Without Hats forever has that association for you, which was a painful one for a few weeks, but now you only remember that Melanie was right that the little romance had run its course, and besides, you started dating Sherry Brock three months later, and Sherry was truly your first love, and so you remember Melanie only fondly now, and when you hear that little coy 10cc whisper "Big boys don't cry" or hear "Safety Dance" and recall its video, in which the singer frolics with a little person in a field as if both were in search for a Renaissance Festival, you feel a bittersweet reflection that only those songs can bring you. Only songs have this particular power.

The way our brains are wired certainly plays into all of this. "As soon as we hear a song that we haven't heard since a particular time in our lives," writes Daniel J. Levitin, in his book *This is Your Brain on Music: The Science of a Human Obsession*, "the floodgates of memory open and we're immersed in memories. The song has acted as a unique cue, a key unlocking all the experiences associated with the memory for the songs, its time and place." Your brain on music, Levitin tells us, is all about connections.

Making a similar point about music and concert memories, a *New York Times* article quoted Dr. Andrew E. Budson, co-author of *Why We Forget and How to Remember*

Better: The Science Behind Memory, along with Elizabeth A. Kensinger, and a professor of neurology at Boston University, as saying about a song "it encourages you to be thinking about that memory and retrieving that memory not just for a few seconds, like looking at a picture might, but for a prolonged period of time."

Plus, songs just have a logistical advantage over all other creations of art. When you got married, even though the two of you originally bonded over your love of *Four Weddings and a Funeral*, your best man didn't announce at the wedding reception, "OK, everyone, because our new favorite couple has always loved *Four Wedding and a Funeral*, we're all going to huddle up together so that everyone can watch the movie together." Instead, it was a song that you told the DJ or wedding band you and your new bride would be dancing to as everyone sat around and watched, feigning feeling emotional. And that song wasn't a song released five months before your wedding, or two years before. It was an old song because of all the years that song had built up its emotional weight for you. Maybe it was Percy Sledge's "When a Man Loves a Woman," or Al Green's "Let's Stay Together" or Berlin's "Take My Breath Away." All I know is, it was old.

And we can reach for songs anytime, anywhere—on iTunes, Spotify, or YouTube, or by grabbing the CD or pulling the record out of its sleeve—as easily as we reach for mints. Wherever we go, music is always around us, like a photo album that takes us back to who we once were, what we once went through.

Your favorite songs from the past are still your favorite songs still today, and they are always playing somewhere because—I have to break it to you—they're also so many others' favorite songs, too. Our list of favorite songs tends to not much evolve as we get older, even as new music comes out all the time. Twenty years ago you might have said your favorite TV show of all time was *Twin Peaks* or *Hill Street Blues* or *ER*. Now you say it's *The Handmaid's Tale* or *Breaking Bad* or *Ozark* or *Girls* or *The Bear*. Which doesn't mean you don't love those older favorites anymore. You just don't watch them like you used to. Instead, as you got older, you kept watching the new shows, and you're glad you did. They gave you so much to talk to your friends, co-workers, and family members about. And we're in the Golden Age of Television—it's easily the best it's ever been. But with songs our loyalty is fierce and forever.

Oh, you might check out the new album by the Foo Fighters, Adele, the Black Keys, Kings of Leon, or the Weeknd, and for a few weeks it's what all the music press and bloggers and podcasters are dissecting to death, and maybe you try to listen to it intently for a few weeks because you understand you're supposed to love it—it's supposed to be the best album they've put out. Everyone is saying so. And you either come to believe that, too, or you just accept that without actually feeling it yourself—without *letting* yourself feel it, maybe. But in a month's time or less, it's as if that big album never dropped at all, and you go right back to listening to everything that came well before it, and it never finds a place in your playlist closest to your heart. Because you have Night Ranger on your playlist.

◎ ◎ ◎

So why can't songs from this century, like the Strokes' "You Talk Way Too Much," the White Stripes' "Black Math," Soccer Mommy's "Last Girl" or St. Vincent's "Save Me From What I Want," get in on all the action that these songs from the '70s and '80s have? The great songs that came after Pearl Jam arrived on the scene too often bounced off us like dandelion seeds because the songs that came before them got so coded into our DNA—by an almost sinister level of monotonous programming carried out by those who believe that repetition is what we need from music most. And this finite number of songs ended up being the soundtrack to our lives that not all of us agreed to have compiled.

Part of our current musical conundrum is, when you're hearing the same songs over and over—as your pharmacist is explaining how to take your medicine, say, or when a salesman says, "Unfortunately, we don't have that in the pink" right over Stewart Copeland's great drum fill on "Every Little Thing She Does is Magic"—we don't experience the music like we once did: turned up loud in our dorm rooms or coming through early headphones, the size of dessert bowls, as we sat in our bedroom and stared at the gerbil running through its red plastic tunnels. The effects of hearing these songs in places where we don't instinctively think, "I wish I was hearing that song from Flock of Seagulls right about now" change our relationship to the music—and changes our relationship to music in general, what we once wanted from it and what we were supposed to need from it in the first place.

Great music has always been able to comfort, but it was never supposed to just be comfort food.

A lot of people who remember watching *Battle of the Network Stars* ("Gabe Kaplan takes the lead!") believe that the songs from this century haven't nearly had the same afterlife because they're vastly inferior to the songs that came forty years before them. And you'll hear from those folks in the pages ahead. But you also can't rate what you've never heard.

We used to want so much from music. More than anything, we wanted it to feel new. We wanted it to feel like a riot, and we wanted it to be as still and safe as a church. We wanted it to make sense, and we wanted it to leave us utterly baffled. We wanted it to be gorgeous, and we wanted it to be raw. We wanted it to tell us stories, and we wanted it to tell us what to think. We wanted it to impress us, and we wanted it to not try too hard. We wanted it to console us, and we wanted it to push us away. We wanted it to make us feel like we needed saving, and we wanted it to make us feel it was too late for that. We wanted it to feel like a miracle, and we wanted it to be deeply cynical about miracles. We wanted it to rage, and we wanted it to whisper. We wanted it to feel like our secret alone, and we wanted to share it with the rest of the world.

In the new music we wanted harmonies that soared like condors. On stage we wanted the musicians to be stripped down to nothing—just wearing socks on their privates was fine!—and we wanted them to be adorned in crowns, capes, and outfits that glittered like a stadium. We wanted guitar solos that opened up like the sea, and yet we were done with all the pretentious soloing. We wanted choruses so sharp we could belt them out to the heavens. But most of all, we just *wanted*. The act of wanting the music was unlike wanting anything else—food, water, sex. Wanting the music was almost as good as the music itself.

And so we waited and waited. Word was, the band had been in the studio for months. Wait, the band had fired their producer! The band was moving to New York to record. No, Switzerland. The band was going back to those songs from the scrapped sessions. No, the band was bringing in an outside writer. The band was going back on the road, but the album was done. It was going to be their best yet! It was going to be their most experimental. No, it was going to be their most back-to-basics album since their debut. Everyone was saying the chemistry in the band had never been better. No, the band had almost broken up over the direction of the album. It was going to be a double album. No, the band was torn about releasing a double album! Whatever it was going to be, the new album was going to the most incredible album ever.

And then. And then. And then the wanting—that kind of wanting—just started to drain out of us. But who were we if we didn't want music like that anymore? We had all we needed, didn't we? Now we just wanted that same music over and over and over and over again. How many new albums were we expected to keep buying, anyway? Besides, the music had done everything it could do, been everything it could be. All the genres had been mixed and swirled around until there was no more mixing and swirling to be done. Folk rock. Country rock. Blues rock. Dance punk. Power pop. Funk rock. And on and on and on. We'd heard it all, and nothing new could possibly come along that we hadn't already heard.

Here we are now, but don't entertain us anymore. We're all set.

The desire to see live music wasn't fully extinguished in us, though. During the early days of COVID, musicians disappeared from the live stage, of course, but by the fall of 2022, touring had ramped up to resemble what it had been before the virus shuttered the industry, with many artists trying to recoup the money they couldn't make in those two years. In fact, according to *Pollstar*, the trade publication for the live music industry, there were 59.2 million concert tickets sold in 2022 versus 57.7 million in 2019. And among the big tours of that year were Genesis, with the now-customary lineup of Phil Collins, Tony Banks, and Mike Rutherford, who hadn't released any new music since the Gulf War. Guns N' Roses played stadiums in 2022 and 2023, and they last released a new album the year Sarah Palin said she could see Russia from her backyard. (That is, if you were among the many diehards who thought of the Axl

Rose—only quagmire that is *Chinese Democracy* more in the vein of the short-lived *Baywatch Nights* and thus not really *Baywatch*, or Guns N' Roses, at all.) Billy Joel sold out each of his monthly Madison Square Garden gigs in 2022, and his last traditional album was 1993's *River of Dreams*. (He released an album of compositions in 2001 called *Fantasies & Delusions*, but it was all classical instrumentals on piano, and even then he got someone else to play the piano, making it at least an important milestone in musical outsourcing.)

The Eagles were headliners in 2022, too, and their last new work came out the same year Britney Spears shaved her head and jousted with a paparazzi's car using an umbrella.

There were, to be sure, lots of newer acts playing new music to the masses in 2022 as well—Bad Bunny, Harry Styles, and The Weeknd among them. But all in all, nostalgia looked pretty good on the old Jumbotron in 2022. And more blasts from the past shelling no new music roamed in 2023. Lionel Richie! New Kids on the Block! Lynyrd Skynyrd, who not only didn't have any new music, but no longer had any more original members. Queen + Adam Lambert! Bryan Adams was playing arenas, too, though he released a new album in 2022— *So Happy It Hurts*. But to go by his setlist at the Indianapolis Motor Speedway in the spring of 2023, it looked like his fans could count on being more happy than hurt—only two songs played from the new album.

And what would a summer be without the Beach Boys—that is, Mike Love at eighty-two and still in a hat playing with a bunch of hired musicians, plus the frequent and still-odd appearance of actor John Stamos. But be warned: they were sure to play their latest hit on this tour. That would be "Kokomo," released in 1988. Which was covered by the Muppets.

I don't come to all this throwing CDs at glass houses. I both love the experience of new music and can sometimes be wary of it, too. I still play the music I grew up with—Yes, Santana, the Beatles, Pink Floyd, Peter Gabriel, the Police, Genesis, Prince, the Kinks, Led Zeppelin, the Who—alongside music just as old that I got around to later in life: Joni Mitchell, the Band, Steely Dan, the Allman Brothers Band. But as I've gotten older I've continued to listen to new music in every decade.

My methods of listening to music are decidedly old-school: CDs and vinyl, though I take as much comfort in the existence of my iPod as I do my 401K. I don't like to stream music because I believe in giving an album a true chance, and I will only do that if I've actually paid for it. If I stream a new album, it feels to me like thumbing through a new book at a bookstore to judge its value, which I also don't do. How can I really know what I think from two minutes of perusing? The act of purchasing a new work—the leap of faith that requires—still remains important and thrilling to me.

But I'm in the minority on that score. According to a 2023 year-end report from Luminate, on-demand audio streams—that is, music that consumers chose directly versus songs that were part of a playlist or came up within some "since you like Coldplay" algorithm—surged globally 22 percent from 2022.

And if you look at any of the records on Spotify, which comprises 40 percent of all streaming—such as the most-listened to songs, most-streamed albums in a single day, longest running No. 1 songs—it's almost exclusively artists of the twenty-first century

Given all that, you ask, how the hell did I publish a book arguing that we don't really want to hear new music? Digging further into other data by Luminate, though, presents a fuller picture of what's going on.

In 2022, 72 percent of the overall consumption of music, which includes streaming, radio play, and purchased downloads, came from catalog shares (defined as any music older than eighteen months). That doesn't necessarily mean it was all Doobie Brothers and Blondie or Grand Funk Railroad that were dominating and could include pretty recent music by such contemporaries as Katy Perry, Dua Lipa, or Billie Eilish. But what is not dominating our collective listening is new music.

Based on a sample size of nearly 4,000 listeners thirteen and older, Luminate reported that the most popular genre listened to in 2022 was rock music, with a rate of 51 percent, but the next category, surpassing hip-hop/rap, pop/Top 40, R&B, and country, was catalog, or "oldies." From the 1950s to the 2020s, the most popular decade to listen to was not the current decade, but the 1990s, which 57 percent of listeners said they preferred, with the '80s a close second at 55 percent. The current decade came in third at 53 percent. So while we might have learned to chillax in the twenty-first century, it's the music from the last one that we're still getting jiggy with.

The situation wasn't much different in the U.K. According to an early 2024 report from the BBC, "new music was largely absent from the year's top 10 best-selling albums." The Weeknd held the No. 1 spot with his two-year-old greatest hits compilation, and No. 2 went to the 2022 Taylor Swift release *Midnights*. It went on to note that new releases by artists such as Olivia Rodrigo and Ed Sheeran were all outsold by "best of" collections from Elton John, Eminem, Fleetwood Mac, and ABBA.

Luminate also reported that the combined digital consumption of audio streams and video streams of "current" music released in the last eighteen months or less was down 13 percent. By contrast, the streaming of "catalog" music had jumped, in 2022, a whopping 19 percent from 2021.

Boomers were listening to more music from the '70s than from any other decade, which was no surprise. Both Millennials and Gen Xers preferred '90s music. Only Generation Z preferred the music of this decade. Also this: only 63 percent of boomers liked it when their favorite artists even released new music. New Aerosmith? New Kansas? New Pat Benatar? Mostly the boomers preferred new knees.

According to a *Billboard* article in July 2023, rock artists had sold 11.2 million more units in 2023 than they had at the halfway point in 2022. But—and here's the real takeaway—"That growth, however, is almost entirely from catalog—10.3 million of it, compared to 900,000 units of growth from current releases."

The incredible blitzkrieg that is Taylor Swift was part of the explanation of the sales increase—not only had her Eras Tour proved to be the most successful tour ever, but she had also re-recorded all her albums (so that she could own the master recordings) and re-released them with bonus tracks, and as I'm writing this sentence, she had eight of the 30 albums in *Billboard*'s 200 chart. No artist has ever dominated like this before. But my contact at Luminate, Jimmy Harney, also told me, in an email, that artists were selling their music directly to fans at higher rates than ever, and that "fans, especially younger ones, are showing more enthusiasm to support their favorite artists by buying multiple vinyl, CD, and cassette products."

But even Taylor Swift fandom has been a deep study in nostalgia, even though Swift is all of thirty-four and her first album came out in 2006. In those concerts she was treating fans to a career retrospective—thus the name of the tour. Swifties turned up in outfits based on their favorite album covers. This was no conventional tour supporting her most recent album, but rather, it existed to remember all of Taylor's albums, to take fans through her evolution from early country singer to full-on pop star to the turn of a folkier Taylor. All those Swifties swimming deep not just in Taylor Swift nostalgia, but also for who they had been and what they loved over the last fifteen years or more.

One major development in recent years that will have a profound impact on the music we'll be hearing in the future—where and how—has been the massive acquisition of artists' catalogs for songwriting, recordings, or both. When the pandemic took hold and it was clear no one was going on tour for who knew how long, musicians had to think about what to do not just with their time, but what this meant for their revenue. In the early days of all the confusion and chaos, some musicians tried to soothe us, and themselves, by performing live via their Instagram accounts. They strummed their acoustic guitars in their kitchens and home studios and on their porches, often covering other artists' songs, perhaps as a way to remember better days. Some made what would be referred to as their COVID records. And others hatched new plans with their royalties and started having meetings with investors. While musicians went back to writing music and waiting out the pandemic to resume performing, these companies would have plenty of ideas—ideas the musicians would never have dreamed of—about how to reimagine the use of their music. And to keep it alive for future generations.

These sales seal that we'll be hearing so many old songs in an even more constant rotation: in commercials, on TV and in movies, in video games and in sampling, or for cover songs. The companies' musicians have sold their catalogs to will also be cashing in on the artists' licensing rights, future royalties, brand deals, and other revenue streams still to be imagined So the prevalence of music from artists ranging from Bob Marley, Stevie Nicks, Bob Dylan (estimated at more than

$300 million), the Beach Boys, Paul Simon, Bruce Springsteen (estimated at $500 million), Neil Diamond, Genesis, Frank Zappa, Sting, Huey Lewis and the News, ZZ Top, and numerous estates of deceased musicians, such as David Bowie and Ray Charles, is only going to increase. Vastly so.

I'd hardly been alone in pondering how our musical past had become such a dominant part of our present, though. In *Retromania: Pop Culture's Addiction to Its Own Past*, Simon Reynolds is in full lament about how stuck we've become, and his book came out in 2011. These many years later, we're in DEFCON 2, but Reynolds was also making a different kind of argument in his book. He was ruminating on how music being made in the twenty-first century was so short of ideas, of innovation, of new life. "Where are the major genres and subcultures of the twenty-first century?" he wonders. Reynolds is laying at least part of the blame on the musicians today for lack of innovation. But I say that the musicians creating music now could be making the most extraordinary music ever created and we wouldn't even know it because of how uninterested we are.

Music writer Ted Gioia was focused on the reign of old songs in his blog, *The Honest Broker*, of January 2022. "Never before in history have new tracks attained hit status while generating so little cultural impact," he wrote. "In fact, the audience seems to be embracing en masse the hits of decades past. Success was always short-lived in the music business, but now it hardly makes a ripple on the attention spans of the mass market."

Gioia also had a clear culprit in his target sight, and it wasn't today's musicians, who, collectively, he assented, were creating good music. Rather, "The people running the music industry have lost confidence in new music," he wrote. "The moguls have lost their faith in the redemptive and life-changing power of new music—how sad is that?"

It was plenty sad, sure, but did we even have moguls anymore? Did we even have a music industry in the conventional sense? All of this was bigger than any kind of executive decision making. This was about who we were now and what we wanted—or didn't want.

Does the music being made today have the same potential for future revenues as these catalogs going for hundreds of millions? For now it was only to wonder, but I had my suspicions. No song stayed No. 1 on *Billboard*'s Hot 100 chart longer than 2019's "Old Town Road" by Lil Nas X, with help from Billy Ray Cyrus. At least in one way, you could say it was the most popular song ever recorded. Take that "Bohemian Rhapsody," "Yesterday," and "Billie Jean"! And yet, why does that crowning achievement seem entirely forgotten just a few years later? A billion people have watched "Old Town Road" on YouTube, but who now talks or thinks about a song that broke one of the biggest records in music? Was it just a dream we had of Lil Nas X riding his horse through the neighborhood? I don't even hear it anymore. What I do hear all the time, though, is "The Final Countdown" by Europe, which came out in 1986. That song broke no records, nor has anything about it ever been final.

On the other side of the spectrum from Lil Nas X, a new
Metallica album is always big news in music, and in April 2023
the band released 72 *Seasons*, their first studio album in seven
years. In the U.S. it debuted at the No. 2 spot on the *Billboard*
200 albums chart, and at No. 1 in more than fifteen other
countries. Metallica was everywhere promoting the album:
five appearances in a week on *Jimmy Kimmel Live!*, a long
interview on the *Howard Stern Show*, interviews in so many
music publications and websites. And Metallica was the first
rock band to create American Sign Language videos for every
song on an album. Within a month, though, 72 *Seasons* was at
No. 69 in the chart—behind Fleetwood Mac's *Rumors*, which
came out in 1977 and was at the No. 37 spot that week but
had been on the charts for 528 weeks. A greatest hits album by
Creedence Clearwater Revival occupied No. 48 and had been
on the chart for 641 weeks, and at the No. 42 spot Queen's
Greatest Hits had been on the chart for 542 weeks. These days,
it seemed like there was always another new album by a huge
act biting the dust.

Still, what convinced me more than anything else that
we don't want new music occurred way back in 2014, accompanied by hand-wringing and global bemoaning like
nothing I could remember in music. The incident in question wasn't that Live had put out their first album without
singer Ed Kowalczyk (who would later have his revenge when
he eventually re-joined the band, then fired everyone else.)
It wasn't that Mötley Crüe had signed an agreement that
they wouldn't tour together again (which they didn't stick to

anyway). It wasn't even seeing the footage of Beyoncé's sister, Solange, attacking Jay-Z in an elevator. Whatever your relationship to any of those artists, that wasn't the incident that reached the nadir of music-related outrage for the year. Instead, that award went to a band that was only, in their view, trying to do something generous and grand: It was U2 giving the world their new music for free and the frothing vitriol that greeted them.

U2 had started recording a new album in 2010, in stops and starts. Bono told *Rolling Stone* that the band had recorded up to 100 songs, but as they kept at it, they realized they weren't much excited about what they had. So they decided to go off and write even more songs, with various producers coming and going—studio guru Danger Mouse among them. "Eventually, the group found themselves with a collection of songs they felt stood up to their best work," Andy Greene wrote about the album. And with that excitement came feelings that the very delivery of the album should be different—and bigger than anything U2 had done before.

This was a time when album sales were already in a serious slump. No one had really cared about U2's bland previous album, *No Line on the Horizon*, though *Rolling Stone* hailed it as the best album of 2009. Sure, it had peaked at No. 1 all over the world upon its release, but it generated no hit songs or classic U2 anthems, and sales of the album were the worst the band had seen in a decade.

Eventually those Irish lads who had stuck together like no other band of their generation had an epiphany. "We wanted to reach as many people as possible," the band's manager, Guy Oseary, told Greene. "We brainstormed and brainstormed. Apple has hundreds of millions of iTunes accounts—giving it away just made sense."

On September 9, half a billion people woke up surprised to find that there was a new U2 album on their devices, and they had received it for free. Free! Who had ever done that? Not Coldplay! Not Maroon 5! Not Green Day! Those selfish bastards. Wow, U2, thank you! But we didn't get *you* anything! This gift of an album was called *Songs of Innocence*. It just happened, though, that untold millions were apoplectic. This was new music they didn't want. Forget that they hadn't paid a dime. Who wanted new U2 music in 2014?, the masses wanted to know.

The complaints came at Apple like the Orcs trying to overtake Helm's Deep.

"Your free U2 album is waiting for you in iTunes like some hoary creep who you didn't invite to the party," tweeted one irate fan. "I think 99% of apple users hate the fact they have a free u2 album and then theres my dad who was close to tears of joy," said another.

The presumptuousness of the marketing gesture was part of the indignancy; there were endless analogies of the discovery of the uninvited album feeling like an invasion. To me, this reaction would have been less mystifying if it had been a divisive artist—someone like Marilyn Manson, or going the other way, Five for Fighting. But in U2 we're talking about a generally beloved band that has won more Grammys than any other.

U2 stole our hearts at Live Aid, in 1985, when during their set closer "Bad," Bono spent two days trying to get from the stage to one particular woman in the crowd he felt strongly about holding and dancing with for about three seconds—in a stadium of 72,000 people. U2 had filled the airwaves for decades with amazing songs that only ever sounded like them. Despite a recent turn toward irrelevancy, U2 was still easily one of the biggest bands in the world, and the objection that *Songs of Innocence* took up valuable device space—a constant complaint in the early days of the debacle—was like arguing that one oversized Dorito had thus blocked the space for more Doritos in the bag.

To exacerbate the problem, as people from Algeria to Zambia found out, this U2 album couldn't just be easily deleted like any other album. *Give me liberty or give me death!* The very next day, trying to quell the furor, Apple got out the word for how to erase *Songs of Innocence.* But even that was a shambles for many, and some unhappy recipients just resigned themselves to keeping the unwanted album but refusing to listen to it. U2 had ultimately produced the first album to have squatters' rights.

There wasn't much of an album cover for the digital release—essentially a plain wrapper—but the cover of the physical album and CD, released the following month, depicted the band's drummer, Larry Mullen Jr., right in front of a shirtless boy's crotch and looked in every way like he was about to give him head. Hmmm, not so innocent, U2. Not judging. It's just that . . . anyway.

All these years later, what happens to my wife Kim every time she starts her car and has her phone plugged in is what happens to many others, I've learned. The opening seconds of the album's first song, "The Miracle (of Joey Ramone)," comes on, and so does that image of Larry Mullen Jr. ready to give head on her phone.

In 2020, another commentator: "Bro that shit still living in my phone. Rent free."

The world sent a tough and telling message that fall of 2014. U2 had proven to be one of the most dynamic and influential bands in the history of rock, and even though they wanted to keep making new music, that didn't mean we wanted to keep hearing it. Music is deeply personal for most of us, and free or not, the music on our devices got there because we chose it. *Songs of Innocence* might have been dreamed up as a gift, but it felt more like a flier for some congressman running yet again for re-election put underneath our windshield wiper— only this flier was literally glued to our windshield, and it was a headache to dispose of.

But really, new music was so twentieth century.

The same old songs are everywhere we go, and that has been the case for so long that it's easy to be completely oblivious to it. But it wasn't always this way.

In part, we can thank Muzak. It was Muzak that produced those string-drenched, generally high-fructose versions of pre-viously recorded songs intended as a soothing background for those in their place of work, and eventually (supposedly) pleasant listening while in banks or sitting in a restaurant. The musical equivalent of watercress sandwiches. Or as Joseph Lanza writes in *Elevator Music: A Surreal History of Muzak, Easy Listening, and Other Moodsong*, "an artfully contrived regimen of unobtrusive harmonies and pitches; metronomic repetition; melodic segments that overlap into tonal wash; a concatenation of hypnotic violins, harps, celestes, and other instruments connoting inherited concepts of how heaven sounds."

Muzak produced its first recording in 1934 with a medley of "Whispering," "Do You Think of Me?" and "Here in My Arms." In the ensuing decade its popularity swelled like the songs themselves, and by the end of the 1940s the nation's capital, Lanza writes, was transmitting the music in the city's buses and streetcars. Decades later, the range of artists being covered by Muzak expanded with the times—the Beach Boys, the Doors, and Led Zeppelin all got their elevator treatments. Muzak would start to peter out during the 1980s, struggling to distance itself from a name that had come to epitomize any cartoon caption that reads, "Zzzzzzzzzz." In 2009 it filed for bankruptcy but was bought by a company called Mood Media in 2011, which specializes in creating soundtracks for businesses or whole industries like retail, restaurants, grocery stores, salons, and financial institutions. Euro-beats, exultant-sounding pan-flute, classical guitar, Zydeco odysseys. (Mood Media also filed for bankruptcy in 2020 because it was impossible for employees in the corporate office to not continually fall asleep on the job. OK, that's not why. During COVID no one was coming into stores, and revenue was tanking everywhere. But Mood Media recovered immediately from that bankruptcy—a judge confirmed its new reorganization plan the next day. I like imagining that in celebration, the Mood Media offices were flooded with the exultant-sounding pan-flute music, but that's just me.)

I was born in 1967, and I remember the presence of Muzak in department stores and grocery stores—I could pick out songs I was familiar with, but I don't remember it as being overbearing so much as it was curious. If nothing else, I understood that the arrangements I was hearing sure took the rock out of the rock songs it covered.

It was when my family joined our first swimming pool that I began to be more aware of hearing actual songs I'd heard on the radio in a public setting. I was seven when we bought a membership to the Holiday Swim Club, and that experience was distinct for two reasons: One, the pool had a crumbling floor, and I was constantly bringing up jagged piece of concrete from the shallow end to the lifeguards; and two, it had a jukebox. The Holiday Swim Club and its sedate swimmers had a great fondness for soft rock: In our relatively brief membership what tended to get played the most, as my brother, John, and I remember it, were Player's "Baby Come Back," "Afternoon Delight" by Starland Vocal Band, "Summer Breeze" by Seals & Crofts, and "Miracles" by Jefferson Starship. There were, though, seemingly a couple of funkier Holiday Club members who were forever opting for the slightly older selection of

"Brother Louie" by Stories—it was a cover of a song originally recorded by the band Hot Chocolate.

I couldn't have understood it then, but I was already forming emotional associations with those songs, and today, all these decades later, it's impossible for me to hear any of those tunes and not recall how quickly I moved through the men's bathroom to the pool area, hellbent on dodging fathers nonchalantly changing in or out of their plastic swim trunks with all the modesty of a colony of nudists enjoying a day at the beach.

A couple of years later, my family upgraded from the Holiday Swim Club to the Moose Lodge, which brought a decidedly different brand of public music. Instead of scores of families and frolicking children, at the Moose Lodge there was a dearth of parents around, and it carried a distinct hint of menace—with a harder musical backdrop to match. The teenage boys who populated the place wore the hardened expressions of juvenile delinquents. They made coarse, barking sounds when they laughed, their Marlboro cigarettes teetering between their lips, and tended to swim in cutoff jeans as I piddled uneasily about in the water. When they stood on the edge of the diving board, someone would inevitably call out for the nutcracker to be performed, and so the divers would dutifully fling themselves into the air while gleefully grabbing their nuts in mid-air and make a splash that emptied exactly one eighth of the pool.

What was forever coming out of the Moose's jukebox was Boston's "More Than a Feeling," Bad Company's "Rock 'n' Roll Fantasy," but Styx's "Renegade," from 1979, played exactly every nine minutes. It began with guitarist's Tommy Shaw's a cappella, introducing the listener to a narrator voicing fear of the law, then after the rest of the band joins the harmonies, there's that *bum-bum, bum-bum* beat of the bass drum, then the snare splat like an axe thrown into a tree, followed by a rebel yell that kicks off the jam. "Renegade" was Styx bringing the heavier stuff, and long after my mother picked me up again from the Moose Lodge I could feel the song in my ear like water trapped that I couldn't get out. And as with the songs from the Holiday Swim Club, I can't hear "Renegade" and not immediately think of guys grabbing their nuts in mid-air.

Still, just as they were at the Holiday Club, these were songs chosen the democratic way—with members' quarters. The community, such as it was, was playing what it wanted to hear. But soon after my days at the Moose, it was nearly impossible to go somewhere and hear music that wasn't selected by someone who thought he or she knew what we all wanted to hear.

"I want my MTV!" The Who's Pete Townshend demanded in the ad campaign conceived to spur more momentum for the channel. The Police and Pat Benatar and David Bowie called for it. Mick Jagger and Cyndi Lauper, too. In his spot Billy Idol added, "Too much is never enough." But we're still feeling the effects of too much MTV, these forty-plus years later. The

overexposure that all those songs got had the opposite consequence of what overexposure usually ushers in: Instead of
burning us out on those songs, as adults now making our way
through the challenges of the early AARP years, we embrace
those same songs all the more.

In 1981 the Buggles' "Video Killed the Radio Star" was
the first video on the channel aired, of course. Video didn't
kill the radio star, though, so much as it remade music as
an instrument for endless, numbing repetition. When MTV
debuted, there simply weren't a lot of music videos available,
since music videos weren't yet a ubiquitous part of the business. Bob Pittman, one of the founders of the channel, estimated there were about 250 in the beginning, but it was a
twenty-four-hour-a-day channel. In those early months you
could see the same popular video multiple times a day.

A lot of artists didn't have any interest in making videos—
at least not in the beginning. Tom Petty's Heartbreakers
hated making them. Billy Joel didn't like them, nor did Bruce
Springsteen or Bob Seger. R.E.M. didn't initially embrace
making videos until they more fully embraced the artistic
possibilities. But a whole slew of artists who arrived on the
scene during the advent of MTV—groups such as Duran
Duran, Culture Club, and Madonna—saw the music video
as a whole new canvas to work with and paint themselves
onto, and many of them happened to have the right look and
sound to catapult them to video stardom.

The implications for the purely musical efforts were
inevitable—and often harsh. As Devo co-founder Mark

Mothersbaugh says in *I Want My MTV*, "MTV was swiftly followed by CDs, and all of a sudden instead of a well-crafted album of ten songs, you had to put all your bets on one particular song, and that's what people heard or saw from you. The rest of the CD was filler. So MTV created this all-or-nothing syndrome in pop music that made for CDs full of *shite*, with, like, one strong song."

Through music videos we experienced a whole new way to get attached to songs, with often bizarre, nonsensical imagery or snippets of some kind of plot. When Big Country's "In a Big Country" came on the radio, you could no longer just think about how the guitars sounded like bagpipes or how that song was playing when you saw that car back into another car at the Taco Bell drive-thru and the driver who got hit jumped out and asked with incredulity, "Dude, are you fucking buggin'?" Now it was also the song in which, thanks to the video, you thought of Big Country going after some kind of treasure and nearly getting blown up before they go snorkeling and scale a mountainside.

New images were being imprinted on our young brains at an astonishing clip. Of tears and kisses; of sequined gloves and corsets; of hair like bolts of electricity, troll dolls, or neon signs; long beards, baggy pants, and short skirts; oversized suits and leather jackets; spandex and ballgowns; eye shadow and eye patches. There was dancing on islands and boats, in garages and on balconies and in diners; dancers coming out of manholes; dancers on stoops and rooftops, in castles and churches. There were fast cars and morning trains and sunglasses at night; mic stands with scarves and whips being cracked; berets and porkpie hats; bodybuilders and beaches; shiny happy people and dark-clad sad people. There were robots and werewolves and owls and eagles and doves and rats and tigers and panthers and snakes; forklifts and motorcycles and convertibles; white weddings and hazy gray funerals; bathtubs and halls of mirrors. There were angry phone conversations and parents who just didn't understand. And an astonishing amount of jumping and rings of fire.

The bands or artists played their instruments in clubs and on concert stages and in the studio, and also at carnivals and on mountaintops and in barns and houses. In loading docks and in infernos and on oil derricks; in school libraries, and also on bars of soap.

There were some clear, interesting narratives, and others that were chaotic and confusing from beginning to end. Some were rousing, some infuriating. Others were just dull and devoid of any ideas or direction whatsoever. But whatever they were, or weren't, and no matter which ones we liked or didn't like, in those early years as teenagers, most of us just watched for so long that not just the songs, but all the particular details of the videos took up permanent residence in our young and impressionable brains.

I was in on MTV pretty close from the beginning because my friend Matt Reid's father was the attorney for the local cable company, and Matt was the first friend I knew who had it. As far as he could remember, he had it from the very beginning, starting in August 1981, right before we began high school. All these years later Matt is the athletic director for a middle school in New Bern, North Carolina, which meant he also taught PE and coached the football, basketball, track, and soccer teams. He and I hadn't talked in nearly ten years, but I reached him one January evening in 2022, after he'd finished with practice. I wanted to know what his relationship to new music was like these days. Whatever his answer, I wanted to know if he felt that the constant repetition of MTV had had any lingering effects.

"A lot of the stuff they were running, we'd never even heard of [those] bands," Matt recalled. He was referring mostly to the British bands who came out with debut albums around the same time MTV launched and whose exotic looks the channel was eager to showcase. "I can remember the world coming to a dead stop when they said, '*MTV World Premiere Video*,'" Matt said. "And we would sit fixated. At the time, we'd never seen anything like that."

Matt and I agreed that MTV gave us a deeper connection to the music because it was so immediately a profound part of the culture. Neither Matt nor I liked everything they played on MTV, of course, but we were bowled over that music could have a visual identity like this. For Matt, part of the impact of MTV being such a big presence in our lives then was that he ended up DJing at the high school dances.

"Whenever I hear songs from the '80s, that's what I think of," he said.

We also talked about all that music we grew up with be-fore there was MTV, and by way of addressing that, Matt reminded me that his son, John, is a guitarist. "A hippie with long hair," he said, and laughed. John was still in college, and music had been a major bond between them. Matt had weened John on classic rock, just as I had my two sons, and John had enjoyed all of that, Matt said. Matt was always into the blues-based bands and artists, and he'd taken John to a slew of his favorites: Robert Cray, George Thorogood, Buddy Guy, ZZ Top, and the Rolling Stones. And they caught Van Halen, five years before Eddie Van Halen died.

John had enjoyed his dad's music, but he was into new bands, too. Matt told me they were having a conversation just the other day about Matt's always listening to music from when we were growing up. "Dad, that's all you listen to," John told him. Matt replied that that was because rock music had stopped with Guns N' Roses. "If it's not Zeppelin or AC/DC, you know, I'm good."

Given that Matt didn't listen to new music anymore, I asked him: How do you know it's not just as good as it was from the '70s and '80s?

"I don't, man," Matt said. "That's the whole point, Dave. I don't." He wasn't embarrassed by that stance; he just had a gut conviction, and that was enough. He had a right to that belief, obviously, but I couldn't help but be troubled by that, because I already knew so many people of our generation felt the same way. The less we seek out new music, collectively, the less artists will be compelled to make it, and they'll settle for touring for a living. That's even more the case as more and more artists settle for residencies in Las Vegas versus tours that grind on for six or eight months. And without new music to promote, are those acts going to play anything but greatest-hits sets?

When I asked Matt how far back did he have to go when he'd purchased an album of new music by an artist or band, it sent him into a deep cataloging. After a moment I said, "More than ten years ago?"

"It probably has been more than ten years ago," he said.

Matt and John were two people who cared deeply about music, but there was a natural generational divide between them about music, too. As there probably should be between a father and a son. "He will also argue that—that in fifty years no one's gonna listen to—a lot less people are gonna listen to Led Zeppelin," Matt said. And he parroted something John had told him: "'My friends don't even know who Led Zeppelin is.'"

To that, Matt said, "I tell him the same thing. I said, 'Son, "Stairway to Heaven"'s gonna be around for one hundred years.'" We laughed at what seemed the undeniable truth in that, even the understatement of that. "Stairway" was as permanent as the Washington Monument.

Or maybe that's just something Matt and I needed to believe.

Naturally, not all artists who made videos saw their videos getting played. Meatloaf, for example, felt like MTV had no interest in him, and other veteran rock acts faced with the need to adjust to the video era and ride the new wave were similarly

MIA. Peter Frampton? Toto? Ted Nugent? Those artists were
barely seen at all on MTV. But other long-established artists
like Steve Winwood, Rod Stewart, Peter Gabriel, and Heart
successfully reinvented themselves for the decade awash in a
new and confusing world of fashion and identity while producing music that, if nothing else, fit in with this ultra-pop
sphere pretty seamlessly.

In the '70s, Heart stood out from the rest of the bands
around them. With Ann Wilson on lead vocals and sister
Nancy on guitar, their music showcased a wide range of styles
and moods—searing rock anthems, folky rock ballads. And
they managed a string of hits that reigned on FM radio in the
'70s. By the early '80s, though, Heart was in a sales slump,
and their new record label, Capitol Records, had convinced
them to work with outside writers for the first time in their
career. The result, a self-titled album in 1985, stripped away
some of Heart's earlier sound—very little acoustic guitar, for
starters, which had been a hallmark of their music. That album also scored four top-10 hits in *Billboard*'s Hot 100 chart,
which I still hear as often as the daily weather forecast.

That turn started with the first single and power ballad
"What About Love?" which expertly followed the pop-rock
blueprint of that period: first, the tender vocal over a low
synth line, then the punch of drums and guitar chords as the
vocal builds, over a few minutes, to a screaming crescendo.
In the video that played around the clock, the band prances
about in a place that appears to be part-dungeon, part-gold-
manufacturing hellhole, where flames are constantly shooting

off and gold bars are being stacked. Are the members of Heart prisoners or managers at Fort Knox?

Interspersed with a performance of the song, Ann emerges from doors straight out of Kong Island, clutching a sledgehammer and dressed like she's in a production of *Oliver* costumed by Victoria's Secret. (Later she handles a blowtorch.) At one point liquid gold is poured into a mold from which Nancy emerges. Later, a group of brooding, sooty-faced men carry a seemingly unconscious Nancy over their heads. What any of that had to do with the song itself, which is simply about the need for love, is to fully misunderstand what the '80s were about.

The Wilson sisters have talked about how they hated being made up the way they were in the "What About Love" video—the huge hair, heavy makeup, chokers, a corset for Nancy—and the ones that followed, though they didn't mind the payoffs: all the new fans the new music brought or playing in big arenas again. By the mid-'90s the hits were again gone, but Heart carried on. In the twentieth century they released three studio albums of new material and one largely of re-recorded versions of older songs that they thought needed some re-vamping. They were also inducted into the Rock and Roll Hall of Fame in 2013, and in 2023 Ann and Nancy received the Recording Academy Lifetime Achievement Award.

But there had been tensions between the two sisters. While on tour in 2016, Ann's husband assaulted Nancy's 16-year-old twins for letting the dogs out on Ann's private tour bus; he was arrested and later pled guilty to assault charges and received a suspended sentence. Heart finished that tour, but the split over that incident put the band on hiatus for several years. Ann released solo albums and toured on her own in that time, and Nancy toured with a new group, Roadcase Royale, then put together a new band. Those bands didn't get much attention and got opening-act stints for groups that had been Heart's peers—Bob Seger, Styx. But in 2021 Nancy released her first proper solo album. Given all that, she was an ideal musician to talk over these ideas I had about new music, since she had seen every stage a musician can have.

I first asked Nancy, who was talking to me from her home in Santa Rosa, California, if she bought the notion that we were stuck on our favorite songs from decades ago and that we were really beyond being open to new music today. She said that the most loyal Heart fans are "wonderfully attached to these songs"—Heart classics, she meant, such as "Magic Man," "Crazy on You," and "Barracuda"—and that was part of the reason she did a lot of Heart songs in her current band, Nancy Wilson's Heart. Heart hadn't toured since 2019 when we spoke.

"The songs themselves, they create their own authenticity," Nancy said, "and they create memories and sense memories for you in your life, especially when you're a younger person. You know, your brain is just forming, and you're imprinting and grasping the stuff that's emotional. Because it's not easy to be a teenager. It's not easy to be a twenty-something or even a thirty-something. It's hard stuff. I mean, it's difficult emotional stuff to navigate. The songs are what I think help us navigate those years, and, you know, find our way through."

Finding songs now, of course, is an entirely different process from the time Heart was originally creating theirs. Nancy thought that the ability to buy albums with the press of a button had refashioned attitudes today about buying and listening to new music.

"There used to be a cultural identity around, like—the new Beatles album would come out; you'd literally stand in line to be the first person at the store to get the album and take it home and put it on your turntable, you know?" She laughed—at far how away that felt, perhaps, or how quaint-sounding. But she believed something sacred had been lost in the very experience of getting new music.

"Now there's just so much, like, static that you just have to kind of deflect all the time because everything is overkill, and it's hard to know what to pick and choose from it all. Or if you care about any of it."

"But on the other hand," she said, "there's lot of newer stuff that I fell in love with." She was talking about *Folklore* by Taylor Swift, which came out in 2020—and its follow-up, *Evermore*. In fact, she had a lot to say about that Swift and *Folklore* in particular. "There's so much actual depth in those songs, and the songs are so well-crafted and performed and meaningful the way she puts them across," she said.

The Wilson sisters have always embraced the folkier side of themselves, and for all the hard-rocking songs Heart is known for, they also have their soft, acoustic ballads, such as "Dreamboat Annie" and "Dog and Butterfly" and "Love Alive." In Swift's pandemic-era *Folklore*, Nancy appreciated that Taylor had "gotten out of her pop self and had gotten into her classic, folk-rock self." She felt like Taylor had "sort of found a way to grow, I think, emotionally" with *Folklore*. The album gave Nancy "hope," she said:

> For me that was really vindication that music
> can survive and listeners can still hear the new
> stuff. So it's really lovely to see somebody like
> Taylor Swift win the cultural attention that [she]
> deserves, you know? A lot of stuff's very ice-
> cream-cone-pop music. It melts in ten minutes,
> and then it's gone. So what Taylor Swift has
> helped the culture realize is some things do stick.

Nancy, too, had produced a pandemic record—her first—in the form of *You and Me*, a 2021 album that had a few covers but also a range of new, enchanting mid-tempo songs, and with Nancy's assured vocals, the songs were at least likely to appease Heart fans. She was really pleased with how the album came out, but she acknowledged the challenge it had in today's marketplace.

Now she was working on a new Heart song. It wasn't clear if this new song, she explained, was going to lead to a new Heart album, though she thought it could, or maybe there'd be a new live album down the road with some new music sprinkled in. But she and Ann were in talks for a big tour in 2024 then, and they both liked the idea of having a couple of new songs possibly to play. For Nancy and Heart, a couple of new ones might just be enough.

The new song, which she was calling "North Star," "is kind of an exercise in, you know, tipping my hat to the structure of Heart music as it existed in the past, as well as tipping the hat to the new generation of Heart fans that have been showing up in droves the last few times we've been out. So I think the stuff from the past also informs the [new] stuff that the new generation might respect or admire."

Nancy was sympathetic, though, to the older fans who just wanted to hear all the Heart songs they already knew— songs that came out when the Fonz was skiing over a shark on *Happy Days* and before the discussion of politics was all embodied in Matt Gaetz's stupid, pinched face. She was in no way sick of the old Heart music, she told me. "They mean a lot to people. I still love playing these songs."

"Your fan base, they grow up with you, and they get older, and they have families, and they don't listen to a lot of new stuff anymore because their lives are pretty full. They want to put on those comfortable shoes and the comfortable sweatpants, you know, and watch their comfortable little show. Or listen to the comfortable music that they remember. So, I mean, there's no harm in that. It keeps those songs alive, too."

At this stage, it only made sense that Nancy had to prioritize legacy over the satisfaction that playing new music could bring. She and Heart have had a formidable career. Tours around the world, a slew of Top 40 hits and classic-rocks staples, over 30 million records sold. In the end, new music, whether it was

a luxury or an indulgence, might always be calling, but the
Wilson sisters had made plenty of great music already. They
had put in their time, and it had paid off amazingly. So if they
ended up performing just a couple of new songs on that new
tour, if it happened, they'd more than earned that right. The
fans might just applaud politely, or maybe they'd be really
moved by the new stuff. That was the thing: Until the music
got heard, if it did at all, you never really knew for sure.

In the weeks and months that followed my conversation with
Nancy Wilson, I felt all the more grateful for her insights,
since almost no other musician would speak with me. And
maybe that even made a certain sense: Essentially what I
was asking, in the emails I sent to the musicians directly or
their publicists or managers, was, *So I think no one wants to
hear any new music from you, and can we talk about that?* I
should point out that when you never hear back, you don't always know what the reasons are. Did the email ever even get
to that person? I reached out to a broad range of musicians,
from Beck to Metallica, Seal to Stevie Wonder, Aimee Mann
to Elvis Costello, Billy Joel to Carlos Santana, Kenny Loggins
to Neil Finn, Lucinda Williams to Sheryl Crow. Some of their
reps who got back to me said the artist was in the studio, or
getting ready to go on tour, and thus unavailable, and I have
no doubt some of them were. In other cases, the musicians
might have just thought the idea was preposterous, or stupid,
and rejected it outright. Who knows?

But some of the PR folks and managers confided in me. "The book sounds really great and close to my heart on the sentiment," wrote one when I first reached out. In the end he had to pass on behalf of his client. "Best of luck, it's a great idea for a book," he wrote.

"Very interesting premise—and one I agree with whole-heartedly," wrote a founder of his own PR firm when I'd asked to speak to two of his clients. "At some point about ten to fifteen years back, I just hit a wall with regards to new music. Like a hard drive that reached capacity."

But then no one from Spotify would talk to me, either. Or Sirius XM. Companies like that have big PR departments; their job is to deal with people like me. Was I getting at something they didn't want to acknowledge? That didn't really make sense to me, but as a journalist for more than twenty-five years who was used to getting people to talk to me eventually, I hadn't encountered anything like this before.

And that brings us to McDonald's, of all places, because I like to work at McDonald's. To be clear, I've never manned the fry station at the fast-food giant or been a Crew Team member. But I've had a long habit of going there to write—the combination of Wi-Fi and endless refills of Diet Coke keep me going. For the first six months I was working on this book I sometimes parked myself in a McDonald's booth in Pittsboro, North Carolina—a small town that happens to have a very tidy McDonald's featuring a leather couch I have never quite had the nerve to try out.

This McDonald's—and almost all of the McDonald's

I've ever spent multiple writing sessions in—gets plenty of young people coming in after school or sports practice, and they also get a lot of grandparents who are trying to kill an hour or so watching their grandchildren until the parents can take over again. That's a lot of people in their '60s and '70s, and at least here in Pittsboro they look for any point of connection to strike up a conversation. Construction crews on their lunch break, UPS workers, mothers with fussy toddlers, the white-collar workers unashamed to be stepping into a Mickey D's because the McRib is back. It's the American tableau united by golden arches: all people, all colors, all sizes.

I'm telling you this because this McDonald's plays music, as do most of the McDonald's I've ever stepped in. Music happens to be something I don't need from a McDonald's. There I'm at the mercy of someone else's ideas about good music, so that already puts me in a state. Plus, I like to listen to music when I want to really listen.

On the other hand, a McDonald's with no music makes it too easy to listen to other people's conversations. Do I want to hear why Lucille thinks Ronnie ought to take the job at the plant, or would I prefer yet another airing of "You Spin Me Round (Like a Record)" by Dead or Alive. OK, all it took was to type the name of that song. I'd rather hear at length Ronnie's inclination to hold out for something better. The pros and cons, how it impacts Lucille. Everything.

Theoretically, music at a McDonald's has to be playlist for all, right? Given the broad crowd that comes in each day, you'd think that the music being played in 2023 would be as general a mix imaginable—Beyoncé to the Band, Rhianna to Reba McIntyre, the Wallflowers to Morgan Wallen, Puff Daddy to Poison—the aural equivalents of a menu that includes the Big Mac, the Egg McMuffin, the Shamrock Shake, McNuggets, a McFlurry, and the everlasting Filet-of-Fish. But curiously—and then, not curiously at all—in this McDonald's it's all '80s music all the time. Maybe it wasn't even surprising that the most visited restaurant on the planet wasn't playing a single song from this century.

I was pondering all of this when the Power Station's "Some Like It Hot" came on. The Power Station featured two members from Duran Duran—bassist John Taylor and guitarist Andy Taylor—who, in 1984, apparently needed at least a creative breather from the day job. They first recruited drummer Tony Thompson, who had toured with David Bowie and had a long run with Chic; Thompson knew all about the groove. Eventually they asked got Robert Palmer to carry the singing duties; this was some months before he had the biggest hit of his career with the hooky but deathly repetitive "Addicted to Love."

The best thing about "Some Like It Hot" is John Taylor's funk-slapping, rumbling bass line and Thompson's drums, which come off as sonic thunder claps. The melody is only serviceable, and lyrically it's pretty typical of throw-away '80s fare:

Some like it hot, but you can't tell how hot 'til you try
Some like it hot, so let's turn up the heat 'til we fry

Still, the song had some seductive shimmer, and on the *Billboard* Hot 100 chart it reached as high as No. 6. But as I think of it, it's just one more '80s song that inexplicably never faded away.

When the song came to an end, I decided to write down what followed. Maybe I was testing myself to see how easily I could identify the songs—I did, after all, go through high school and college in the '80s—but maybe I wanted to make a point I couldn't yet articulate. In the weeks that followed, I found that I couldn't stop thinking about these songs—as a collection, as individual singles, what they mean today, and also what they don't. They all charted on *Billboard*'s Hot 100, so they were at least notable in one way. In some cases, in only that way.

After "Some Like It Hot," here is what followed:

"Cruel Summer" by Bananarama
"Time (Clock of the Heart)" by Culture Club
"Fresh" by Kool & the Gang
"Will You Still Love Me?" by Chicago

(In the '70s, Chicago's distinct sound was anchored by its hard-swinging horn section and Terry Kath's flowing guitar lines, but by the '80s, with Kath having inadvertently killed himself with a gun in 1978, their music got dressed up in a pastel suit. It's not easy to go from "25 or 6 to 4" or "Does Anyone Really Know What Time It Is" to the treacly greeting card "Will You Still Love Me?" but this one, as the lead single from the band's fifteenth album, was a smash for them. Old Chicago fans might not have still been loving them, but plenty of others did.)

"When Doves Cry" by Prince
"Don't Know What You Got" (Till It's Gone)" by Cinderella

(Heavy metal bands with pop tendencies were a huge part of '80s music—Poison and Mötley Crüe made it work better than their contemporaries, but most others didn't have comparable songwriting chops. Some of the most popular hits in this genre were the tender power ballads, which seemed to exist so that in the videos, as in this one, one of the members could be passionately playing the piano out in nature while wearing a headband.)

"I Want a New Drug" by Huey Lewis and the News
"The Politics of Dancing" by Re-Flex
"Just Like Heaven" by the Cure
"Wild, Wild West" by The Escape Club
"Everybody Have Fun Tonight" by Wang Chung

(The lyrics of this one feature the band's name as a verb: "Everybody Wang Chung tonight." We can be thankful that this was an idea that bands before or after Wang Chung never fully embraced, as we were never asked to Foghat, to Yo La Tengo, or to Crosby, Stills, Nash & Young anything.)

"When I Think of You" by Janet Jackson

"If You Leave" by Orchestral Manoeuvres in the Dark

"No One is to Blame" by Howard Jones

"Chains of Love" by Erasure

"Pink Houses" by John Mellencamp

(If you listen to "Pink Houses" and Mellencamp's output from this century, his vision—musically and lyrically—has been remarkably consistent. The rootsy strumming acoustic guitars, the handclaps and gospel-inflected background singers, the storytelling and social and political commentary informing the lyrics. Mellencamp meant "Pink Houses" to be a more biting reflection on the state of the country—not a celebration of America. It's been misunderstood in the same ways Springsteen's "Born in the USA" has been. Whatever we can say about the '80s, we weren't exactly at our sharpest.)

"White Wedding" by Billy Idol

"Walk of Life" by Dire Straits

"Just a Gigolo/I Ain't Got Nobody" by David Lee Roth

(Hearing the singer of such Van Halen classics as "Runnin' With the Devil" and "Atomic Punk" doing this kind of vaudeville schtick was sad enough back in the '80s, but yet another airing of this mashup of two songs, written in 1929 and 1915, respectively, and originally put together and performed by Louis Prima—was that much harder to confront in 2023. "Sad and lonely, Sad and lonely" indeed.)

"The Finer Things" by Steve Winwood
"Magic" by the Cars
"Walking on Sunshine" by Katrina and the Waves

(As with any decade, the '80s had a plethora of one-hit wonders, and the emphasis on visuals led to signing so many acts who were as colorful as an ice cream store but had no capacity for writing music people wanted to hear over the course of even a brief career. If you were going to only have one major hit, though, as this band did, you could be proud to have a song that worked so earnestly to make people smile. From the opening snappy drum kickoff to the singer Katrina Leskanich's little yelp, the song jumps into joy right from the start and never lets up. "Sunshine" is simple a celebration of being loved: "I feel alive / I feel the love / I feel the love that's really real." Unfortunately for Katrina and the Waves, America only loved them this one time, but the song's afterlife has been extraordinary. This song has shown up in a plethora of movies, TV shows, and commercials promoting everything from Claritin to Fisher Price toys, Nescafé Original to Applebee's, and been covered by other artists—including Dolly Parton. It's as widespread as sunshine itself.)

"Nothing's Gonna to Stop Us Now" by Starship

(Whatever else you say about this song, you can't argue that the boast of the song's title was insincere. Starship had previously been Jefferson Airplane and played Woodstock and helped define the trippy, darker sound of the late '60s with their psychedelic romp "White Rabbit." But by the time the band had morphed from Jefferson Starship into Starship and had made "Nothing's Gonna to Stop Us," they resembled the original band about as much as the 1968 New Jersey Americans ABA team resemble the 2024 Brooklyn Nets. Today, re-branded as Starship featuring Mickey Thomas—the vocalist who took on lead vocals for Jefferson Starship and stayed on with Grace Slick for what became Starship—carries on at casinos and state fairs near you because there are still people who will deliriously thrust their hands in the air at the first vocal cry of "We Built This City." Only reporting what's true.)

This block of songs—running just short of two hours—pretty much encapsulated what the '80s music scene was about. Madonna, Duran Duran, or the Eurythmics didn't materialize, or Springsteen, or Michael Jackson, but there were other '80s mega-acts to stand in for them. The list also captured how much English synth bands—Erasure, Orchestral Manoeuvres in the Dark, Escape Club—ruled the day.

A lot of acts in this set managed a long string of hits throughout the '80s, but for those that made it through the '90s and beyond that string had ground to a halt. As I researched all these artists, I was amazed to learn how many of them still existed in some incarnation today. Seven of the bands seemed to be defunct. Of course, Prince was no longer with us, and Ric Ocasck and Benjamin Orr of the Cars were also dead, so the Cars were off the road for good. David Lee Roth performed last in 2020, and while Steve Winwood hadn't toured in a few years, he would be opening for the Doobie Brothers in 2024. Otherwise, the rest of these acts were touring the summer of 2023. Far fewer had released new music in a long while, but that only made sense. Touring was how they made a living at this point. Still, learning that this many of the acts I heard that day in McDonald's were still around to tour was like learning that *Alf* was into its thirty-eighth season.

Within that list of songs, there were, as I hear them now, several songs that transcend the decade and hold up really well today—songs that we should hear alongside classics from other eras. "Pink Houses," "When Doves Cry," and "Walking on Sunshine," for example, aren't hampered by the sound of '80s production values. In the '80s new technologies in music were often prioritized over the craft of songwriting. Synthesizers, for example, such as the Yamaha DX7, were a ubiquitous tool in the studio—and pumped out those drone-like bass lines that were everywhere in the decade. Sampling had emerged, and the use of MIDI (Musical Instrument Digital Interface) equipment was becoming much more frequent as well. MIDI relied on its own "language" that allowed various pieces of equipment—computers, keyboards, samplers—to be connected and talk to each other, sending messages in code and triggering sounds. One of the benefits of MIDI that was that it made music editing easier than ever before.

And drums had never sounded bigger or punchier than they did in the '80s. The technique known as gated reverb—which was first employed when Phil Collins was playing on Peter Gabriel's album commonly referred to as *Melt*, made the drums sound like the footsteps of Godzilla, and that style of recording drummers was rampant throughout the decade. Electronic drums had reached a new level of viability as well. And there was a leap in drum programming—drum machines that both replicated familiar drum sounds and patterns and created new ones. (You can listen to those songs from that McDonald's list and guess pretty accurately how many don't feature a live drummer.)

Vocals were doused with a ton of reverb and delay in the '80s, which, added to some of these other technologies, could give the music an even more synthetic feeling. Plus, the singing itself was often incredibly dramatic—beseeching choruses that came blaring out of the speakers like air raids. All of these elements led to the big '80s sound. And even through the often-crappy speakers of boom boxes of the decade the music sounded dynamic.

Technologies in music kept advancing, of course, but because of those advancements, the music of the '80s often feels like a musical daguerreotype to me—it can possess its own beauty, but I find a lot of it to be really hard on the ears.

That set of songs at McDonald's also served as a reminder to be grateful that the '70s music hadn't been hampered by the obligation of music videos. Imagine if Steely Dan had had to clown around bug-eyed in videos for "FM" or "Deacon Blues," like Hall and Oates did, or if Carole King had been all dolled up for a video to promote "Will You Love Me Tomorrow." Thankfully we just have the experience of those songs as songs.

On the one hand, hearing all those '80s songs at
McDonald's was like hanging out at a McDonald's back in
the '80s, which, inevitably, did stir up memories of my teenage years. And on some days that's a more welcomed set of
memories to tap into than others. But more importantly, that
afternoon would have been like going into McDonald's in the
'80s and hearing these songs from the 1940s:

"This Land is Your Land" by Woody Guthrie

"Pennsylvania 6-5000" by Glenn Miller and His Orchestra

"Boogie Woogie Bugle Boy" by the Andrews Sisters

"Pistol Packin' Mama" by Al Dexter and his Troopers

"As Time Goes By" by Dooley Wilson

"I'll Be Seeing You" by Bing Crosby

"Paper Doll" by the Mills Brothers

"(I Love You) For Sentimental Reasons" by the Nat King Cole Trio

"Some Enchanted Evening" by Perry Como

"Mairzy Doats" by the Merry Macs

"Let the Good Times Roll" by Louis Jordan

"Love Somebody" by Doris Day and Buddy Clark

"The Gypsy" by the Ink Spots

"Lover Man (Oh, Where Can You Be?)" by Billie Holiday

"The Honeydripper" by Cab Calloway

"Just Kidding Around" by Artie Shaw and His Orchestra

"Why Don't You Do Right?" by Peggy Lee

Where was Beyoncé or Ye, before he became unhinged, or Jack White or Green Day or Harry Styles or Miley Cyrus or Adele or Coldplay or Taylor Swift? Where were Lizzo and her flute, for God's sake?

Matt Ingold is the director of operations for that McDonald's, and five others in the area, and when I reached him by phone and asked why all the '80s music, what I heard, in part, was one more reason I was in the process of moving back to North Carolina after almost twenty-five years of living just outside of Washington, D.C.

"Yes sir, I'm with our technology gentleman right now that's with our organization. Gimme one second."

"OK," I said.

"And we're discussing that. But give me one minute and we'll have an answer for you, OK?"

I could also add I was moving back to North Carolina for the barbecue, and there would be truth in that, too, but really, you can't beat a civility like Mr. Ingold's, of which there is no shortage in this fine state.

That's what I was thinking during that moment of waiting, and then Matt came back on the phone and said, "Okay, very good. So I got some clarity on it. I wanted to make sure I had some information correct before I called you back. So we have Mood Media. So right, so it's not just our radio station or anything we pick up locally. It's Mood Media. We pay for the service. And there's multiple different selections with Mood Media. And that's probably just the one that happened to be programmed in first when we set it up. And it's located in our office, out of reach of our crew and managers. So they really don't mess with it. But there is an option that you can select '50s music, '60s, '70s, '80s, '90s music, etc. Or I believe on there there's just a mix of songs. So that one might be better for us to choose. I'll be happy to have our technology guy with our organization take a look at it and just do more of a mix within the store."

I was alarmed that Matt thought I had reached out in complaint, so I assured him the reason I'd called him was purely anthropological. And I ventured, perhaps to eliminate any sense of judgment, that my experience was that '80s music seemed to be a great comfort for people—even for people who were born in the 2000s, though I spared him why I was also so confounded by that.

"Yeah, absolutely, David," Matt said. "That's 100 percent right. It just happened to be when we set it up—that's sort of been there for a number of years. It's probably been on that one the whole time. I can just tell you this: We haven't had any complaints from it, so as long as you're OK with it, we're going to keep it as is."

To be clear, Matt Ingold said that last part without a hint of sarcasm or irritation. He told me he appreciated that I'd reached out and thanked me for calling.

I wanted to talk to corporate McDonald's about how they saw music in relationship to their restaurants, but they wouldn't return my calls or emails. Still, the way the McDonald's in Pittsboro was set up was how most of McDonald's in the country seem to be set up—with franchise owners left to handle such matters, as long as they're working with Mood Media. There was no reason to think that some of the McDonald's didn't play today's hits. I just hadn't found one yet that did.

A few months after that, Kim and I bought a house that was still close to that McDonald's, but there was another one even closer, in Chapel Hill, and I found myself setting up shop in that one just as regularly. That one plays only '70s music.

◎ ◎ ◎

Of course, it was entirely possible this lens I had, this conviction that we didn't really want to hear new music anymore, wasn't just unreliable, but entirely wrong. Or maybe there was just another way to see it, and if so, that other way would be valuable for me to hear. When I'd last spoken to Ben, the former music critic for *The New York Times* and the author of several books on music, we were talking about Peter Frampton's talk box and the ways its use on the live version of "Do You Feel Like We Do" had changed the trajectory of Frampton's career. When I caught him this time, at his home in the Bronx, New York, he was telling me about a new book he was writing—about listening to music when running and how, during the pandemic, while running and listening, he was hearing music with more clarity than he ever had before.

Ben sure wasn't listening to the songs I'd become so irritated by during these runs—no Thomas Dolby's "She Blinded Me With Science," no Cher's "If I Could Turn Back Time"— so first I wanted to know if he thought the long afterlife of those '80s songs is as problematic as I do.

Because Ben teaches classes on music and cultural criticism at NYU and interacts with young people all the time, he was a little more hopeful than I was about "our" relationship with the current music and music in general. "I want to believe that people are more interested in the present," he told me. Still, he wasn't dismissing that there were challenges to being open to the music being created today, but he sketched out a much larger context than I'd thought of. "So one thing is that this is an unsettling time in human history," he said. "And so, there's a lot of discussion right now around how people in general seem to be having a harder time imagining the future, or any future, than they did in the past. You know, which has to do with war, and natural resources, and capitalism, and stuff like that. I guess if you can't naturally and automatically imagine a future, then that means you can't get excited about a future. Which means that you only have one choice, which is to go backwards and get excited about your past."

He didn't think that theory had only to do with music, though, and mentioned that there had been a lot of books published recently that were essentially about rereading: memoirs in the form of books about books, what we can learn about ourselves about the books from the past. "But there does seem to be this reflexive tendency toward looking at your own path as a listener," he said. He thought that could lead to an overly tender kind of reflection, and "I worry that the tenderness becomes a bit morbid." All this got him thinking about the British author Mark Fisher, a scholar and music writer whose deeply influential blog, *k-punk*, examined the culture at large.

Fisher killed himself in 2017. "His argument was that nothing was new anymore and there was a reason for that. And that was because people couldn't envision a future."

Then he asked a question that particularly interested me: "What would it mean to hear a new song, or a new musician who really excites us and makes us, like, want that in our regular rotation? As opposed to, you know, an old Neil Young record?" I thought about new bands or artists I'd gotten onto this century, and my mind first went to the National, who formed in 1999 and who had put out two studio albums in 2023. When it comes to music I gravitate toward, it's always the music first, and lyrics tend to be low down on the list of what's important to me. The way I see it, I have literature to turn to for words and ideas and storytelling, but you don't hear a great Duane Allman solo by reading *The Sun Also Rises*. The National's songs, though, get my attention for the moody baritone of Matt Berninger and the lyrics' sharp sense of imagery—someone talking to a shark in Kentucky aquarium; a love interest driving her car into a garden and apologizing to the vines.

(In May 2023, the National's album *First Two Pages of Frankenstein* debuted at the No. 14 position on the *Billboard* 200 chart. The following week it had plunged to No. 186.)

Ben said, "If I'm hearing new work by somebody who's new to me and I feel very excited about it and I want to listen to it again and again, it's a little bit more than just scratching an itch and finding satisfaction. I think that I'm imagining being part of a listenership just starting. You know? That has not become closed. So in a way it is a kind of imagining a future—a future in which you join the listenership of this musician. And you don't even know who the other listeners are yet. You're just like, *Wow. They must be out there. They're my new people.* And it's a very future-y kind of thought, you know? It fills you with hope."

Nancy Wilson had also talked about finding hope through today's music. Was that a comment specifically about today's music, I wondered. Or as two people who had devoted their lives to music—albeit in very different ways—maybe it was only natural that as they got older, like the rest of us, they wanted to believe that music could still go in some exciting new directions.

I wanted to think about the future of music, too, but the hold of music from the past had me asking more questions. Take a song like "Don't You (Forget About Me)" from 1985 by Simple Minds. It was one of endless examples I could throw out of a song that I didn't dislike—that I thought was perfectly fine—but was it natural that I heard it as often as I did? Should I hear that song out in public so much more than I do, say, "Loser" by Beck (1993), which still sounds so fresh and original and unlike any other song I know—although I guess a lot of stores like Target might not be high on a chorus that goes: "I'm a loser, baby, so why don't you kill me."

"I mean, like, the whole country was just drenched in that song," Ben remembered of "Don't You." He wasn't quite as leery of the song as I was, though. "It's an evocative song," he offered, but then said, "I mean, the degree to which it's evocative may not equal the degree to which it's good."

"Don't You" was a huge song for one of the most decade-defining movies of the '80s, *The Breakfast Club*. (Have you ever checked into an Airbnb and *not* seen *The Breakfast Club* on a shelf of DVDs?) But did we possibly hear it so much because so many people are endlessly nostalgic about that movie, and in hearing that song, they are really reliving what it was to watch that movie for the first time—and then over and over?

"I don't know if anybody is raising their hand and saying, 'We want to hear Simple Minds,'" Ben added. "Do you? I mean, isn't that decided for us?" By that he meant, "The reason that we keep hearing it in banks and stuff is, you know, because somebody keeps putting it on a list of songs that customers like." Data sets, he meant. "Based on their age, their income bracket, their blah, blah, blah. It doesn't sound to me like anybody actually, you know, did interviews with normal people and said, 'What are the songs you love to hear when you're in the bank?' It just sounds like the result of data crunching and old data."

He wasn't sure, of course, that it was an algorithm and said it could be a music-furnishing service of some kind that, for the theoretical bank, focused on mood and tempo. That got us on a discussion of Muzak, and Ben cut to—and possibly through—the heart of these ideas. He was reflecting on what it was like to be young again, as Nancy did, and simply have the time to just absorb yourself in something, to be so immersed as to go into your room, close the door, and just listen and listen. "But after you round the corner of your mid-twenties or whatever, you have less of that self-absorption time."

This got him thinking of his mother-in-law, who was in her eighties, and he imagined the music she most wanted to hear probably predated 1962. So wasn't this just what happened with every generation, he wondered. Was I really describing some shift in the time-honored impulses?

I made my case. "I am basing it on how those songs follow me wherever I go," I concluded. "And I think: Why haven't they been replaced by like, the song that was Song of the Year in 2004?" I wasn't remembering what song that was when I said that, but I looked later, out of curiosity: That song happened to be, well, "Dance With My Father," by Luther Vandross and Richard Marx. And I might have given another example if I had realized that, since I didn't want that song following me, either.

Ben thought about that—not "Dance With My Father"—and said, "The fact that so much of America and its culture is calibrated to our own interests" maybe all played into it. If Amazon saw that you bought this CD, then surely you would like this one. If you followed this music writer on Twitter, he explained, then she's going to keep telling you about *this* particular kind of music she's known for writing about, but probably not a lot about any other music outside of her purview. It had, Ben believed, become numbingly easier to find yourself siloed based on your earliest expressed interests than to be exposed to something fresh. "I do think that's a big change," he said. Earlier generations had their challenges, but this was a monumental one.

This led him to what he characterized as an ugly thought. "Every once in a while I get in a snit, and I do think new music sucks. 'It's just bad, man.' You know? It's like, 'I don't care. It's not good anymore.' I will get in that mood every once in a while, even though it's stupid." And that thought, when it comes, takes him to this idea: That for all the music from the '90s that maybe felt corporate or, as he put it, "rolled out," for "all the evil that record companies have been a part of, they did build very meticulous products, with a certain kind of quality control." He was talking about that stretch of music in which artists who were either very new on the scene or who, in the studio, hadn't really hit their zenith yet and were paired with notably seasoned producers. He was thinking of such pairings as Alanis Morrissette and Glen Ballard for *Jagged Little Pill*, Bob Rock and Metallica for the *Black* album, Butch Vig and Nirvana's *Nevermind*, Steve Lillywhite and the Dave Matthews Band's for *Under the Table and Dreaming* and *Crash*, Mutt Lange and Shania Twain for the colossal *Come on Over*, and Rick Rubin and the Red Hot Chili Peppers' *Blood Sugar Sex Magik*. Those were all some of the biggest albums of the '90s, and whatever you thought of the music, it was undeniable how good it all *sounded*— how bright and clear and sharp and just how *attended to* each song felt in the production, in the very execution of everything that made up those tracks.

A "weird sort of top layer of wisdom being placed on the music that came out," is how Ben described that period. And given how much the big labels had fallen apart or were in such decline since, he ventured, "I wonder if what you're saying is a result of that change." That is, maybe our current era of music didn't sound as big and as smartly realized and put together as others had, that the artists didn't have the songwriting toughness or the producers to hold them accountable as maybe they needed to. And, as a result, if the music of this era was failing by these measures to be as impactful, there was a reason it wasn't showing up alongside the old go-to's. It was a theory, at least.

Where Taylor Swift's *Folklore* had wowed Nancy Wilson, Ben pointed to Beyoncé's 2022 *Renaissance* as the kind of release that could keep him believing in the future of music. For Ben, "Those songs are just stuffed with fascinating detail. It's so meticulous. There's so much for your ear to grab onto."

With that, Ben said, "Then here we are, back to the idea of the future. The idea of the future is a projection of time."

After we talked, I started reading Mark Fisher, at Ben's recommendation, and here is one idea that really stood out. "The fact is that nothing ever really dies, not in cultural terms," Fisher wrote in his *k-punk* blog in January of 2006. "At a certain point—a point that is usually only discernible retrospectively—cultures shunt off into the sidings, cease to renew themselves, ossify into Trad. They don't die, they become undead, surviving on old energy, kept moving, like Baudrillard's deceased cyclist, only by the weight of inertia."

I didn't originally follow the last part, though—I had no idea who Baudrillard was, so I looked him up. Jean Baudrillard was a French sociologist and a cultural theorist. He wrote a lot about postmodern society, and in his work he focused on this notion of "hyperreality," in which we become unable to distinguish reality from the simulation of reality. But who was the deceased cyclist? Fisher was referring to a 1902 novel, *The Supermale*, by French writer Alfred Jarry, and one of the plot points in that book is a 10,000-mile bicycle race, including a team of five cyclists, and during the race one of the cyclists dies from exertion, presumably. But instead of falling off, the dead cyclist stays on the bike and just keeps going from the momentum—and in fact passes the other team members. Why Fisher referred to that character as Baudrillard's cyclist versus Jarry's, I'm not sure, but Jarry, a philosopher who had his own critiques of French society, was an influence on Baudrillard. Anyway, the larger point Fisher was making was about carrying on like a zombie—dead but not dead. Old energy keeping the parts going.

I could see us all on that bicycle, pedaling away as the Walkman's headphones pressed into our demised ears the sounds of Loverboy's "Hot Girls in Love."

As it turned out, my friend Bob Funck had a new gig to play. It was at a tiny club called The Cave, in Chapel Hill, which bills itself as the town's oldest bar. Since its opening in 1968, it's become a legendary haunt in the state. The Avett Brothers, Arcade Fire, R.E.M., Superchunk, and Lyle Lovett had all apparently played there early in their careers.

Bob greeted me outside his house in flannel pajama pants

and a T-shirt that read, "Los Pollos Hermanos"—the famed chicken restaurant in *Breaking Bad*. Inside the modest living room his coffee table was crowded with vapes, loose change, a candle, a lighter, a plate with ashes, and a small speaker. On his mantle was a sculpture of a Native American looking grimly out into the distance, and a lamp with a Native American man riding a horse. There were three books up there, and I was moved—but also a little sheepish—to see that two of them were ones I'd written.

It had been seven years since I'd accompanied Bob on that tour he put together, and he figured he hadn't played more than twenty shows since then. He'd played a couple of shows in Raleigh a year ago at the same establishment—a "noisy, chatty, socializing kind of place, you know." And one baby shower.

The Cave gig had come about because a musician friend was booked to play there with his band and recommended Bob for the opening act. Bob hadn't put out any new music since releasing his first CD in 2015, *Waitin' for the Rain*—under the moniker of the Bob Funck Band and which he'd financed himself: This wasn't for lack of material, though. He had a bunch of new songs he wanted to record—this time just him on acoustic guitar and vocals. He didn't have the money to finance studio time to record them, though, so he decided he'd go the DIY route.

A couple of years ago he'd outfitted the room off his living room for recording. He had a four-track and eight-track mixer in there, along with a tangle of chords, an amp, two other guitars, and speakers. On the walls he'd affixed foam pieces to help with the sound, and he'd spent a lot of time, in fact, getting the room ready for this recording. But a problem hovered over him—quite literally: A family lived upstairs. Bob had great affection for the family, though only the daughter spoke English, and so his interactions with her parents consisted mostly of waves of the hand and simple greetings. The mother sometimes made dinner plates for him. But the family was almost always home, and Bob was forever hearing their footsteps on the hardwood floor as they went from room to room. And he worried that this would mar the recordings. He'd tried to record here and there when he thought they'd left for a while, but then they'd come back again, and he eventually gave up.

The songs were going to get a proper airing at the Cave, though—a venue no bigger than Bob's living room and the small room with his recording equipment, and with a ceiling so low it could make people feel claustrophobic immediately.

Over the purr of a window-unit air conditioner, Bob said he was still tidying up the new music—he hoped he could play about ten songs during his set, and seven of those would be new. With two nights before the show, though, there was a new worry. "My voice is fucked," he said. Summer allergies were taking their toll.

Still, he was eager to perform again, though he wasn't honestly sure what kind of audience he'd have, since he was the opening act on a bill of three. The main act, Fleabath, was a D.C. band that, on its website, referred to itself as "Primordial, ragtag, and firing on all cylinders." They were promoting their EP *F Is For*. That crowd wasn't exactly Bob's ideal audience.

For now, all he could do was hope that some friends would turn up at the Cave. A few of them might have heard a couple of these songs here and there, as I had, but otherwise, if there was a crowd when he kicked off, they'd be hearing them for the first time. But Bob had no manager, no label, no audience to speak of. No message board on Reddit devoted to him with posts like, "Is Bob Funck ever going to release a new album. WTF?"

What he did have, though, was a deep need to keep writing new songs, as he had been—especially during the last few years. There was no telling if he'd ever get them recorded and put them out in the world in the usual ways—Spotify, Apple Music, etc. If he did, someone who played James Taylor's *Greatest Hits* or Joni Mitchell's *Blue* on Amazon Music wasn't going to get a recommendation that said if you liked James Taylor or Joni Mitchell, you might enjoy Bob Funck. Bob was realistic about that. But he wrote new music because that's what singer-songwriters do.

Yes has always been my favorite band. Founded in 1968, Yes was one of the leading progressive groups out of England; along with cohorts such as Genesis and Emerson, Lake & Palmer, they created elaborate, intricate music that owed more to classical music than the blues-based rock that came before them. Yes's lyrics were no more conventional than their music and tended to deal with such pop staples as, well, harmonic convergence, the seeking of knowledge, and the power of the sun.

Just to give you a sense of just how deeply Yes's music runs for me, I once wrote for *The Washington Post* about listening to a new box set of seven full Yes concerts culled from three weeks during their 1972 *Close to the Edge* tour, and each of those shows had the exact same set list. The collection offered more than twelve hours of performances—and I listened to all of it in one day.

"As I'm driving," I wrote toward the end, having taken to the road late that night for the last recording, "I am having the most intense listening experience of my life. To my fellow drivers, it might look like I am trying to dislodge something from my throat. [Steve] Howe is positively shredding it in the final bars, and I am pumping my arm in ecstasy. I am 48 years old, and rock music—Yes music—has never felt more vital to me than it does in this moment. I am 16 again, 22, 30. And I am also 75. Yes has been the biggest musical constant in my life—and always will be."

These days, Yes has no original members left, though guitarist Steve Howe played on all the seminal Yes records of the 1970s—*The Yes Album*, *Fragile*, and *Close to the Edge*, among them, and in concert today, there are few songs they play that aren't taken from those three albums. He wasn't in Yes when they made their comeback with "Owner of a Lonely Heart" on their *90125* album in 1984 (when he was away from Yes, he played in the band Asia), but since then Yes had gone through more lineups than *Cats*. Howe was back in the fold by 1995, and now with singer Jon Anderson out of the band for going on sixteen years, and bassist Chris Squire and longtime drummer Alan White having passed away, Howe *was* Yes, essentially.

I'd interviewed Anderson, Squire, and White before, but when Steve came on the screen in a Zoom session in rural England, I got a little verklempt. In our conversation, Steve, dressed in layers, with a corduroy jacket on and sitting in what appeared to be a cellar, echoed some of the things Nancy Wilson told me, but unlike Heart, whose recording future was at least uncertain, Steve had Yes continually creating new music under his watch—they'd released three studio albums in the last ten years.

I started off by saying, "We have such emotional connections to the music from earlier parts of our lives, and as we get older, we're not allowing the possibilities of the same kinds of connections. So that's the premise—that's the book. And first, I would love to just hear what you think about that because you may disagree completely."

He nodded in agreement. "I'm with you on both sides," he said. "I mean, when we're in our teens, you know, we pick up a lot of the music that we'll always like, and then in the twenties you kind of, like, get a bit broader, and you think: *Hey, you know, that's nice! That's nice!* So you get this lovely well of music. But you're right, when you get to forty and fifty, you start thinking: *Oh, this new music that's coming out is a bit like*"—he laughed—"*it's a bit disappointing.*

It's not for me. You know, it's for the people who are, um, fifteen to twenty-five, say, just to generalize." He thought about that, then added wistfully, "And I still love much of the music that I got involved with, you know, from *fifteen to twenty-five*."

He then said Yes had a new record coming out that spring, and he was hopeful about that, though certainly realistic. Of the Yes fans still with the band, he said he was "hoping they won't turn to what we call a blind ear to—" the album, and laughed again. "You know?"

"We're still under the appraisal that the '70s music was some of the greatest Yes music that we can ever make," he said. "We were young whippersnappers, and we were very adventurous. We were ambitious, and we were fairly talented. So we basically put all that together and kind of created sort of a—almost something we've got to hold on to. But that's not the case. It's not holding. I love playing that '70s music, too."

"In a way, we can't help being who we are," he said, then added, "which is a good thing." When you've toured all over the world, influenced legions of musicians—in Yes's case, from Rush to Tool to Dream Theater, Phish, and the Flaming Lips—and sold more than 30 million albums and have been inducted into the Rock and Roll Hall of Fame, you get to make such a declaration.

He got back to talking about the new album. The album itself was always a key concept for Yes—more so than most bands, I'd argue. I mean, in 1973 Yes released a double-album consisting of four twenty-minute songs, *Tales From Topographic Oceans*, whose central concept was based on a footnote in *Autobiography of a Yogi* by Paramahansa Yogananda. Not exactly the stuff of 45s. Then Steve paused to reflect on how much the state of the album had morphed in this century. "The idea of an album got lost. 'What's an album?' I mean, you ask a young kid today. 'An album? What, forty minutes of music, or fifty minutes of music on a piece of vinyl, or even on a CD?'" He was acknowledging what we all know now—that it's about individual tracks, not albums as a whole. He was also lamenting this because Yes's records had always featured more elaborate and longer compositions alongside shorter pieces; different moods conjured from occasional acoustic passages woven into longer extended jams, all meant to be listened to in sequence as one big musical statement.

As Nancy remembered waiting in line to buy the new Beatles record, Steve remembered going into a record shop asking the salesclerk who the guitarist was playing on a particular Dizzy Gillespie record. (In that particular memory, it was Les Spann, who, Steve was amazed to learn, also played flute on that same album.)

"Yes are an album band," he said, "and our new record that's going to come out in May, it is attempting to break the barriers that restrict people from considering a whole event of music together." For Yes, that meant more epic tracks, like in the glory days of Yes—fourteen minutes for this one, he said, ten minutes for this one. "We've been here for over fifty years, so, you know, we're going to be around. We've proven that we've got a longevity. So what we do is only try better."

"We want to be seen as the musicians we are, that we can create something very vital right now, which maybe is quite unusual, you know?" It was heartening to hear Steve Howe, now at seventy-five, suddenly talking with the brashness of a young musician in a new band, insisting a record executive, or the buying public, give them a chance. "There is this stigma, and it's almost 98 percent true"—he laughed—"that the older bands won't have success with their newer records. It's usually very, very true. But there are exceptions to everything."

As I was asking Nancy, I wanted to know from Steve his thoughts on the other reality of recording new music—playing that new music for fans in concert. And here his view was quite aligned with Nancy's and Heart's. "Well, you know, we can always hope that this new album does have an effect, and in its own right it does stand out, and therefore there's a good chance we'll be playing more than one tune from it. So, you know, that's the way we look at it. You know, total optimism. Complete belief. It sounds overly egotistical, but as about as much belief as one can have"—he laughed—"we've got."

In the U.K album chart the new Yes album, *Mirror to the Sky*, peaked at No. 30, but plunged pretty quickly. In the U.S. it never cracked the top 200.

When I saw Yes in Greensboro, later that year, at a new and decidedly smaller venue, it was only at about two-thirds of the 3,000 capacity. (When I saw them in 1984, they filled

the Greensboro Coliseum, with more than 20,000 in atten-
dance. They also played all nine songs off the new album
that evening.) In 2023 they played just one new song from
the new album.

◎ ◎ ◎

Perhaps out of all the '80s artists who made it big, Tracy
Chapman was the one who sounded like she was plucked
from the '70s, or even the '60s. The African-American folk
singer went from playing the streets of Harvard Square to a
debut album, in 1988, that earned her three Grammys. The
concerns in Chapman's earnest, social-conscious lyrics were
so far removed from the songs dominating the airwaves then—
Def Leppard's "Pour Some Sugar on Me" or Billy Ocean's
"Get Outta My Dreams, Get Into My Car"—and her voice,
sometimes a whisper, sometimes the cry of an anguished an-
gel, wrapped around her acoustic guitar in ways that made her
seem like an important, but tentative, messenger from the past.
Chapman's "Fast Car" was an '80s song that never went away,
and we could be grateful for that.

In May of 2023, I read the latest blog by Bob Lefsetz, who
for a time worked in the entertainment industry as a lawyer
and now writes a popular blog about a range of issues in the
music business but also about the music itself and why it matters. He'd come across a Tik Tok video of country singer Luke
Combs in concert telling the audience what Chapman's "Fast
Car" had meant to him both growing up and ever since, how

he remembered his father introducing the song to him and Combs learning to play the song on guitar. The clip ends before he begins the actual song.

Lefsetz noted that "Fast Car," which Combs had recorded and released on his album *Gettin' Old* (if I was in the marketing department of Columbia's River House label, I'm pretty sure I'd have said in that initial meeting about the album's launch, "So, I'm just *wondering* if we could test a few possible other titles before we *definitively* say *Gettin' Old* is it"), was now huge on Spotify, and when I looked up his version, it had nearly 54 million streams—the second most on the album. (Chapman's original version had, impressively, nearly 676 million streams then.) But Lefsetz's larger point was how the companies that acquire publishing music rights "don't account for a cover of 'Fast Car' decades after its initial release when they value a catalog, they look at the past, not the future." The implication was that Tracy Chapman was missing out on what had become a goldmine for Luke Combs, though Lefsetz didn't interview Chapman. Lefsetz dismissed the aspect of nostalgia playing a role in the cover's success, asking, "What are the odds Combs's audience is familiar with it? Low. It's brand new to them!" Instead, Lefsetz was focused on lost opportunity in the music business.

I guess Leftsetz believed that Combs's fans were either too young to have heard "Fast Car" before or that because they're country fans, they couldn't possibly know a folky ballad that was a huge pop hit that was also nominated for Song of the Year, Record of the Year, and was one of the most iconic and distinctive songs of that decade. And maybe he's right. But I'm quite sure that Luke Combs fans once had parents who played for them music that they happened to like and grew up on, so I don't easily accept that that the song couldn't have been known previously to Combs's fans. I was born in 1967, but I know "Night and Day" by Cole Porter, Duke Ellington's "It Don't Mean a Thing (If It Ain't Got That Swing)," and "Isn't It Romantic?" by Richard Rodgers and Lorenz Hart—all of which came out thirty-five years before I was born—because they're also iconic songs.

Anyway, at least part of that little Luke Combs video was, for me, just another sign of the '80s grip, though, in this case, it was a cause I could get behind, since "Fast Car" is a transcendent song. Combs's version is practically a note-for-note copy, except for some layering of electric guitar, so as an homage, it felt a bit too on-the-nose. But if Lefsetz was right that none of those Luke Combs fans knew it, then good for Combs for shining a light on it.

What also got my attention in that Leftsetz blog was this little note about the number of streams for the song "Africa" by Toto: "Turns out 'Fast Car' is forever. Like Toto's 'Africa,' an afterthought on the album that has 1,423,651,528 Spotify streams in its original iteration, never mind the 75+ million of the Weezer cover and the multiple versions on YouTube. There's money there . . . A LOT of money." (In 2018, the band Weezer had put out their own version of "Africa," which appeared on Toto's 1982 album *Toto IV* and is among the crown jewels of soft-rock hits.) So was Weezer just having a laugh covering such a song? The catalyst was, according to *Vice*, a fourteen-year-old girl in Cleveland who played guitar in her own band and created an account called @Weezerafrica. She kept tweeting Weezer's official Twitter account about it, daring the band to record the song because, well, Weezer is to mockery what Led Zeppelin was to sex. Finally the band gave in. "i jokingly told weezer to cover africa and now it's my thing," the account boasted. NPR, in covering the story, wondered if the Weezer nod was, "ultimate evidence that life online has destroyed both logic and human intuition?"

The covers of "Fast Car" and "Africa" told two stories that made the same point: We couldn't escape the pull of '80s music, but we could go about it one of two ways. We could either embrace the reality of that with sincerity, as Luke Combs had, or we could smirk our way through it as Weezer had. With "Africa," Weezer had a song in *Billboard*'s Hot 100 for the first time in more than nine years, and their first No. 1 song on *Billboard*'s Rock Airplay Chart. It had 2.8 million streams in the week it was released. The video featured "Weird Al" Yankovic—of course it did—standing in and over-emoting for front man Rivers Cuomo—lest anyone miss the joke.

But the joke, really, was that we responded to it with such predictable nostalgic rapture. Having Weezer cover Toto was like James Earl Jones playing Fat Albert. Sure, they could do it, but what was the value in it? What we needed from Weezer was another great Weezer song. Instead, we got "It's gonna take a lot to drag me away from you."

◎ ◎ ◎

Jason Hanley, the vice president of education and visitor engagement at the Rock and Roll Hall of Fame, in Cleveland, had lots of thoughts about the grip of the '80s music in particular. And he both understood why I was a little obsessed with being so worn out by the same old songs, but also like Ben Ratliff, he was not as convinced that this was such an exception to what happens in music and in life with every generation.

Jason, fifty-two, had been at the Hall for eighteen years. He has a PhD in musicology. He spends his days overseeing the teams that provide a broad range of educational curriculums to students as well as the live music programming and onsite artists interviews that happens at the Hall. He listened patiently as I sketched out my thoughts about where we were in our relationship to new music today, as I kept adding more examples of my reasoning. Finally I said, "What do you say to that assertion?"

He laughed and said, "Whoo, David, that is a very good, loaded question! Because there are so many layers to it, right?" Then he dove in. "Music, in general, is an incredibly nostalgic art form. And there are scientists who have proven this." That much I knew by now, but Jason got to see how that manifested more than most, given where he came to work each day. "When you experience that nostalgic sort of euphoria over a song, it also brings back all of the memories, smells, tastes, touch, emotion that was connected to those moments in which that song became grafted on your neural consciousness. People will sit in the Rock Hall of Fame, at our exhibits, and hear the music and see the artifacts and story we're telling and cry and be emotional. It might remind them of a loved one who's passed on or key moments in their life."

As we began to talk about the '80s, Jason had other thoughts about the power of nostalgia. "Even at that time, there was this sense of nostalgia for the past. If you look, that's when the Rock and Roll Hall of Fame begins, in 1986, because it's looking to honor the previous generation of the greats of rock and roll. Elvis, Little Richard. And you get bands like the Stray Cats, who are saying, 'We're gonna play rockabilly.' Or you get Joan Jett covering Tommy James and the Shondells ["Crimson and Clover," from 1968]. A lot of covers. You had this way by which musicians in the '80s were also tapping into a nostalgia for a previous era and a previous generation, but they were doing it covering songs that would both connect them to maybe an older audience but also was generating new audiences at the same time."

"And think about songs that were written," he said. "I'm thinking Joan Jett, you know, 'I Love Rock and Roll.' 'Throw another dime in the jukebox.' Already by the '80s that was sort of an anachronistic thing to say. Or Billy Joel 'It's Still Rock and Roll to Me,' and it's him reminiscing about being a greaser and the whitewall tires he references in the lyrics, right? By the '80s, nobody had whitewall tires anymore."

He also pointed to the trend of artists from the '70s and '80s hitting the road and getting attention for playing whole albums—in sequence. Yes had done that in recent years, and Peter Gabriel had played *So* all the way through a few years ago. Seal was touring the summer of 2023 by playing all of his first two albums in the same way. I'd seen the Who play all of *Quadrophenia* back in 2012, and in their final tour, Pink Floyd performed all of *The Dark Side of the Moon*. The Doobie Brothers, Cheap Trick, The Cure, and Rush, too, among so many others, had played their classic albums and promoted their tours that way.

Jason said that sense of nostalgia had to be seen in the context of today, and what he meant by that was, "We are bombarded by the new." Back in 1981, for example, on a Friday night at 8:00 p.m., you had your choice of network shows to watch, and the options may have been dull, depending on your kind of television, but it wasn't exactly dizzying: NBC's *NBC Magazine With David Brinkley*, CBS's *The Incredible Hulk*, or ABC's *Benson*, and that was it. Now think of the choices you have today, between Hulu, Apple TV, Amazon Prime, Max, Netflix, an exorbitant array of cable channels, as well as the network options—at any time of the day or night. "There's a massive output of stuff—" in contrast to that earlier, monolithic culture "in which everybody watched Michael Jackson's premiere of [the] "Black or White" [music video] on television at the same time together," for example. "And that was the only new Michael Jackson album you might get for years," he added.

In other words, through today's lens, the media world of the '80s was hardly the blitzkrieg of stimulation that it is today, and so we could think of that time as being mercifully quaint. There was no Twitter, no all eighteen episodes of season three for a Netflix show that just dropped. No live streaming of anything, no deep fake videos. (And because his name came up when I searched deep fake videos to see if a hyphen was appropriate, and because he has had the audacity to publish more than ninety books, starting in the late '80s, I will also say: no Deepak Chopra, either.)

Jason was remembering the world premiere of "Black and White," which, when it debuted in 1991 in more than twenty-five countries simultaneously, was the largest premier of a music video, because everyone could watch it at the same time and talk about it the next day, and what came from that was a feeling of connectiveness. Maybe you loved it, maybe you hated it. Maybe you wanted to better understand why Michael was dancing with Zulu hunters in Africa. But the next day it wasn't being dissected in endless blogs and podcasts and social-media. Quieter times. As a reality, Jason was arguing that that was something people could be nostalgic about.

"I think because there's so much new music and so many different things," he said, "it can often be hard for people to find an entryway into that. Whereas in the past, there was only maybe a couple new records put out each week. And you picked the one you liked and you spent a lot of time with it."

That change has plenty of consequences for why today's music, even the best music, doesn't stay very present, unlike the neighbor who is always out in her front yard every time you step out your front door and waves a little too eagerly with each hurried jaunt you make to the car, who is always ready to resume the very same conversation about not very much and somehow manages to ask as you are managing a load of groceries, "Do you know what day they're supposed to pick up leaves from the street?" And yet we do take a certain comfort in knowing that that neighbor, despite being annoying sometimes, is always around. That neighbor, of course, is REO Speedwagon's "Keep on Loving You." Very unlike that really cool neighbor down the street who is so aloof, who doesn't seem to be around much at all anymore and—come to think of it, did she just move away completely? That neighbor, of course, is Lorde's "Royals."

It's because our daily life is so saturated—with everything—that Jason agreed with me that albums didn't have the same kind of cultural impact they did in the twentieth century. "The pace of society is so quick," he said. "We consume things at a rate that is unparalleled in the history of humanity. Where *Dark Side of the Moon* might've been the only album that I could afford in a six-month period." He laughed at how antiquated that felt in this age of Spotify.

Not only did we sit with the same albums for weeks and months, he was saying, but the way we listened had eroded, too. "I was sitting with someone the other day and listening to some music, and they immediately started skipping. I said, 'What are you doing?' They said, 'Well, the song's almost over.' I said, 'Yeah, but this album, like, listen to the end of this song and where it ends and the beginning of the next song.'" But apparently letting an entire song play through was asking too much.

But mostly Jason saw this draw the '80s music had on us as something we'd gone through before. "I do think that this happens every generation," he said. "I do think there's a sense of always looking back and a nostalgia for the past." Particularly from the twentieth century onward, "that rapid change of society, I think, has heightened that sense of nostalgia. And I think it's heightened it in a lot of ways."

Jason could see change coming in ways I hadn't. The boomer generation was, well, only getting that much closer to the Great Gig in the Sky. "I think the baby boomer generation held onto its youth for so long," he said, "and it dominated society with both its size and population and the culture, right? This is why people are still going to say the Beatles are the best band ever. I'm not going to argue with that—I love the Beatles. Now there is a sense that Gen-X is becoming the sort of elder generation as the baby boomers' culture is beginning to fade a little bit."

In that way, Jason was arguing, there could come the time when the Beatles are seen in an entirely different light than what we've always known—they could be viewed as less important, less influential, theoretically, than Pearl Jam, Kings of Leon, or Arcade Fire or Artic Monkeys. No one stayed on top forever.

"I think you will see that clock click forward," he said. "And at some point, you mentioned it's going to be the Gin Blossoms—" I had wondered earlier in our conversation if the companies that acquired artists' catalogs would eventually get around to '90s bands like the Wallflowers and the Gin

Blossoms—"and then it's going to even move its way forward beyond that. And I fully believe that in thirty years from now, McDonald's is going to be all Taylor Swift and The Weeknd." Can't wait!

Of all the bands or artists likely to produce new music in 2023, the Beatles and the Rolling Stones weren't exactly topping anyone's list. The Beatles broke up in 1970 and never reformed. With John Lennon killed in 1980 and George Harrison dying in 2001, even the most delusional fans didn't cling to hopes of new Beatles music.

And yet here it was in the form of the song "Now and Then." For the Beatles Anthology project that came out in 1995, Yoko Ono had given to the surviving Beatles three demos, on cassette, of John Lennon singing and playing piano sometime in the late '70s. With the capacity of audio technology at the time, George, Paul, and Ringo were able to take two of the songs, "Real Love" and "Free as a Bird," flesh them out musically and sing alongside their departed friend. All of this played out as something a bit miraculous at the time. The songs couldn't be compared with any of the Beatles' best music, or even the catalog's middle of the pack, but "Free as a Bird" won a Grammy in 1997, and both songs were hits in the U.S. and UK.

Though they'd tried, Paul, Ringo, and George hadn't been able to make the third song, "Now and Then," work because John's vocals were too inaudible over the piano. (Another version of the events is that Harrison simply disliked the song, calling it "rubbish," and didn't let it be completed as a Beatles song.) But as director Peter Jackson worked on his "Get Back" documentary—a greatly expanded and buoyant rebuttal spin to the original documentary that captured the making of the *Let it Be* album—based on all the footage shot for the original film in 1969, his crew had developed a technology that could isolate and extract individual parts of a piece of music and clean them up sonically so that they sounded remarkably clear. That technology gave Paul and Ringo a second chance at "Now and Then." Paul added a bridge in the middle; they rerecorded their parts (bass, drums, guitars, additional piano), kept George's guitar from the earlier session, and added some soaring strings, with Paul working in a slide guitar solo meant to conjure George's slide guitar work.

The lyrics are relatively simple by Lennon's standards— no elliptical word play, no quixotic imagery.

Similarly, the melodic structure of the song is straightforward as well—no "Strawberry Fields" leaps, no "Tomorrow Never Knows" epic ambitions. It begins with a series of A minor chords, and the song never sheds that heavy feeling of melancholy, despite the late-song orchestral swell. No Beatles' solo music, tellingly, sounded like the Beatles, and to my ears "Now and Then" still feels like a John Lennon song despite all the layers added to it; it's missing that Beatles majesty that Paul's and Ringo's playing couldn't ultimately give it. Still, "Now and Then" was the Beatles' thirty-fifth Top 10 hit on *Billboard*'s Hot 100 chart. Whatever your feeling about the song itself, its existence could feel like a wonder, or it could feel ill-advised or even indecent, given how it came be.

Meanwhile, the one true rival of the Beatles, the Rolling Stones, had survived all the decades the Beatles hadn't, and now in 2023 the Stones had a new full-length album, *Hackney Diamonds*, their first album of original songs in eighteen years. At least, "survived" seemed a fair way to put it, given the tragedy of Altamont, the drugs and the drug busts, the departures of Bill Wyman and Mick Taylor, the deaths of Brian Jones and Charlie Watts, all the tensions and endless fighting between Keith and Mick. In this century there had been just the one Stones album of original material, *A Bigger Bang*, in 2005. And that album had no legacy of its own and was quickly forgotten.

However, when the band released, in 2016, an album of blues covers, "Blue and Lonesome"—songs from their blues heroes, such as Howlin' Wolf, Willie Dixon, and Little Walter—the reviews were, on the whole, deeply admiring. "It's the most honest music the Stones have released in years," a review in Pitchfork read, "not because the source material confers it with the patina of authenticity, but because the entire blues-covers concept is a tacit admission that they don't really give a shit about being a contemporary concern anymore, so they're just going to do something that feels good." But then, for the Stones an effort like this was also about as arduous as blowing their noses.

Hackney Diamonds, on the other hand, was a chance to glimpse what was left between Mick and Keith as writers as well as performers in the studio. The album had plenty of guest appearances: Elton John unfurling some boogie-woogie piano on a couple of tracks. Lady Gaga belting it out and Stevie Wonder on a variety of keys bringing us to church on another. Bassist Bill Wyman was back for one song, appearing on one of the two tracks that had Charlie Watts's drums, recorded several years ago. Even Paul McCartney was on hand for bass on one track.

In fact, the Stones confirmed they were already working on a next album. The madness!

I was interested to hear what Mike Edison, author of *Sympathy for the Drummer: Why Charlie Watts Matters*, had to say about *Hackney Diamonds*, though, having read his book, I already had a suspicion what that might be.

Mike, who is also a drummer and music teacher, let me know he shared my disappointment that the Stones had moved on without Charlie. "I don't think it's the real deal at this point," he said of the trio of Mick, Keith, and Ronnie Wood carrying on as the Stones. "I think it's too far removed from the original." He also didn't believe that anyone could replace Charlie's incalculable spirit. On *Hackney Diamonds* Jordan's drumming "just didn't crack and snap, crackle and pop the way Charlie Watts always did," Mike lamented.

Given how much he loved the Stones of old, I asked him about the Stones recording new music in the first place. Was he even open to it?

"It would be a weird thing for me not to want new music—if they came out with something, I'm always going to listen to it," he said. Then Mike asked me whether I was familiar with the Jewish tradition of *Dayenu*. I wasn't.

It's a Hebrew word, he said. "It means: It would have been enough." *Dayenu* is a song traditionally sung at Passover, with fifteen verses, all expressing gratitude for fifteen gifts God bestowed on the Jewish people, but it's also a way of thinking and seeing. "It's like, wow, if God had [only] brought us to the promised land, it would've been enough," Mike explained, remembering one of the verses. "And if He had [only] given us the manna to feed us, it would have been enough," recalling another. "And if He had [only] gotten us out of slavery, it would've been enough." On and on the song goes. "It's like, all these blessings on top of all these blessings," Mike said.

Mike was telling me this because *Dayenu* was a way he thought of the Stones in their golden period—which informed, in part, how he considered the Stones' latter decades. He was reflecting, specifically, on their string of three albums, starting in 1969, that some people believe is the best string of three straight rock albums in history. Had it only been *Let it Bleed*, he said, "it would have been *Dayenu*." Next came *Sticky Fingers* in 1971. And then *Exile on Main Street* in 1972. Which was its own miracle, Mike said. To have an album like *Exile on Main Street* exist at all was, perhaps, supposed to temper our expectations for what else might have followed.

About *Hackney Diamonds*, Mike previewed his feelings about it by saying, "You know, maybe they're running out of miracles." He then went on to say that he had listened to the album and was thoroughly unimpressed. "Like, where's the swagger?" he asked. "Where's the danger, where's the sex?" He thought "the whole thing sounded plastic" and wished they "would just go in and make a rock and roll album," though many critics felt like they'd done that, frequently declaring it their best album since *Tattoo You*, in 1981. But Mike was undeterred.

What felt true to me was that it was impossible to hear either recording outside of the lens of nostalgia. Listening to "Now and Then" I could see George Martin's crisp suits and the Abbey Road crosswalk and Ringo playing in his girlfriend's coat during the rooftop concert and George's sitar and Paul's beard and hear John's "Julia" once more. But did we *need* this song? Did we need to be reminded of the Beatles as a brand? Their greatness? Was "Now and Then" truly good enough to exist as new Beatles music? Or was it simply good enough to keep the incredible love of and fascination with the Beatles going until the next Beatles project materialized, whatever that would be?

Likewise, *Hackney Diamonds* had plenty of echoes of the Stones' own astounding history. The crunchy riff by Keith on "Get Close" immediately conjures his opening riff on "Can't You Hear Me Knocking," or Mick's breezy vocals on the sweet shuffle of "Dreamy Skies" brought to mind his honeyed delivery on "Factory Girl."

Of course, Mick, Keith, and Ronnie had every right to do whatever they wanted to, and I admired that they had it in them to write and record new music. And unlike Mike, I had enjoyed *Hackney Diamonds*. But it was hard to conclude that all of this music didn't ultimately exist to take us backward. That felt especially true with the Beatles' "Now and Then," which was more about what technology could do versus searching for inspiration. At least the Stones were looking for that inspiration or had found it—depending on how you heard the record.

I kept thinking about what Mike told me about *Dayenu*, though. And what occurred to me, in trying to find a more optimistic way to think of the Beatles and Stones' new music— the blessings, if there were any—were that a new generation could, for the first time, hear new Beatles music and Rolling Stones music along with everyone else. Everything old kept finding ways to be new again—*that* wasn't the blessing—but maybe there was just a glimmer of *Dayenu* in young listeners experiencing new Beatles and Rolling Stones music on their own, contemporary terms. They weren't dependent on dad putting in a CD on the drive to school and then delivering a long lecture on Paul's slide solo vs. what George might have done with the solo, and maybe they could tune out Mom swooning to the track on the family road trip and declaring, "See, I don't care what anyone says—music today just doesn't have this kind of classic sound like the Beatles."

Instead, young people today could hear this music streaming on their devices alongside the latest from Beyoncé, Dua Lipa, Jack Harlow, Ariana Grande, Ice Spice. New Stones and Beatles music, or new-*ish*, for new listeners. Maybe that, too, in these confounding days of music, was enough.

◎ ◎ ◎

For reasons I couldn't yet articulate, I wanted Chris Richards, who had been the pop-music critic for *The Washington Post* since 2009, to be my last interview for this part of my exploration. I didn't know Chris terribly well, really, but I was a big admirer of his writing because within music—concerts, albums—Chris saw all of life's dramas playing out. In a review of a Rolling Stones concert in 2019, he was struck not just by the invincibility the four principal Stones—Mick, Ronnie, Keith, and Charlie—had shown that night, but also by what his careful study of their bodies in motion revealed about their awareness of themselves at this stage of still being the Rolling Stones—and also as individuals who happened to be in the Rolling Stones. "This band sounded *alive*," he wrote. "Not 'still alive'—a phrase that can feel patronizing and rah-rah—but totally alive, completely present, sweating out songs in real time, elegantly pushing rude noises into an unknowable future. This wasn't a band of survivors reenacting their once-greatness. This was the greatness."

Our connection wasn't hurt by the fact that his wife, Caitlin Gibson, a reporter for the *Post*'s "Style" section, is a dear friend of mine and a writer I'd had the great pleasure to work with for nearly twenty years.

When I reached out to Chris about getting together, he said he was determined to work in 10,000 steps each day and that our discussion would happen as we traipsed around his neighborhood that evening. When I arrived at their house they had just put their five-year-old daughter and three-year-old son to bed, and both Chris and Cailin gently eased out onto their front steps so as not to wake them. As we were catching up, a child's caterwauling drifted over us, and Chris thought to check on the children until Caitlin assured him the cry was coming from across the street. A few minutes later, the same moment played out again until Chris had to be sure for himself and ducked back in. Still the child across the street. For a man who listens intently and expertly for a living, his hearing was momentarily on the fritz.

Chris, in black pants and a T-shirt, supplied with water for him and me, and I had the edgy giddiness to jump into the deep end of a subject we'd loved our entire lives. I explained what I'd been writing and wrestling with and talking to others about all these months, and I sketched out what I believed the impact of nostalgia had on our listening habits these days and then asked what he thought about that. "The pandemic, for me, really forced me back into a nostalgic place because the present was not an option," he said. "You know what I mean?" I smiled knowingly because Ben Ratliff and Chris are good friends who will text each other out of the blue about an Otis Redding song or a Norma Tanega album, and this idea already had echoes to what Ben was saying when we spoke.

"You couldn't go out into the nightlife and see something new," Chris said as he steered me through unfamiliar streets. "So you know, in my case, I was home with a record collection. And it really drove me back into the past, into my memories, into the formative music that I really cared about. But I found that to be personally kind of like a finite resource that I burnt through really quickly. And then what happened was, I began exploring all this music that was contemporaneous to my adolescence that I hadn't checked out.

"In hardcore punk, you can say there's a tree trunk that you could call, like, Minor Threat and Black Flag and the Dead Kennedys and SSD. And then, you know, by like 1987, the tree starts going in all these different branches. So I grew up on a very particular branch. And I didn't want to know about all these other kinds of hardcore music. So after I kind of dredged through my past—every time I was like, 'Well, what about all these things that I kind of ignored or dismissed when I was younger?'—I found myself getting into that. So it was kind of this weird, different nostalgia because it wasn't going back to my own experiences, but back to a time where I was getting turned on to new things."

It's worth noting that Chris was a guitarist and singer for a seminal punk band in Washington, D.C., called Q and Not U, who were revered for their more danceable vibe and catchy melodies within a musical constitution shaped by the D.C. hardcore bands before them. They put out three albums between 2000 and 2004 on the famous Dischord Records label, which Ian Mackaye, the singer in Fugazi, one of the most important and influential punk bands ever, had started, along with partner Jeff Nelson, and put out all their music on. Q and Not U toured intensely, including jaunts in America, Europe, Japan, and South Africa before, eventually down to a trio, called it quits in 2005.

But back to nostalgia. "I'll listen to music from the past,"

Chris said as we established an easy walking pace, "but I always want to be more engaged in the present. I kind of shudder when I meet someone who thinks that music died the day they graduated high school. Which is a lot of people. Just as a music critic, I find myself just implicitly—like, part of the job is fighting against that. Music is perpetual, you know? Get out there. So I fought nostalgia tooth and nail for the first forty years of my life."

I asked him if that was generally an easy thing to do.

"Yes," he said, "but the thing that I realized about nostalgia was the good of it and the power of it and reclaiming parts of yourself from the past. And in my case, hardcore punk, when I discovered it as a teenager, it was incredibly empowering. It made me feel like I had a voice. It made me feel like someone was speaking out against the injustice of the world on my behalf. You know what I mean? I could align myself with it. And at forty, forty-two, however old I was when this pandemic started, same kind of thing: We're powerless. We're angry at the government." He laughed at the old inclination to still think like a punk.

In talking about identity and music, Chris was describing what happened—or could happen—to people who were discovering the power of music for the first time. All the people who don't want new music anymore because they found their identity—whether through music or some other facet of their community or culture—a long time ago and didn't need music for that anymore, that's the very large group of people I was trying to understand, the group that worried me.

I wanted to know Chris's thoughts on streaming's impact on our relationship to new music/old music, and as I brought it up I realized I was leading the witness. I knew we could make endless discoveries if that was our aim, but I wanted to know if Chris thought streaming had, at least in part, proven to be a means to the opposite of that—that streaming could keep us playing what we already knew in the form of our playlists.

"One hundred percent," he said. "It's really easy to get into your silo where the algorithm figures out what you like. It definitely wants to keep you there. And that's just a corporate mechanism at play. And that's changed the way that new music even sounds. If you think of artists like Drake, he releases these albums that are many, many, many tracks. And there are no dramatic left turns. It's all very, like, unified."

In my naivete I asked, "Do you think there's an intentional, larger purpose?"

"I would say that is 100 percent intentional because you want the listener to enter this trance state and keep the streaming numbers racking up," he said. And no streaming numbers mattered more than Spotify's.

Spotify's payments to artists are broken down between recording royalties and publishing royalties. That means money goes to whomever holds the rights to the recording or the owner of the recording, which is usually the label or a separate distributor; similarly, money is paid to the songwriter or songwriters of the song or the owner of the composition, typically through some third-party agency such as a music publisher. Based on Spotify's payment model, artists can reportedly expect to receive between $0.003 to $0.005 per stream. For a great many musicians on Spotify that amounts to extraordinarily little money, and for a very long time there has been a consistent complaint from musicians that they aren't fairly paid from streaming revenues. Part of their ire speaks to their contracts with their labels and the labels' deal with Spotify. These days, labels are seeing healthy profits from the biggest hits on Spotify, and musicians have argued that their share of those earnings is unacceptably small.

The Spotify reality, for megastar artists such as Drake or Dua Lipa, though, whose songs can have millions or even billions of streams, is quite different. When I checked last, Dua Lipa's "Don't Start Now" had more than 2.5 billion streams, but what amount of that payout Dua Lipa would actually receive would depend on such factors as additional collaborators on the song (she and three others received songwriting credit) and whether Dua Lipa owns the song or her label for the album featuring "Don't Start Now," Warner Records, owns the rights. (In late 2023, it was reported that Dua Lipa had acquired publishing rights to her catalog of songs, so she would, in theory, receive publishing royalties as well.)

In late 2023, Spotify posted a blog entry about a change in its payment policy. "Today, Spotify hosts well over 100 million tracks," it read. "Tens of millions of them have been streamed between 1 and 1,000 times over the past year and, on average, those tracks generated $0.03 per month." Now, Spotify announced, "Tracks must have reached at least 1,000 streams in the previous 12 months in order to generate re-corded royalties." That means a musician could have five songs that were close to 1,000 streams at the end of that year but not even have pennies to recoup. Yet Spotify contextual-ized this move as an effort to send an "additional $1 billion in revenue toward emerging and professional artists over the next five years."

"Streaming is all that matters now for artists," Chris said. "That's where the money is coming from. I mean, there are concerts, of course. But streaming numbers are huge. And then, yeah, of course, album sales. [But] there's something about scoring uniformity [in] an album because it keeps the listener from changing the channel. I definitely think that if any album sounds same-y, that's what's going on."

Chris thought about that a moment. "Now granted, there's an art to that, too. Did the Ramones sound same-y? Did AC/DC sound same-y? Yes they did. And that was the point. So if you love Drake, you're very happy because you get twenty-five songs that all sound pretty much the same. A lot of records, there's just no left turns or a sudden shift in tempo that feels dramatic. You don't want to shake the listener from that kind of narcosis state."

We'd been walking a while now, and I asked Chris what I said would be one of my last questions of the night. I don't know why I thought this would be a simple answer, since Chris thinks about music in complex ways, but what he had to say about it said so much about the ways music can gets its grip on us so early on that I want to repeat at length what he said. It didn't speak only to the powers of nostalgia, but to the crux of the various ways we can love a particular band for the rest of our lives.

"Has your favorite group now basically been your favorite group for much of your life?" I asked.

Chris laughed. "This is where you've nailed me." He didn't mean that I'd been trying to catch him in some kind of hypocrisy, but rather, that it might stand to reason that a pop music critic's favorite band might not be the same one from his youth because the critic evolves, the critic grows in his or her discoveries, and maybe Chris believed the answer he was about to give me went, on the face of it, against that idea.

"The answer is probably yes," he said. "Okay. A girl moved to my school, freshman year of high school. I was wearing a Pearl Jam shirt on the first day of school, and she said derisively, 'You *like* them?'" He laughed. "And I said, 'Yeah,' and she goes, 'Well, do you know about this band, that band, the other band? She just moved to town. She looked like she had come from another planet. She had all these punk patches all over her jacket. I'd never seen anybody like her. And then immediately she started schooling me on stuff. We rode the same school bus, so, like, by the end of the first week of school she gave me a Black Flag tape and a Fugazi tape. Life-changing moment, for real. Like, the course of my life shifted. Black Flag was amazing. They're probably one of my favorite groups of all time. Fugazi, though, actually, existed at the time, and were also forty-five miles down Route 50. I grew up in Annapolis, and I was, like, 'Wow, this is happening now and here.' Then when I found out you could go to the show for five bucks and some people that I knew could go up on the stage and be behind their amps and stuff, I was like: *This doesn't happen at the Pearl Jam show in Seattle, I'm pretty sure.* It definitely doesn't happen at the Metallica show. I was like, 'This is for me.'

"So it's not just like they were my favorite band," Chris said. "This band became my culture."

"It was the way you judged all other music, probably," I suggested.

"Yes," he said. "I feel so fortunate to have born into that. The music of Fugazi made me more curious, and more exploratory, and [I] wanted to hear more things and give more things a chance. They just made life worth living. And there had to be others that did the same thing. My religious belief system, whatever, that's because Fugazi makes sense. This is the thing about scenes and communities: When you are a member of a scene or community in music, you're really invested in it, and you're participating in it. You are far more likely to be a better guest in other people's communities. You know what I mean?"

I did.

"Like, you will know something about what it means for people to come together around a sound. And I think that's really valuable, and I think it's really important to think of ourselves as listeners, as community members, not as customers. We're not streaming service subscribers. We're not users. We are members. We are participating."

This, too, was what Ben Ratliff had been saying. And he and Chris were right—music can exist without listeners, but it can't thrive without our participating. The music from the past didn't *need* participators like it once did. It had gotten plenty of that over a long period of time. But new music—not all of it, obviously, because we're not going to like all of it, but *some* new artists, or *some* new music from older artists—needs us. And it always has.

SIDE TWO

IT GOES ON
AND ON AND ON:

JOURNEY, TRIBUTE
BANDS, AND THE
WORLD THEY MADE

Those of us who truly love music need an experience that goes beyond just hitting play on our devices. So we venture out to the theaters or clubs or bars featuring live bands, or we see our favorite acts at the vast stadiums where, if you had to swim to the stage from your seat, you just might drown.

Sometimes that primal need to belt out our favorite songs alongside other hardcore fans—and forming a temporary but intense sense of community, just as Chris was talking about—for a couple of hours can prove to be some of the happiest memories we have. When we're teenagers or in our twenties, we're still learning about the power of live music—what can make a great performance you'll remember all your life, what goes, or doesn't, into a performance you'll remember absolutely nothing about seven weeks later. And then, as we start to make our own families, the concert experience tends to be one of the first things that drifts away. It's the expense of babysitters, for one, or maybe it's not feasible to drive the three hours to see Dave Matthews the way it once was. Or maybe you get content to just catch glimpses of your favorite groups on YouTube and save yourself all the hassle—the parking, the guy behind you who, every time the music turns quieter, turns to his friend and loudly resumes the conversation about Erin wigging out at the Hamptons. Maybe standing up for two hours isn't as easy as it used to be, or maybe you resigned yourself to staying seated, but then you can't see anything because the younger people in front of you are standing. Damn the younger legs! Maybe you decided you'd seen all the opening acts you ever need to see. Maybe the music got too loud. Maybe you got confused about the direction that band you used to be crazy about was going in. Their music got too heavy, or it got too country. Or the band started believing they were Steely Dan. Maybe the band had so many musicians in and out of the lineup that it became akin going to see the Harlem Globetrotters.

Or maybe the idea of seeing your favorite bands age is too painful. The sudden emergence of a cane on stage that just doesn't scream "Rock on!" The vocals that now quiver as much as they shimmer. The emergence of stomachs, the lack of hair, teeth maybe not meant for screens that big.

Or maybe live music simply doesn't mean as much to you as it once did. You're older now, and your life is full without any more concerts. Now it's readings at the bookstore, or Chess Night at that new pub. Maybe it's better to stay home and watch Netflix and Max, and the idea of going to see live music again makes as much sense as digging through your parents' attic and finding those puppets you once had and putting on a show for your partner.

Or possibly it's none of that, and once or twice a year, despite the outrageous price of concert tickets these days, you book a date with what constitutes the Eagles, AC/DC, or the Who. The problem can be, though, that the big acts who were in their prime during Watergate might go on tour in the same intervals as Joe Biden used to run for president. Or maybe now your band mostly just keeps a Las Vegas residency, and a trip to Vegas just isn't in the cards for you. (Oh, Rod Stewart, will you ever visit Duluth again?)

The good news is, you can still hear your favorite J. Geils Band songs from the live stage pretty easily, but in one scenario, the stage will be a little smaller than when you saw them last at the Boston Garden. OK, the stage might be as big as the area where you keep your trashcans and recycling. The light show will be decidedly less dynamic, true. Maybe there won't be actual seats, per se. But when was the last time you were this close to the stage? Since you caught Tori Amos on her first tour? Or does it go back to the B-52's Cosmic Tour, on the wave of delirium when radio couldn't get enough of "Love Shack"? Now you're this close again, and OK, the musicians themselves are both entirely familiar-looking and somehow just a bit off, the closer you gaze at them. Well, it's J. Geils Band-*ish*. It's Whammer Jammer—a Tribute to the J. Geils Band, or Bloodshot: A Tribute to the J. Geils Band, or Raputa—J. Geils Tribute Band. Because you've stepped into the sometimes complicated, sometimes exceptional, often widely available and occasionally highly lucrative world of tribute bands, that group of generally exceedingly competent musicians who never quite managed to be in a band that signed with Capitol Records or Columbia or Atlantic but who also never lost their determination to rock out and decided, eventually, that playing someone else's music is entirely better than working at Whole Foods. And they're playing the songs you've never gotten enough of.

These bands mostly sound like and resemble, if you're watching from a good fifty yards away, such acts as Alabama, the Beatles, and the Carpenters. Kiss and the Who and Led

Zeppelin and Van Halen. Prince and Elton John and Jimmy Buffet and Rick James and Stevie Wonder, Eric Clapton. The Eagles, the Bee Gees, and Mötley Crüe. The Grateful Dead. Santana, Sublime, the Smiths, the Scorpions, Starship, Styx. AC/DC, ELO, and ZZ Top. Hall and Oates. Genesis, Tina Turner, Cher, the Doors, Heart, Metallica, the Dave Matthews Band, and Linkin Park, Chicago, and Earth, Wind and Fire. Oasis and UB40, Poison and Pearl Jam and Pantera. Joy Division, the Talking Heads, Blondie, the Ramones, the Drifters, Stevie Ray Vaughn, Glen Campbell, the Blues Brothers, and the Tragically Hip. If it's Bread you're after, look no further than TOAST—"The Ultimate Bread Experience." And basically every band who had recorded an album in the years *CHiPs* was on the air, letting us relive our glory days of spandex, lighters, and power ballads.

These bands play the songs the way we know them and want them to be—no jazz odyssey going on here—except, well, they aren't the same musicians, of course, so the shows feel like sitting on a mall Santa's lap as an adult: No one is being fooled, but it can still be comforting. Or it can also be weird. And the ticket prices aren't like a Paris honeymoon, either, with parking lots as big as speedways. These tribute band shows let us step back into who we were thirty years ago, before the subdivisions, the kids in therapy, the divorce, the singing fish plaque you got at the office Christmas party.

Is going to see a tribute band like going to see an exhibit of fake van Goghs? Or is it no different than going to see a regional production of *Grease*? Can we learn something about the music we love by seeing it performed by a tribute band trying to replicate it exactly as we first heard it? Does it inspire us to better appreciate the original, or does it alter our musical appetites so that the result is like learning to love meatless hamburgers?

I was wondering about all that, but also I was thinking this: Seeing a tribute band is the most guaranteed way there is to avoid hearing new music. And by talking to the musicians who played in these bands and the fans who showed up, I wanted to better understand our ever-distant relationship to new music and our unquenchable desire for the old.

Somehow it's not surprise that the state that brought you Mar-a-Lago, the world's largest collection of fossilized poop, and a state lawmaker who tried to *repeal* the law banning dwarf tossing ("All we really did by passing that law was take away some employment from some little people," Rep. Rich Workman told *The Florida Current* in 2011) boasts a disproportionate number of tribute bands in the country—maybe more than any other state besides California. In Florida you can catch, as of this writing, All Fired Up, a name that doesn't immediately prepare you for the Pat Benatar experience, but that's what All Fired Up gets you: all the Pat Benatar songs you could hope for, sung by a woman who kind of looks like Pat Benatar. Or maybe John Mellencamp is your favorite. Quick, get tickets for

Mellenchamp! "Mellenchamp is a truly international act with members hailing from the USA, Great Britain, Japan, and Venezuela," the booking agent's website reads. OK, so it's a global initiative John Mellencamp experience. There is every tribute act waiting for you in the Sunshine State because in Florida, the music of our past is always playing somewhere.

And then there are the Journey tribute bands—Florida boasts eighteen, according to Billy Lindley, who for ten years fronted Never Stop Believin'. Not to be confused with Odyssey Road, the Infinity Project, or Chain Reaction to name just a few other Florida Journey bands.

Journey didn't sell the most albums in the 1980s, nor did they win any Grammys—they were nominated just once, in 1996, for their lame "When You Love a Woman." Journey never had the critical praise that other acts that dominated the '80s did, like U2 or Peter Gabriel or the Smiths, nor did they star in their own autobiographical movie like Prince did in *Purple Rain*. They weren't featured in a Michelob commercials like Steve Winwood or Genesis. What they did have was massive airplay throughout the decade, with nineteen songs that cracked the Hot 100 chart, though none went No.1. And their terrible videos were always on MTV. But beyond all the record sales and commercial success, Journey was a total embodiment of the decade. What were all those '80s teen flicks—from *Sixteen Candles* to *Pretty in Pink* to *Say Anything*—but odes to love and heartbreak? In the unnuanced '80s, we seemed to be either in love or heartbroken. There was no "I'm doing me" kind of thinking back then.

Love or love lost: Journey owned and conveyed those feelings better than any other musical act in the decade.

To inhabit the Journey world was to always be lying beside you in the dark, drifting apart, finding open arms but also going separate ways, being all right without you but also being forever yours. Their lyrics were generic enough so that anyone could see themselves in them—Journey didn't write songs with the kind of character-driven specificity like Billy Joel's "Only the Good Die Young" or Bob Dylan's "Hurricane." Instead, Journey wrote the everyman, the everywoman songs.

Journey was to the power ballad what Henry Ford was to the automobile, which is to say, they didn't invent it, but they sure knew how to write a power ballad for the masses. But Journey also knew how to rock, and being proficient at both let them do something few other '80s bands did as well: They appealed to males and females equally.

They weren't a particularly pretty band, so in the '80s Journey wouldn't have looked right on that sailboat that Duran Duran rode on in their "Rio" video, but Journey could have easily passed as the crew that serviced the boat. Journey seemed to shop where we did, tending toward jeans in concert, not the Boy George muumuus or the Hussars military tunics of Adam Ant. After the '70s Journey was mostly done with the big afros, and their hair was akin to what you might find in your morning shift at the local fish hatchery at the time— longish, mullet cuts; it also didn't change colors. They didn't wear eye shadow or streak their faces with rouge. The bassist and drummer could have sat behind you at a football game screaming about the ridiculous penalties being called, and even when you turned around to give them a look, as if to say, "OK, can you guys maybe tone it down about the penalties?" you wouldn't have realized it was Ross Valory and Steve Smith. In a pet store filled with exotic, electric-looking fish, Journey was a tank of five mackerels. But this was all part of their appeal.

Another part was the combination of Steve Perry's soaring vocals, which carried clear soul roots and an unbelievable ability to convey emotions, and Neal Schon's huge, ringing chords and hypersonic bluesy soloing style that was no less expressive than Perry's voice. With that dual level of musicianship fueling songs built so expertly and undeniably hook-laden, Journey's success was a blueprint of rock success in its first twenty-five years.

Journey's *Greatest Hits* album, released in 1988, may have only peaked at the No. 10 spot, but it has remained on the *Billboard* 200 chart for more than 800 weeks. *That* is cultural impact. That is how you dominate a decade. So let us tread carefully—and respectfully—here. And let's just note that that Journey never had anything like that commercial success again in this century, and that is also why I was focused on Journey's music: the old versus the new. That and the fact that there were more Journey tribute bands in America than Arby's.

Journey had been a lot of things to a lot of people, but they didn't have the mystery or chops of Led Zeppelin; they didn't go off and bring Ladysmith Black Mambazo in for an album like Paul Simon did; and they didn't go off searching for their America in a documentary film like U2's *Rattle and Hum*. They weren't on *MTV Unplugged*. New, younger bands didn't talk about how Journey influenced them. It was rare to spot a Journey T-shirt in this century—people didn't even wear Journey T-shirts ironically.

The band has always been our Chef Boyardee of rock bands. Easy, no surprises, always works in a pinch. Enjoyed by millions! In 1998 Perry left the band, and thus began a series of replacement singers. A lot of fans moved on, too—for a while.

By the late '90s and through the early 2000s, Journey's glory years were well behind them, and it was easy to forget that they were even still around. But Journey also found new ways not to just hang on, but to come back fully into the public's heart.

Despite all the kinds of music that grew and evolved in the '90s and beyond—grunge, rap-metal, hip-hop, for instance—and despite all the lineup changes, the diehard Journey fans kept listening to the hits. They got married and had kids, and they raised their kids on Journey's music. That old narrative trajectory is true for lots of bands, of course. Having my sons listen to the Beatles' *Revolver*, Yes's *The Yes Album* and the Allman Brothers Band's *Live at the Fillmore East* was as important to me as getting them vaccinated. For those of us who love music so much that we want it to be just as important to our children, all that time we're driving them to soccer games and play dates and summer day camp, we use that time to talk to them, sure, but we also use that time to have them listen to our music, to teach them how to be quiet and just try to absorb it. So there was a whole new generation who grew up on "Stone in Love" and "Girl Can't Help It" and "Separate Ways."

Journey's music also found new ways to reach us. "Don't Stop Believin'" played almost in its entirety over the final minutes of *The Sopranos* finale, in 2007, when Tony Soprano, sitting at a restaurant booth, selects the song at the table's mini-jukebox as the family joins him one by one, with the deeply foreboding sense that at least Tony is minutes away from getting whacked. *The Sopranos* was one of the most iconic and influential TV shows ever made, and a Journey hit being the last notes heard on *The Sopranos* went a long way in the reviving the band's status. It went a long way in intimating that Journey might even be cool.

Then, in 2013, a documentary called *Don't Stop Believin': Everyman's Journey* was released in theaters and told the story of how the band plucked the latest Steve Perry replacement, Arnel Pineda—from Manila!—after seeing him sing on YouTube. The movie focuses on the pressures on Pineda, who was coming from total obscurity, a whole other culture, and also a period of homelessness to fronting the massive machinery that is Journey. These days, finding a replacement to your singer that way is a pretty common and natural occurrence, but in 2007 that still made for a notable story.

Journey was eligible for induction into the Rock and Roll Hall of Fame starting in 2000, but for fifteen years they didn't show up on the nomination ballot. That said plenty about how the rock establishment saw the band, since the selection committee was made up of other musicians, music writers, and industry figures. Instead, during Journey's fallow period with the Hall, the Lovin' Spoonful, the Dave Clark Five, the Hollies, and Donovan got inducted. Not exactly the Justice League of rock. However, when Journey got nominated in 2016 they sailed right in. And tellingly, their induction was saved to close a show that also included Pearl Jam, Yes and the Electric Light Orchestra. The whole narrative of Journey felt like it was being rewritten.

There's always been an idea that rock music was supposed to come with a snarl, a twist of the lips. The attitude more dangerous than happy. Rock was a fist in the air, or the devil horns, or simply the middle finger. But Journey was different. Journey simply held out its hand. And that impulse proved to be their salvation.

The current incarnation of Journey was headlining arenas as if they'd stepped right back into their commercial peak, despite not having a hit in ages. You could see that as a triumph— timeless music still buzzing through big venues, despite being performed by only two of the musicians who helped make it— or you could see that as a sign of a deeply broken artist eco-system, in which a slew of bands who came well after Journey had failed to break through to a similar level of popularity not because of a lack of talent, but because by the time they were emerging the industry was such a shell of what it had been.

Here are some of the bands from this century that weren't, in 2024, playing the kinds of venues Journey was: the bands whose first album got serious radio play, but by the third album the label didn't hear any hits and put no money or energy into promoting it. The bands that had, in their second album, experimented boldly with their sound, and a decline in sales or downloads or streams led the label to cut ties. The bands whose music was hard to categorize with easy labels. The bands who were paired with the wrong producer for their first effort and never got a second chance to make a great album again.

Whatever you thought of Journey still being a major concert draw today, their regular touring boded very well for the Journey tribute bands. In 2020, when I was just starting to think about what the rise of tribute bands said about our relationship to new music, I talked to three members of a Journey tribute band called Never Stop Believin', based in Boca Raton, Florida. The band had originally named themselves after Journey's biggest song, "Don't Stop Believin'," but Journey didn't like that, Gary Bivona, the longest-standing member of the band, the musical director, and de facto manager, explained to me over the phone just as the pandemic was starting to take hold in America. He said Journey's lawyers threatened legal action against the band. So Don't Stop Believin' changed their name to Never Stop Believin'. But that didn't pacify Journey either, Gary said, and eventually Journey suggested again they would take legal action. "They keep picking on us," Gary said. But when Never Stop Believin' failed in trying to trademark their name, he said Journey left them alone after that.

As a teenager, Gary got into music when his father brought home the pump-organ the church was retiring. It turned out Gary was a natural. He hoped playing the pump organ would impress his father, since "we had no relationship," he said. But his father was indifferent to Gary's pump-organ work. For Gary, though, the pump organ represented his calling. Through high school Gary continued playing keyboards, and he'd picked up the bass, too. He was also writing music of his own.

After high school he started making money in cover bands in the Long Island scene. And then his big break came in 1987, when he joined a band called Marchello, which signed with Sony Records. Gary believed he was on his way. The band put out two albums—he described the music as harder-edged than Journey's, and Gary played synthesizers. Marchello had big hair, but not big luck, ultimately. They had a minor hit called "First Love," which saw some rotation on MTV, but no more hits followed. The band was dropped after four years. Gary quit soon after.

"I just thought better things would happen," he said. In other ways, they did. He soon had a daughter with his wife, and he started teaching keyboards at a Yamaha school. And then the '90s came, with the Seattle grunge scene in full roar, and suddenly keyboards were as in vogue as safari wear. Gary recorded an album under his own name, which he financed; the gigs were few and far between. "But, you know, it was a good little living," he said of teaching. "Then I started having problems with my wife." They eventually divorced.

In 2008, and with full custody of his children and living

in Florida by then, Gary's then-girlfriend came across an ad online that changed his life. "She goes, 'Hey, you want to be in a Journey tribute band?'" Gary knew Journey's music, and he was particularly taken with the way Jonathan Cain, who replaced original keyboardist and singer Gregg Rolie, had helped craft all those pop-rock hits of Journey's golden era.

At the audition, Gary met Don Chamberlin, the singer pulling the band together. The idea was to sound like Journey, dress like them, look like them. "Our first gig was at a [minor league] baseball stadium on July 4th, 2009," Gary told me. "Over 5,000 people there. We started off with a bang. I mean people just wanted Journey." Gary estimated that there were only six other Journey tribute acts in the country then. "Then three, four years later, there was probably fifty of them."

Four years into the band, Don discovered that he had polyps on his throat, and his singing days were over. Gary took over running everything, and first he had to find his new Steve Perry.

Billy Lindley's path to Journey was similar to Gary's, in that he was originally shooting to be in a rock band with a record deal. Born in Memphis, in 1972, he was raised with music all around him; his dad was a prominent bass player on the scene. "That's how I got into music," he told me, when we first spoke. "I was just kind of born into it."

Billy ended up fronting a band called Black Sun, whose music was squarely in the rap-metal vein. They opened up for Insane Clown Posse, Mudvayne, and Limp Bizkit, he said, but Black Sun never got signed. Billy worked as a computer technician for a while, then found work in a studio as an engineer. He ended up in Iowa, where he worked on snowmobiles. He had four children by this point. Joined another band. Followed a woman to Florida, got some gigs in a cover band.

Despite playing exclusively Journey music, Never Stop Believin' kept getting calls for Bon Jovi songs. None of the members were big Bon Jovi fans, but they also wanted to make money, so they sometimes played sets broken into half-Journey tributes and half-Bon Jovi tributes. The biggest difference between the two, besides the music, was the wigs. The Bon Jovi wigs were bigger.

When Gary caught Billy at an area gig he wondered if he could be part of the Bon Jovi tribute. By this point Billy was nearly forty, and in Gary he recognized a seasoned musician who was professional and knew how to make steady money playing someone else's music. Gary heard an elasticity in Billy's voice that made him think he could handle the Bon Jovi gig, but he wasn't initially sold on Billy also being ready for Journey.

"Steve Perry is tough," Billy said. "I mean, he is truly one of the toughest vocalists I've ever tried to emulate." But he was determined to get the gig. "I said, 'Give me a chance. I'll become Steve Perry as much as possible.'" Gary was eventually won over.

What appealed to Billy in the beginning of his days in Never Stop Believin' was less the songs but the impact the songs the music had on people. "When people come up to you after a show and they say, 'I close my eyes, and you took me back to that time with my husband,' or 'That time back then, it was just like being there.' That says to me, I did my job."

Even though he'd been doing the Journey gig for years when we talked, Billy told me, "I learn every day how to be a better Steve Perry."

By the time the pandemic had cleared in substantial ways and I could get to Florida, in the winter of 2023, Gary had found a new singer, but he was letting Billy sing through April. Billy just wasn't selling the Journey dream enough anymore, Gary told me. The stage patter had drifted too far away from Journey. Gary expected Billy to talk about Journey being in the Rock and Roll Hall of Fame and how great that was, or Journey's beginnings—how the band was formed by ex-Santana bandmates Neal Schon and keyboardist Gregg Rolie. But no, Billy, just wasn't bringing forth the full Journey focus, Gary felt. This wasn't all the tumult for Never Stop Believin': Their guitarist had left to be the bassist in a Van Halen tribute band. Gary had had members leave before, though. He was all about keeping the gig going.

As musicians, the COVID years had been tough to get through, and as relieved as Gary was to have the band getting more gigs again, these weren't the rosiest of days for Never Stop Believin'. They had gone years getting paid $4,000 or $5,000 per show, and they had been refusing gigs that didn't pay that much. But fees were often closer to $2,500 now, he told me, and other Journey tribute bands were taking those gigs. Never Stop Believin' was losing out. Now Gary believed it was time to take those gigs.

There was plenty of tumult in the real Journey band, too. Steve Perry had been gone for decades, but longtime drummer Steve Smith and founding member and bassist Ross Valory were booted out of the band (again!) in 2020 because they were allegedly trying to take ownership of the band's name (a complicated affair involving lawsuits and counter lawsuits). By the time I saw Journey in 2022, in Greensboro, there was only one original member left from when the band formed in 1973. Or another way of putting it: Journey had one more original band member than Never Stop Believin'.

In 2022 Neal Schon filed a cease-and-desist order against Jonathan Cain—who was still in the band—insisting that he stop playing Journey's music while hanging out at Trump's Mar-a-Lago. A video of Cain performing "Don't Stop Believin'" with Marjorie Taylor Green, Kimberly Guilfoyle, and failed GOP Arizona gubernatorial candidate Kari Lake supplying backing vocals at the resort had gone viral. Cain then fired back that Shon had recklessly used the Journey credit card (who knew such a thing existed?) and that Schon's wife had been part of that spending, and then Schon basically said it was Cain and *his wife*—Paula White-Cain, who is Trump's spiritual advisor (*Wha?*)—who had spent Journey funds on . . . stuff. Right before the tour commenced, Schon teased that maybe Gregg Rolie should show up on the tour with them. Then Schon announced that wouldn't be happening. Schon's wife, Michaele, then posted on the Facebook page she shares with Neal: "Let's pray for forgiveness for those who hurt Gregg Rolie and hope they learn what spirituality is someday."

In the days before Kim and I saw Journey perform in Greensboro, singer Arnel Pineda tweeted that Journey "can fire me anytime . . . and don't lecture me about spiritual BS." No wonder my requests to interview Neal Schon had gone ignored. I had only wanted to ask him about Journey's music and how it had permeated the American consciousness, not all this *Real Housewives of Journey* drama.

Going into the Greensboro show, I was thinking about Journey and also Gary's Journey band. I was wondering when we're paying tribute to Journey, what is it we're paying tribute to, exactly? The songs alone? The era in which these famous, beloved songs reigned? The need to be unselfconscious about love and heartbreak? Being misunderstood? Or maybe I was really just thinking about that moment in the "Faithfully" video in which Steve Perry stares gravely in the mirror and contemplates shaving his moustache. And then does.

Inside the Greensboro Coliseum, before opening band Toto started up I talked to Maria Russell, from Kannapolis, North Carolina. Maria, forty-one, said, "We've listened to Journey for a long time"—she and her husband Kevin. "Just listening to it growing up from my dad, and so, like, deep into Chicago and Journey and all those bands. So I grew up listening to it, and it just stuck."

When I asked her why those songs had such power for her still, she said, "Nostalgia, probably."

"But also, we've passed it onto our kids, too," Kevin told me. "Like, they are just as excited when it comes on the radio as we are." Their kids were eight and twelve. In those moments, Maria and Ken would start singing along, he said, and "that excitement was just infectious."

They had not seen Journey before, but "this was on my bucket list," Maria said. She hadn't heard anything off the latest Journey album, *Freedom*, from 2021, and hadn't sought it out. But now they would, they told me. "On the way home," Kevin said, and then they laughed because—as I took it—that was definitely not what was going to happen.

In the next section over, Ruth Briles, sixty-nine, was with her date Bill Spaugh, sixty-seven. They had attended the same high school but went decades not being in touch. Bill had lost his wife, and Ruth was divorced. "I found him on Facebook," Ruth told me, "and I said, 'Billy, call me,' first time to speak—"

"After fifty years," Bill chimed in. They were dating now, Ruth explained. They planned on getting married. (And they did.)

Bill called Journey's music "make-out" music.

"They did it all," Ruth said of Journey. "I mean, you could dance to it."

"Understand it, sing along," Bill added. He said he thought those songs were timeless and lamented the music of his daughter's generation. "She's thirty-five," he said, and "she's learned our music."

"I feel sorry for our youth," Ruth said. "There's no beat" to that music.

I asked them if they knew that Journey had put out a new album last year.

"Yeah," Bill said.

Had they listened to it yet?

"No," Ruth said, which made her laugh. Then she said she was waiting for it to be on Pandora, though it went on Pandora as soon as it was released.

"OK," I said, and I must have said it suspiciously because Ruth laughed again.

Going back to the Journey music they knew, Bill said there were no stories in the music that came after Journey's great run of hits. And their story was: Life had brought them on a date seeing Journey together, and that felt all the more romantic because Journey's songs were about love and finding each other. Like Maria and Kevin, they'd never gotten around to seeing Journey, either. Now they were ready.

In the row right in front of me, Melissa Ward, forty-seven, and Brett Gerald, forty-five, had driven over from Roanoke, Virginia and were also seeing Journey for the first time, though "She's more excited about Toto," Brett said. Melissa concurred.

When I asked them about their connection to Journey's music, Brett said, "I grew up in the '80s, so I love all that music."

I told them I thought we didn't really want new music anymore.

"I can absolutely agree with that," Melissa responded.

"Yeah, I mean, I have work, I have a kid in school," Brett said, "so it's just, like, you don't have a lot of time to do stuff like that"—by which she meant, to really *listen* to new music. Make the time and sit down with a new recording, try to absorb it. "I love music," she added, lest there be any confusion. Neither woman purchased new music these days but relied on Spotify for whatever they wanted to listen to. Brett told me she had sought out new music on Spotify—mainly New Country, but Melissa said, "I don't. I have a playlist of all old stuff."

"I like all the stuff I grew up with," Brett conceded.

"Old music takes you back to a different time in your life," Melissa said.

In 2023, Toto was boasting one more founding member than Journey—they still had guitarist Steve Lukather and keyboardist David Paich. And from the beginning they delivered a tight, professional set marked by a sense of palpable gratitude to be playing in front of so many people again. In 1982, both Ronald Reagan and Toto had a huge year; Reagan gave his first State of the Union address, and Toto won three Grammys for their album *IV*, including for Album of the Year. When the band played "Rosanna," which won the Record of the Year then, the already-packed coliseum went into immediate pandemonium, as if the idea that Toto would actually play their Record of the Year had been too much to even hope for. A couple found their seats next to us as "Rosanna" played on, and immediately the woman managed to livestream the song, have her and partner pose for a selfie, post that selfie on Facebook, and "love" that selfie, all while Steve Lukather was still playing his guitar solo. You go to a concert to see a band that peaked in the '80s and is still playing today, and this is what you get.

When the band moved into "Africa," there was a little instrumental prelude that didn't immediately signal to the masses that this was what they were playing. But when the keyboard played the main theme, the coliseum shook as if a giant asteroid had just smashed Toto's bus in the parking lot. Who knew a song that still dominated Lite FM today could bring about such violent glee?

After an impressively efficient shuffling of equipment off the stage, Journey came on twenty-five minutes later, with Neal Schon, as he would all night long, taking the spotlight for some hyper-speed guitar noodling to kick off the set. Despite the songs themselves, live, Schon was indulging in that fireball soloing style popularized by heavy-metal deity Yngwie Malmsteen, hammering a multitude of notes per second. After the opening guitar debauch, the rest of the band joined in for "Only the Young," with a mix that mostly favored the snare drum.

Then, just two songs into the concert, something so cosmically unthinkable happened, a development so destabilizing and so utterly unprecedented in the history of live music that it could only be compared, in sheer traumatic terms, to the great San Francisco earthquake of 1906: Journey played "Don't Stop Believin'" as *their third song*! The most famous song in Journey's catalog was neither the last song the band played, nor the first, but the third, for crying out loud! I mean, when Jonathan Cain began pounding those familiar chords on his red piano, the collective gasp was so loud that fans on the floor were sucked up into sections two and three, like alien abductions. Was this some kind of stunning tease in which Cain would play a few measures and then wave it off to be comical, and everyone would laugh and forgive him as Arnel told folks, "OK, Greensboro. Don't worry. I'm pretty sure we're going to get to that one before the night's over." Then the fans who had been sucked into sections two and three would be dropped back to their seats from the deep exhaling.

Journey, why are you playing with our FREAKIN' minds!?

But no, this was happening now, and if you had run to the bathroom or not found your seats just yet, then for the rest of your life, as you came across anyone remembering just how narrowly he or she escaped death on 9/11, you would have a more harrowing story to tell about luck and how Journey played "Don't Stop Believin'" as their third song in the concert and you missed it.

The singalong to "Don't Stop Believin'" was as if all of South Africa was in full voice—and that "Don't Stop Believin'" also happened to be their national anthem. The crowd didn't sing "Born and raised in South Detroit" like it was a lyric to a song but screamed it the way you might scream to a firefighter that your baby is still in your burning house. By any measure, it was remarkable to see a single song inspire so many people to try and strip their vocal chords forever over. If that didn't capture the dying devotion to a song, there wasn't a single thing I knew about music.

More expected FM staples followed. Then Journey played a song from this century—"Let it Rain," from their *Freedom* album. Strange that their fiftieth anniversary tour was called the Freedom Tour, I thought, and that they would only play one song from the album. The bouncy rocker was a fun injection that Schon and Pineda seemed delighted to be pulling out as the singer kept pumping his arms and bobbing his neck to Schon's lead guitar. The ensuing applause was, we could say, polite.

When "Faithfully" kicked off, the entire crowd stood up immediately—dutifully, as if "The Star-Spangled Banner" had started up. "Need help getting up?" a woman behind us asked her husband, but he shook her off. It was another sing-along so deep that every bone in my rib cage introduced itself.

After that, when Journey moved into "Separate Ways," the crowd responded with an energy required for swimming the English Channel. At that point Kim yelled in my year, "Honey, the middle-aged, they're out of their minds."

The concert ended with "Be Good to Yourself" and "Any Way You Want It," and then the lights went on. Journey had played their encores without going through the pretense of leaving the stage and being welcomed back. There's usually a response from a crowd when the lights go on—*Ah, come on! One more!*—but after two and a half hours, everyone seemed sated and content to go get in their cars and complain that no one was moving. *We're just sitting here!*

◎ ◎ ◎

A week later I drove down to Florida. The night before my first Never Stop Believin' gig—and attending my first tribute act ever—I caught Gary playing a solo performance at an Italian restaurant called Zino, located in a strip mall in Estero. To go by appearances, almost all the guests seated at six tables had all lived through the Cold War and the strange preoccupation of trying to stuff as many people as possible into phone booths. Gary was set up at the piano, and the setlist was a collection of songs from the American songbook programmed for smiles and comfort—"What a Wonderful World," "My Way," "The Way You Look Tonight," "Smile"—along with some more contemporary ballads that go down as easy as applesauce. Elton John's "Your Song," Chicago's "Colour My World," Eric Clapton's "You Look Wonderful Tonight," and James Taylor's "Don't Let Me Be Lonely Tonight." Between sets and afterward, Gary made a point to visit each table, since these were all customers who had been seeing him regularly at his Wednesday night Zino gig, clapping shoulders and laughing good-naturedly.

Vinny Ricigliano, the general manager, said he'd seen all the entertainers in southwest Florida—he'd opened several restaurants before Zino—but he had a particular affection for Gary, whom he referred to as "a guy that goes behind the piano and has 1,400 songs in his head."

"Listen, there are better singers," he told me. "There are better piano players. There are better musicians. Ain't nobody better that knows everything he does and performs it at that level."

For his own listening habits, Vinny said he didn't care to hear anything recorded after 1979. "'Cause, music got taken out of the songs," he explained. His complaint about music after that time was that it was "seventy-five percent synthesizers."

Since Vinny, who had live music at Zino six nights a week in season, wasn't interested in anything like new music, I asked him—just like I'd asked my friend Matt Reid—how did he *know* that it wasn't worth listening to? How could he know without listening to it?

"Oh, I've listened to it," Vinny assured me. "I've raised three kids. I've heard all the crap."

On the way to see Never Stop Believin' in Fort Myers, I passed a billboard that highlighted KC and the Sunshine Band's upcoming appearance at the Seminole Casino Center in Immokalee. The first 45 I ever bought was their "That's the Way (I Like It)," at age eight, and the billboard called out to me like a sweetheart from childhood. Had one person devoted more of his or her life trying to get us to shake our booties than Harry Wayne Casey, AKA KC, who was still going funky at seventy-two? What really warmed my heart, though, was that the band logo was still the same all this time later—that plump, '70s-flowing script. Even that font commanded you to *get down*.

I pulled up to the Legends Golf & Country Club and parked toward the back, and when I got out of the car the *plink* of action from a nearby pickleball court greeted me. I strolled through bocce courts, and well beyond that, in the open expanse, Gary, in a hat and sunglasses, stuck out his hand in welcome. Billy, in those clear sunglasses I've never understood and a Harley Davidson T-shirt, was working cables and the sound equipment and greeted me next. The two newest members, Mike Murray on guitar, and Steve Quinto, the drummer, were tuning up.

Gary was unhappy that the club had the band performing for two hours versus the ninety minutes he preferred. He felt like ninety minutes made for a tighter set, and if they were going to play another thirty minutes, they'd have to indulge in more solos, which he didn't like to do. For Steve, this meant he'd be helping out by playing a drum solo. A drum solo at a country club wasn't the most natural occurrence I could think of, but at least members would be in comfortable seats, a long bank of beach chairs maybe thirty-five yards from the stage and divided into three sections for the 600 who'd signed up to attend. There were a lot of bands playing in the country tonight who would have welcomed a crowd of 600. Even an audience of sixty willing to give a listen. I've been to shows when I was among six or less in the audience. But all those shows were by artists playing their own music.

Today's tribute bands, though—the ones who were good— were mostly being spared that old indignity, which was both great for them but also a reason to further reflect on what that said about our relationship to music being made and performed today. Because of our bottomless nostalgia, tribute bands had built-in audiences that other bands playing their own music, in their earliest days, could only dream of.

Before tribute bands existed, bands developed an audience either through their ability to make other people's music sound special, or they got there on the strength of their own music. If they were both talented and caught some breaks, they started playing gigs in nearby towns as well. Then they started traveling across the state. Suddenly they got an opening slot for a bigger band that everyone knew. And they kept at it—they kept writing and became better performers. And that's what could lead, just possibly, to attracting the attention of a label and getting a record made, and that was usually the first step if they were going to have any chance at making it. There was no one way, of course, and no right way. The stories of whoever made it in popular music cover a boundless range of origins.

Sometimes, though, no matter what these bands did, it just wasn't meant to be. Billy and Gary were just two of the countless musicians all over the world who had had to accept that. The rise of tribute bands, though, gave musicians like them opportunities they otherwise wouldn't have had. And the more we kept listening to the bands and artists, like Journey, that made it so long ago and increasingly less to the acts who were still trying to break through, there were going to be more musicians like Gary and Billy and fewer musicians like my friend Bob who were performing their own songs because the opportunities were simply fewer.

Anyone can put their original music on iTunes, Bandcamp, Spotify, YouTube, or other streaming services and hope to find an audience that way. But that way also leads you to a truly endless sea of songs whose depths nobody could ever fully explore. And if that's the only way people can find your music, it's also an increasingly impossible way to get booked into a small venue in Raleigh, North Carolina, or Brookline, Massachusetts, or Winter Park, Florida, or Brighton, Michigan or pretty much any other town in the country with clubs that host live music but already have a slew of local bands trying to get booked there.

It's not today's changed landscape that I'm bemoaning, because nothing stays the same, but I'm bemoaning the consequences of all this change. No one would go to a bookstore reading because someone you'd never heard of was reading *The Sun Also Rises* or *The Collected Stories of John Cheever* or *The Heart is a Lonely Hunter*. You go to a bookstore reading to open yourself up to a new author, a new book, or maybe it's an author you've loved for years, but that author is there to read from his or her new book. Likewise, a movie theater showing *Rambo: First Blood Part II*, from 1985, week in and week out, is not going to survive, but increasingly, a small club only featuring current acts playing original music faces odds closer to the theater showing *Rambo*.

With music we had lost our way so badly, I believed.

◎ ◎ ◎

Billy told me a country club was a familiar setting for the group and that they played events like this regularly. Before the pandemic, though, they also toured all over. He said his first five gigs with the band, ten years ago, were outside of Florida. "Indiana, Minnesota, back down to Oklahoma, Texas, Ohio." The salad days. And they had been booked for a European cruise, too.

"Baltic States," Gary said wistfully as he passed by.

"The Baltic States, man," Billy said. "Yeah. Starting in Copenhagen."

"Yeah."

An Alaska gig had also been squashed by the pandemic. "I fought them forever about money, 'cause they didn't wanna pay us," Gary said. "And then finally, I got them. Remember?"

"Yep."

"And now it's back to crap money," Gary said. Tonight's take: $3,000.

The live-music landscape was still recovering from the pandemic. Billy said business was back to maybe seventy percent. "So if you were coming here before the pandemic there were eighteen tribute bands in Florida alone, just Journey tribute bands," he said.

"I mean, they weeded themselves out pretty quick because, you know, you get what they paid for," Gary said.

For Billy these last upcoming gigs were a farewell to his Journey work, but he had his Tom Petty/Stevie Nicks gig to focus on, which had been in action for about a year. "They call me the Tribute King, mainly because I can sing so many different voices," Billy said. "I do Chicago. I do Eagles. And Eagles, I sing—I can sing like Joe Walsh. I can sing like, um, what's the guy's name? He plays the drums for the Eagles."

"Don Henley," Gary said.

"I do Rod Stewart," Billy went on, "I do—it's better to tell you what I *don't* do. Don't do Brian Johnson from AC/DC"— Johnson whose vocals are like a train screeching to avoid hitting a car stuck on the tracks. Still, Billy was clearly the Rich Little of rock.

Gary and Billy kept tinkering with the sound. Two teenagers passed by in a golf cart, and as they motored by the driver started singing "Don't Stop Believin'" back to the band in a mocking tone to the enjoyment of his passenger.

When the bass player, Kam Falk, arrived, and with everyone's instrument coming through, the band launched into the muscular "Stone in Love." The music carried over the lake beside, to the homes across. Some putters stopped to observe, and a man in a pink shirt walking past, his stomach well in front of him, immediately nodded in approval.

"Sounded fabulous from back there," another man called out as he ambled by.

Gary acknowledged the comment, and after a disciplined hour of knob tweaking, he announced, "Let's get out of the sun."

The band decamped to the clubhouse. Inside they opened a door to a room that looked like a dance studio, with wooden floors and mirrors all around, and in the next room the staff had pushed tables together to feed them. As the band ate their chicken dinners, they explained to me that their goal was to replicate the "classic Journey" lineup on the *Live in Houston 1981: The Escape Tour*. But there were exceptions, since Gary's band didn't play all those same songs in a row. Plus, Gary didn't like how fast the songs were played on *Live in Houston*. He wanted to give fans the songs just as they had been played on the radio—and he wanted to offer as much of the visuals of that show as was possible—or reasonable. So Billy would dress exactly as Steve Perry did that night in Houston, as would Mike as Neal Schon. But Gary didn't dress as Jonathan Cain, which threw that visual dynamic completely. Instead, Gary tried to look like Gregg Rolie. His reasoning was, he sang lead on three tunes Gregg Rolie originally sung, and since no other Journey tribute band Gary knew had opted for a Gregg Rolie look-alike, he thought that might make Never Stop Believin' that much more distinctive.

Over in the corner, I could see Mike's Neal Schon wig on a Styrofoam head, which, with its giant coils, looked like a brunette Little Orphan Annie wig. That prompted me to ask: Did they ever feel like actors?

"Of course," Gary said.

"Oh yeah," Billy said.

"Me, too," Mike said.

"You know who's going to be acting today?" Gary said. "Me, because I don't feel well." Gary had a urinary tract infection. The group expressed their condolences.

"I think my first show with you guys, I didn't have the

wig," Mike said. "And then, you know, I got a wig, and it was—I thought it was gonna be weird. I thought it was stupid." Instead, the wig sealed the deal for Mike. Once he found one and put it on, he said, his feeling was, "Oh my god. I was like, *This is fun as hell!* Because I'm a natural ham."

Billy's reaction to my question went deeper. "I'll tell people: I'm not a musician, I'm a performer. That's how I truly feel."

"Yeah, that's OK," Steve said.

"Do I know music?" Billy said. "Yes, but I'm a performer. I feel like an actor, but not so much that I'm not trying to be, you know, a showman. I'm not a method actor like Daniel Day Lewis."

In his 2002 *New York Times* article about a Guns N' Roses tribute band, Chuck Klosterman referred to tribute acts as "arguably the most universally maligned sector of rock 'n' roll." Twenty years later, that idea had morphed into something knottier—and much less true. Tribute bands were more in demand than they'd ever been, and with so many competing for the same audience—whether that was Blondie fans, Eagles fans, Journey fans—there was more emphasis on authenticity than there ever had been. The right wig, the right sound, the right look—it was all part of what could separate one act from the rest. Billy was speaking to how high the stakes had become in the tribute-band world—how much we cared about how we wanted to experience the music from our past. If you went to see Shakespeare, you wanted the actors to take it as seriously as possible, not giggling over the fact that they weren't really these characters they were portraying. Billy's confession, then, about being a performer versus a musician, struck me not just as honest, but also particularly bold.

Before long, the talk, as it often can with the band, turned back to Journey itself. "Don't forget poor Gregg Rolie, though," Gary said in something of a non sequitur. "The first three albums, he's the lead singer, just like he was in Santana. And then they said, 'Sorry, you're not the lead singer anymore. We're getting Steve Perry in the deal.' I mean, that's, you know. . ."

"That was probably a blow to him," Billy imagined.

"It really was," Gary said somberly. Of course, Perry's arrival starts to result in more hits, but Rolie "also didn't like the direction of the band. But I think it was the *greatest* direction for the band."

There was talk of visiting the band's biggest fan, who lived on the country club property, before going on stage, but Gary bowed out. "Definitely gonna go to the emergency room in the morning," he said. "I'm fucking dying. Like somebody stabbed me in my balls."

Before everyone got dressed, I wanted to know their own relationship to new music in general, to this central argument I was putting forward. Did they listen to new music?

"You know, we have no more capacity to sit and, like— who sits down these days and says, 'I'm gonna listen to this new album that came out'?" asked Mike, forty-six. But, he added, "We're musicians." By which he meant, despite what he'd just said, as musicians they had to find *some* way to listen to new music. Part of what made Mike different from the others was that he was the only one who had a full-time job—he was a fiber-optics splicing technician for AT&T, where he'd worked for twenty-five years. He'd played in plenty of cover bands, but this was the most significant band he'd ever been in in terms of regular gigs—and the best money he'd made.

Steve, though, said he tried to listen to new music every day—a couple of hours or so. Spotify was his means of finding that new music, and he had done that today, for ninety minutes of the two-hour drive to the gig. Then he put on his Journey playlist, just to prepare himself for the evening. "Don't get me wrong, I still listen to the same stuff I used to," he said. But his favorite artist was not from the '60s or '70s, or even the '80s. "Ben Folds Five is my favorite band." Their first album came out in 1995. But Steve was all about making new discoveries, too. "There's some good new music coming out," he said.

The band mused on the prospects of new music for a while, then Mike said, "I think the music industry is just moving back to what it was in the fifties, where it's people writing a song; you put out a song, and that's it. There's not an album to consume anymore."

No one in the band was much up for buying new music anymore, though Steve would buy a new Ben Folds Five album if they put one out, he said. (Their last studio album was 2012.)

Out of the five members, only a few had actually listened to Journey's *Freedom* album.

"I was eager," Gary said.

"I had no eagerness to listen to new Journey stuff," Steve said.

Mike could only give it a cursory hearing. Kam had listened to it but was generally noncommittal to it. Just as COVID was hitting, I'd also talked to Kam at length by phone. He told me he grew up in Chicago studying classical piano and was adept in Beethoven, Bach, Brahms, Haydn, and Mozart. He was a cellist in the symphony, which led to him playing bass. In high school he started listening to jazz and jazz fusion, which blew his mind. After college he went for his master's in jazz writing, at the University of Miami. On the side he played in some Top 40 bands to make money, and like Gary, he also recorded his own music—five CDs worth—financing them himself. "The dream has always been to go out and perform the original music that I'd been writing." It was, of course, essentially every musician's dream—and so often remained just that.

In 2007, Gary caught Kam at a gig and was hugely impressed. He kept seeing Kam at gigs and approached him to join his Journey band. "I really initially expressed no interest in it whatsoever," Kam told me. "I said, 'Look, man, that's just a nostalgia thing.' I never owned a Journey album in my life."

But Gary was adamant that Kam sign on, and once Kam began to listen to Ross Valory's bass work more carefully, he could suddenly see the possibilities for himself. "He's a wonderful bassist, man. I mean, I grew to appreciate it." Upon joining, he also appreciated the steady gigs and income. "It's gone completely the opposite of what I would've imagined ten years ago," he said. "I would have thought certainly by three or four years of playing Journey music I'm going to be ready to move on to the next chapter and be done with Journey all together. Not at all. I'm still digging it."

It was almost showtime. Billy switched to a shirt he'd made himself that was an exact replica of what Steve Perry wears in *Live in Houston*: yellow with black leopard spots, cut in a triangular shape. Billy held his wig in front of him, like Hamlet holding Yorick's skull, and lovingly brushed the black hair all the way down. "You know, I've gone through several wigs," he said. He'd spent up to $300 on a wig. "But this one—it's one of the best wigs I've had, and it's the cheapest wig I've ever bought." Price: $37.

Gary slid on his Gregg Rolie hair, a more shapeless mop that made him look like the caveman from the "GEICO" commercials. He was trying to get into the right mood, but he was clearly feeling miserable. "I've always had a problem with my prostate," he lamented.

Kam put on a blond wig—an early Ross Valory look—that went to his shoulders. Steve, on drums, took a slightly looser approach to the visual aspect. Tonight he would wear a wife-beater tank top and bandana, and Steve Smith doesn't wear that in the Houston show. But, Steve Quinto reasoned, both of them were behind the drum kit. How much did it matter what he was wearing?

From the beginning the band sounded remarkable—and remarkably like Journey. Mike stuck to Neal Schon's playing note for note, and the match with Schon's guitar tone was spot-on. Just like the recorded versions, as they were saying in the dressing room. Billy didn't have much space room to move around, but he was singing in fine form, alternately sounding exactly like Steve Perry and a guy whose job was to sound like Steve Perry. What threw me a little was the stage patter between songs. If you're going to dress, sound, and even move like Journey, it felt strange to me to talk, between songs, like a band *devoted to* Journey. But maybe acting like they actually *were* Journey would have been a step too far. The crowd seemed generally engaged. There wasn't a lot of head bopping, and at times it was just as easy to imagine that these folks were sitting in front of a large screening of the *MacNeil/Lehrer Report* under this waxing crescent of a moon.

The band kept throwing out the hits—"Any Way You Want It," "Separate Ways," "Who's Crying Now"—Gary coaxed the exact keyboard sounds of Jonathan Cain's, and his playing expertly matched what everyone knew. Kam was supplying great backup vocals, as was Mike, and Steve's drumming was on-point in every way to Steve Smith's fills and feel. Having played these songs so many times, it would have been easy, I thought, for the band to just coast or go through the motions, but the constant eye contact between them all, the energy they had in playing this music, wasn't just palpable but impressive. It was a job, sure, but it was one they were doing with great care.

At one point Billy referred to Journey's history before Steve Perry joined the band, and to tell that story, he turned it over to Gary. "Fort Myers, how you doing?" Gary called out. By the tepid response, it seemed as if Fort Myers was ready for a nap. "We just want to thank everybody for treating us so amazing. You guys are great. Thank you so much. Yeah, you know what? We've been doing this fourteen years, and we just love doing this. We always want to tell the story because people forget. Journey's been around for so long, since 1973. But before that Neal Schon, who was fifteen years old, was in Santana with Gregg Rolie. And they had all those hits: 'Evil Ways,' 'Oye Como Va,' 'Black Magic Woman.' All those hits they had, and they were amazing, but by '73, they left and started Journey. And thank God they did. Woo! One-hundred million records later and, uh, Rock and Roll Hall of Fame."

The crowd had grown notably uncertain, as if Gary was giving a lecture on atomic energy. In talking about Gregg Rolie, though, Gary was also explaining why he was about to sing lead, and he then kicked off with "Feeling That Way," his vocals loose and soulful, and "Any Time," which showcased the band's soaring four-part harmonies. (Steve was a singer himself, but since Steve Smith never sang back-up vocals, he held back.)

As soon as Gary played the main chords of "Open Arms," a dozen or so attendees moved to the front of the stage to slow-dance. Just as quickly, that number doubled, and soon I lost count of how many were out there. I was moved by the tenderness on display; some husbands twirled their wives, but mostly the couples just swayed together, hands linked together, or the husbands' hands found the small of their wives' backs as they two-stepped under the starry sky.

After "Lights," a tribute to the feelings of connectiveness to San Francisco, where Journey was formed, Steve began playing an unfamiliar beat behind his kit, and at first I was confused when the other members abandoned their instrument, but this was how Steve was starting up his drum solo. The beat led to some busy tom fills, then his triplets began to pummel the crowd. For the first couple of minutes the crowd was particularly still, and then the occasional whoop shot through. As the solo bult up, there were more whoops. It was the only music of the night that no one knew, but it was winning the crowd over. When Steve brought the percussion demonstration to a close in a hail fire of cymbal crashes, a couple watching from their golf car at the edge of the parking lot honked in approval.

In the second set, the country clubbers particularly appreciated "Wheel in the Sky." The dancing seemed less certain— can you slow-dance to "Wheel in the Sky"? Some tried it, and others moved into a boogeying shuffle to meet the heaviness of the song. About seventy-five minutes in, others had gotten their Journey fill and began making their way home.

To introduce "Only the Young," Billy said there was a particular story to tell about that song, since it was part of the soundtrack for a movie called *Vision Quest*. (It stars Matthew Modine as a high school wrestler who decides he will lose weight so that he can switch to another weight class and take on the undefeated state champion—a process that causes the central drama of the movie—his vision quest.) But as soon as Billy mentioned "soundtrack," he couldn't remember anything more and explained that he was having a "brain fart," so he turned it over to Gary. This was the kind of stage-banter lapse that drove Gary crazy.

After "Lovin,' Touchin,' Squeezin'," Billy, now going off the rails a bit, explained to the crowd that the band was originally called Don't Stop Believin', but that Journey had sued them, and that was why the band had changed its name. From there he got onto the difficulties of COVID and told the crowd, "And the cruise ships haven't come back yet. Nothing in the European cruise ships, but, uh, we are working on them. So look for us out there. We like to do those cruise ships. We're called Never Stop Believin.' We are a national/international Journey tribute band. That's right, we do sail the seven seas, see all the countries in the world. Thank you so much for having us here this evening."

And then they kicked into "Faithfully," which brought back all the couples to dance together so that all the space between the stage and the front row was filled. In the crowd, ten people thought to hold up their iPhones and wave them the way the entire crowd in Greensboro had. When "Faithfully" came to an end, the band got another golf cart honk.

"Don't Stop Believin'" came last, and their carbon-copy delivery carried all the emotional heft of the original. The crowd sang along in impassioned voice, and Billy came close to hitting those last famous Perry implorations as the original song fades out. By now the crowd was insatiable. Billy acknowledged the fervid response, but that was everything they'd planned to play. "We're fresh out of Journey," he told them. The crowd didn't accept this and kept cheering in defiance. The band quickly huddled; Gary called out for Bon Jovi's "You Give Love a Bad Name."

How about Bon Jovi? Billy asked the crowd.

Yes, if it meant one more song they knew so well, the crowd made clear they could handle a Bon Jovi song. Billy told them they would play it as Journey, which he didn't really mean, since he was going to switch his vocal style to Jon Bon Jovi's, but when all of the band except Steve cried out, "Shot to the heart!" the country clubbers raised their spotted fists in approval.

The Bon Jovi hit came through honorably, if a little less passionately, and after the final, blasting chord one country clubber shouted out, "Hell yes!" in a way that almost sounded intimidating. Someone else called out for "Freebird," as if that hasn't happened at concerts in this country 4.2 million times in this decade alone, and yet it still set off a little ripple of naughty laughter.

There had been a turn in the evening, in the crowd's response, and the band felt jubilant. Billy, Kam, and Gary gathered by the stage steps.

"Who has it better than us?" Gary asked them.

◎ ◎ ◎

Given the magnitude of Elvis—the voice, those hips, the sunglasses, those capes—and the way people idolized him, it was inevitable that men who could sing low and grow sideburns would create acts around performing as if they were Elvis. But most people point to the Broadway show *Beatlemania*, which debuted in 1977, as the beginning of the full-on tribute act. That show, which had no narrative or real storytelling elements, instead featured four actors cast as the four Beatles as they performed Beatles music. Each was chosen based on their resemblance to the Beatle in question and also their musical abilities. It turned out to be a huge hit with audiences—for simple reasons. The Beatles had been broken up for seven years, and this was not only the next best thing to seeing them perform again—it was the only way, if you could look past the fact that they weren't actually the Beatles.

It was in the '80s, when some of the biggest bands in the world had already or long-since imploded, died, or stopped touring—the Doors, Led Zeppelin, ABBA, for example—that amateur musicians began to form bands emulating their look and music. More tribute acts in various genres followed, but it was really in the 2000s when tribute acts hit the big time. Basically, if you can name an artist or band, there's a good chance a tribute act for that artist exists. That's what David Victor told me when I reached out to him to better understand the scene and what it all meant.

David is the founder of Protributebands.com, a website that focuses on high-end tribute bands curated by David or his colleagues. Those bands' clips are on the site and a show-case for booking agents or just regular folks looking to hire a tribute band for Dad's seventieth birthday celebration, say, or Todd's retirement bash. It's sort of like a website for es-corts, but instead of perusing for redheads or women with European accents, you're checking out how well a certain band performs "Mr. Roboto."

"I think the interest now is definitely as strong as it's ever been" in tribute bands, David said. "Things really picked up in the early 2000s, and it's been just kind of at a regular peak." (He referred to a Ticketmaster statistic on his website from 2019 reporting that pre-pandemic, tribute bands and cover bands sell an average of 1.7 million tickets annually in the United States.) He mentioned the growth of casinos through-out the country that book live entertainment and how huge that had been for the better tribute acts. He also noted "these concerts-in-the-park thing. I mean, that didn't happen before. Where do the cities get money to pay thousands of dollars to tribute bands to play a Queen show so that people could come out and drink their wine and eat their cheese and have a good June afternoon? I don't know. People decided that that was a thing they wanted to do, and it does attract people."

The biggest tribute acts, David said, could have a suc-cess parallel to the real band. Among those big names were Dark Star Orchestra, famous for playing exact set lists the Grateful Dead is known to have performed; Australian Pink Floyd, and Get the Led Out, a hugely successful Led Zeppelin tribute act. "If you look in *Pollstar*," he said, referring to the trade publication for the live music industry, Get the Led Out's "grosses are up there with a lot of the national acts, even better. They play Red Rocks every year." (Red Rocks is the legendary outdoor amphitheater in Colorado known for massive, majestic slabs of red sandstone all around the stage.) "They play freaking Red Rocks every year, and they crush it! It's as if they *were* Led Zeppelin." He laughed. "It's really nuts."

But how a tribute band, playing another artist's work, aping their appearance, and doing everything they can to suggest the experience of the real band worked from a rights perspective is tricky.

"You enter those legality waters," David said, "and, you know, technically any tribute band could be shut down by [the original band] who is eagerly interested in shutting them down."

Venues that feature live music are supposed to pay a yearly fee for a blanket license—such as a BMI license—that allows an enormous range of music to be performed in public establishments, such as bars and restaurants. (BMI, which was founded in 1939 by radio-industry executives, claims to have more than 22 million pieces of music in its domain.) In those venues, how much money, or what percentage of that performer's fee, Journey, for example, will make from a Journey tribute act will vary, depending on factors such as size of the venue, the admission fee, etc.

David's website also ranks the popularity of tribute acts based on how often someone searches for the tribute act in Google. He began rattling off the list from the first quarter of 2023: Beatles first, then Journey, the Eagles, Queen, and

Led Zeppelin rounded out the top five. Other rankings got my attention for various reasons: The Carpenters and the Ramones were odd neighbors at 50 and 51, respectively. More people wanted a Sublime tribute act, though, putting them at 41. Toto had a respectable showing at 67, just beating George Michael/Wham! at 68. And Genesis was just one slot ahead of folksy nature boy John Denver, at 47 to his 48.

One observation David had about the list was that it heavily favored bands over solo artists. He had Elvis at No. 12 and Tom Petty at 16. David was always a little incredulous about this when the results came in. "Where's Bryan Adams?" he asked. "Bryan Adams had smash after smash after smash after smash. Where is he? I mean, how hard is it to look like Bruce Springsteen or Bryan Adams? Put on a white T-shirt, wear some blue jeans, and play a Gretsch [guitar] or something. The guy who does Super Diamond isn't a dead ringer for Neil Diamond. You know, he's wearing a glittery shirt. He plays, and people hear Neil Diamond songs, and they're happy. [But] Neil Diamond's another one, not even in the top 20 here."

Were there many calls, I asked, for Madonna tributes, given all her hits?

"Nope. Jimmy Buffet's in there, but number 45. Paul McCartney, 55. Bruno Mars, 56."

Bruno Mars? That got my attention. I asked him about how much interest there was in acts whose careers started this century.

"Bruno Mars was the first one that I saw here in this list," David said. "I'm just kind of flicking through it as I talk to you. I mean, it's old bands." But then he spotted the Zac Brown Band at No. 29.

"Dave Matthews at 30," he said, though the Dave Matthews Band had been around since the early '90s.

David noted that there was also a tendency to form tribute bands "in spite of the fact that, you know, people aren't clamoring for them, and I would say Steely Dan is one. There's like a billion Steely Dan tribute bands. It's just not a band that people search for. Where are they? They're not even in my top 81 here." (The distinction of 81 went to Air Supply. In your face, Ambrosia!)

"What do they do with themselves if no one wants to hear them?" I asked.

"They don't work much is what they do with themselves," David said.

David didn't just know about the tribute scene as an outsider. His dream was to make a living playing in his own band. He released five albums of original material, starting in 1991, then more music under the name Velocity. That first Velocity album got regular airplay in Salt Lake City, he told me. "Of all places," he said, "on the new rock station that had just come online." So David and Velocity went out there regularly to play shows. They sold nearly 5,000 copies of the debut album, he said. "You know, it was like we were kind of on our way."

As far as I could tell, the surest way to guide your career to a tribute act was to think that you were on your way with your own original band. If you got signed to a label or you heard your song on the radio or you made a music video that got attention, why wouldn't you think that that, or at least have every reason to hope? If, after all the years spent learning your instrument, finding the right people for your band, learning how to write songs, then writing better songs, and playing clubs, music insiders and label executives started to talk to you about your future, it would only be natural to conclude that you'd put the days of sending out demos and having fliers for your next gig printed out at Staples behind you.

Through the ages, this is not much different from how it's traditionally been for athletes or actors or dancers or visual artists or writers trying to make a career of it. But the digital age—Napster, streaming services, YouTube, the death of radio, and the Amazon surge that helped wipe out the record chains and local record stores throughout the country—proved to be a slow-moving tsunami that particularly devastated the music industry. That's why tribute bands are often made up of members with broken dreams. They grew up idolizing artists whose success stories unfolded well before the collapse of the industry, and in those bands they let themselves see their own future. But their dreams were rooted in the success stories of the twentieth century, and the realities of the twenty-first century were entirely different.

The support for David and Velocity from that radio station didn't last long, once it was bought by a new station with a new mandate, David said. As in: "Don't play new music because new music is not guaranteed to sell."

Velocity lost whatever velocity it had, and with that

window closed and no interest from record labels, David joined a Boston tribute band called Smokin'. "I mean, it was more opportunities to play," he said. "I kept seeing Queen bands and Journey bands, Beatles tributes, and kind of a small subset of classic rock bands. And Boston wasn't one of them."

Part of that explanation, David said, was that Boston hasn't been a very active band for quite a while, and so people hadn't been focused on them. Queen, on the other hand, had had a musical based on its songs that played in multiple countries, he pointed out, and then Brian May and Roger Taylor recruited Adam Lambert from *American Idol* to start touring with them in Freddie Mercury's place. And then there was the Queen movie, *Bohemian Rhapsody*, which was nominated for an Oscar for Best Picture and won in the Best Actor category, with Rami Malek playing the role of Mercury. So Queen's music had continually been out there with runs of fresh energy. After Boston singer Brad Delp killed himself in 2007 (in one of the most bizarre methods for suicides in the history of rock, he'd brought in two charcoal grills into his bathroom and lit them, dying of carbon monoxide poisoning), the band replaced him, over the years, with a range of singers.

After one performance with Smokin' that David felt particularly good about, he put the video of that North Hollywood show on YouTube. Nothing much happened with it for a long while, but eventually that video got the attention of the real Boston, and since Boston needed a third guitarist and an additional singer to round out their multi-part harmony vocals, that's how David came to join Boston.

David toured with the band, worked on one subsequent Boston studio album, and was living the Boston dream. Four years later the gig was over. David, who suffers from a bad case of tinnitus, then merged his passion for music and his interest in digital marketing to become a tribute-band gatekeeper.

As we were talking and looking at his tribute act rankings, I said I was amazed that Nirvana, one of the few groups we can easily say changed the course of rock music, had so relatively few tribute bands.

"Nirvana's at number 32," he noted.

We agreed that just imagining how much Kurt Cobain would have hated the idea of a Nirvana tribute band might have played into that, and that maybe the very idea of a Nirvana tribute band was to miss the point of what the band—as opposed to, say, the Scorpions, at 57—was all about. "Also just the nihilistic sort of nature of that music versus Boston, versus Journey," David added.

After we talked, I spent more time on the website, where he lists the ten best Journey tribute bands. Never Stop Believin' isn't on there. To go through those other Journey bands' biographies, I saw that they were able to make some pretty big claims. There were musicians who had played with David Lee Roth and Ted Nugent, and one had toured the UK and Asia. One band played a show with Styx, and another performed on Disney Cruise Line. One band claimed to have worked with Steve Perry himself! These were bands who performed at art centers and small theaters all over. Infinite Journey didn't even dress up like Journey or wear the Journey wigs, and somehow they had made it to the number ten spot. In one of their videos, they were performing on a huge stage with a high-end light show, and behind them was a large screen with projected colorful graphics. By tribute-band standards, at least, all of that was impressive, but their portly singer had a beard and was bald. Yes, he could sing, but he was performing in black gloves, too. Bald, bearded, and gloved: Come on, Infinite Journey! So not Steve Perry.

I was feeling bad for Never Stop Believin' after looking into those other bands. I was thinking how hard Gary worked to make the band as good as it could be, and here they were getting beeps from golf carts for applause. After all these years of playing, the chances of their getting booked into the kind of venue Infinite Journey had seemed pretty clearly out of reach. But then I remembered something Gary had told me in our first conversation. We were talking about his early days of writing his own music—in high school—and he was remembering when he played a new song for a girl he was trying to impress. He hadn't thought about this in a long time, but now that he was back in that memory he wondered if he could still play the song. He went to his keyboard, and sure enough, there it was for him. I could hear a little melancholy in the otherwise bright, beautiful melody, and then he came back on the phone. The girl, he recalled, was visibly moved when she heard that. "Oh my god, I felt that," she told him.

"I never asked to make a lot of money," Gary said. "I never asked to be famous. I just wanted to make people happy with my music. Guess what? I'm still doing it."

◎ ◎ ◎

The next night Never Stop Believin' was off, but Billy was on again, this time as Florida's own Tom Petty. It was another country club show—tonight was Quail Creek Country Club, in Naples—though with a much bigger stage. But as Tom Petty, Billy wasn't exactly going to be roaming around like Steve Perry tended to do. Plus, as Tom Petty, he'd be playing guitar all night.

The combination of Tom Petty and Stevie Nicks/ Fleetwood Mac songs occupy a different kind of stronghold than Journey's songs. The Petty/Nicks songs are more textured and musically richer, I'd argue, and they transcend the time they were recorded in more than Journey's. Lyrically, they're more varied, exploring more nuanced aspects of love and loss and the overall human experience more than Journey managed. There's also a more poetic approach to the storytelling in that catalog of songs—consider Petty's "Mary Jane's Last Dance" or "Into the Great Wide Open" or "You Wreck Me" or Nicks' "Landslide," "Dreams," or "Edge of Seventeen."

On an endless list of examples of songs from the past that are never really in the past, in 2020 a guy named Nathan Apodaca was on his way to work at an Idaho potato warehouse when his car broke down. He then grabbed his skateboard and, clutching a large bottle of Ocean Spray, kicked his way on to work. With the other hand he opened up his TikTok account on his phone and filmed himself as he cued Fleetwood Mac's "Dreams" to play in the background, a song Stevie Nicks wrote and was recorded in 1977. Apodaca suddenly starts lip-syncing quite expertly. Soon after, the clip became a viral phenomenon, reaching more than 50 million. Was it just how oddly natural this Hispanic man on a skateboard looked singing Stevie Nicks? Was the appeal simply the introduction to the great "Dreams" for a generation who didn't know it? Was it the song juxtaposed with the chill vibe of Apodaca rolling along? Or was the Ocean Spray the defining element that clinched it? Whatever that particular magic was, "Dreams" became the oldest song ever to chart in the Top 10 on *Billboard*'s Streaming Songs that wasn't a Christmas song.

Strolling through the parking lot of the club, I predicted that tonight's show would feature only the songs from the last century, despite the fact that Petty put out four studio albums—with the Heartbreakers and as a solo artist—after 1999, and Nicks had released two studio albums and recorded one Fleetwood Mac album since then. (I would be right about that.) And I thought, too, how those songs were also going to feel just as present here on this balmy winter evening as anything recorded this century.

The band was gathered by the side of the stage when I arrived, along with their booking agent, Paul Easton. He'd been representing the band for around six months, and Paul knew something about what it was to launch a band. His father, Eric Easton, was the Rolling Stones' first manager, along with Andrew Oldham, from 1963 to 1965. He moved the family to Naples, Florida, in 1980. "I grew up in this business," Paul said in his Southern England accent. "I'm sixty-one now. How sad."

Tribute acts were a significant part of Paul's clients, he told me—he had a Springsteen act, a Billy Joel act, and he was just starting to work with a Van Halen band. He also mentioned that he managed the Baha Men. Before I could remember what their big hit had been, Paul dutifully whispered that famous chorus, "*Who* let the dogs out?" and shrugged. "We're doing a whole bunch of shows 'cause it's the Bahamas fiftieth anniversary of independence."

Ambassadorship rarely got so funky.

I asked Paul how the tribute scene was these days. "If you're really good like these guys, you can be doing very well," he said, "and you can graduate from—a lot of tributes play shitty bars. But if you do it right, you can graduate to mid-level theaters." He rattled off some of the biggest ones— tribute acts that played all over the world, then said, "You know, look, Tom Petty is no longer with us, but we have Billy. People want to hear the songs, and they want to hear them done well. And Billy's arguably the best Tom Petty I've seen."

What did people want from a tribute act, I asked him. "They want to relive their youth," he said. "They want to relive the good times. Billy's delivering a feel-good experience. He's helping people relive the best times of their lives."

Billy nodded. "And that's why I do it."

It was time for the group to eat before the performance, and as we walked to the club Paul said to no one in particular—a clear habit of the business: "Rock and roll."

As the entourage milled through the club on the way to the dining hall, the sight of Fonda Cash, the Stevie Nicks singer, petite, and her blonde hair spilling over her shoulders, caused one club member to shriek, "There's Stevie Nicks! Stevie Nicks is in the house!" Fonda, who wasn't even decked out in her Stevie Nicks outfit but in jeans, a T-shirt and in rectangular glasses, smiled and greeted the woman with admirable humility.

When everyone filled their plates, they found a long table in a downstairs conference room. I asked Fonda how challenging it was to sing Stevie Nicks's songs in her distinctive style, and she said, "It's extremely easy and natural because I have just her voice naturally." And this was true. She had that raspy voice even when she was just speaking. "I find her earlier stuff—I feel that I match her '80s voice really good, you know? I'm right on with the '80s, and it takes me a little bit more work on [1970s] Fleetwood Mac stuff."

For all her adoration of Nicks—and the way, really, Fonda had focused her own career on Nicks's—she had only seen her in concert for the first time that fall. "She doesn't hit the high notes and stuff like that [now]. More she just plays it safe. But what I thought was so amazing was her tone and her power. Her tone was amazing." Fonda also admired how Nicks responded to the fans. "Always bowing to them," she remembered. "I was pretty much in tears through the entire show."

In putting her part of this show together, she was much more focused on Stevie Nicks as a solo artist and had been slower to appreciate the Fleetwood Mac chunk of her career. Though the show was largely solo Nicks, she made a couple of exceptions. "The fans would be extremely disappointed if I didn't do 'Gold Dust Woman' or 'Rhiannon,'" she said.

She stopped to eat for a couple of minutes, then she remembered something else. "And Stevie and I do share some common—I have a very bad habit of dating my music partners." At first I thought she just meant in the past, but then Billy, who hadn't mentioned anything to me, offered a sly grin and said, "I'm the bad habit."

Fonda had been in a Stevie Nicks/Tom Petty tribute once before, back in Colorado, she said, and in fact, Billy had been thinking about a Tom Petty act for a while, too. Fonda had caught a Never Stop Believin' performance, and, impressed with Billy's Steve Perry, reached out to him soon after. She had only wondered if he might know someone who could do a Tom Petty voice, she explained, and Billy, telling her he could do a very fine Tom Petty, asked her to send some clips of her doing Stevie. "I was blown away," Billy said. "She's got that Stevie Nicks that no other Stevie Nicks out there has." When you're around tribute acts, you sometimes hear double-talk like this.

After talking about the possibilities for a while, they finally met in the fall of 2020, and they'd been working on the show—and a relationship—ever since.

What seemed novel about the Petty/Nicks idea to me was that though the two stars were close friends, they recorded only a few songs together—with "Stop Draggin' My Heart Around" being the big hit. But Nicks had sometimes also gone out on tour with Petty and the Heartbreakers as a backup singer, and Billy and Fonda had poured over all the footage of the two of them together that they could find on the Internet.

Fonda was proud of her ability to sing in Stevie's octave when Stevie was in her prime, and she thought that was what set her apart from other Stevie Nicks singers. "The Petty that I worked with before, he had to lower all of the keys to the song to do it. To me, it made the tribute not an actual tribute—when you're changing the key. It's not accurate, and you can't. How can you sound exactly like the artist if you're a step lower?"

That question floated over us for a while, and then, before everyone dispersed to get dressed for the show, I asked the group their thoughts on our relationship to the music being made today. Was today's music just not as good? Was it that the songs being written today were every bit as good as what we knew from the twentieth century, but that fact was just eluding too many people? Or was our disconnect with today's music part of something entirely different?

Paul, who had mostly been quiet since we'd sat down, said, "I think there's another twist to this, which is how music is consumed. There are about nine-hundred ways to monetize a song copyright. In the old days, you had three ways to monetize a copyright. So that's why companies want to purchase rights is because the way that they monetize this stuff. They're all smaller slivers, but there are more of them. And the experience of music is very fragmented. So kids generally don't listen to the radio; unless you are a Top-40 artist and your label's gonna put six figures into marketing your song, you're not getting on Top 40. There are only twenty slots a week that a program director is gonna give up, and, you know, if J Balvin drops an album, well, those slots are gonna go to that guy. So [kids] discover them through streaming, algorithmic playlists.

"You know, blah blah blah blah blah," he said. "A lot of referral recommendation. But that's a very different experience. We all grew up with a communal experience. You may not like Barry Manilow, but everybody heard a Barry Manilow song. You may not like so-and-so, but you would hear these songs, and they become part of your life."

"I will say the music's not as good, Paul, anymore," Fonda said.

"I disagree with you," said the band's guitarist, Robin.

"I disagree, too," Billy said.

"All the techno stuff that they make on the computers now?" Fonda said in bewilderment.

"There's a lot of music being made that you'll never hear," Paul told her. "But listen, because I get quite passionate about this: If you just put some headphones on one day, sit on the couch, and everybody else is asleep, and you listen to maybe ten or fifteen songs of your favorite artist, and then let Spotify go into an algorithmic playlist mode, and then as it plays [other] songs, all of the sudden you'll start to see artists you've never heard of, and you would never hear them on the radio. But they have millions and millions of streams and millions of followers. And they're making a living, and they're writing really good stuff."

That led to a discussion about how radio is dead, which everyone agreed to.

"You're not that audience," Paul said to Fonda, referring

to Fonda's distaste for what she heard on the radio. "In other words, when you reach a certain age, unless you're Clive Davis, who apparently can listen to everything until he's two hundred years old and absorb everything, in general, people reach a certain age in their life, and it's almost like the memory banks are full up."

"It's a hard-drive thing—there's no room," Billy said, which was the exact analogy I'd been using with people for years.

"That's right," Paul said. "You'll listen to music differently. I love watching people bitch about the Grammys or whatever. Or the Super Bowl [halftime show]. They're bitching about the quality of the act, and I'm thinking, *Yeah, but you're not the audience.*"

Fonda's father, Bobby Cash, was a rockabilly artist signed to King Records in the early '60s, "So I grew up around music, and I never, you know—well, actually, I never grew up," Fonda told me.

"Instead of going to bed at 8:00 p.m.," Fonda continued about her childhood, "I had to go and stay in nightclubs till 1:00 a.m. in the morning watching my dad, and then I'd have to get up and go to school every day. And at [age] nine, my dad just called me up on stage without any warning, said, 'Ladies and gentlemen, my daughter Fonda Cash.' And I looked around the room, and all of these people were clapping, and I am just thinking, *I'm gonna kill him.*" She laughed about that now. "I don't know what I'm gonna sing. [But] I thought to myself, *If I don't get up and sing, I'm gonna disappoint everybody in this room.* I said, 'Dad, what am I doing?' He goes, 'Just One Look' by Linda Ronstadt. And I guess I knew all the words, and I sang it. And then the whole place stood up and clapped, and I said, 'Okay, I like this.'"

Fonda, who said she dropped out of school by eighth grade, started having children at nineteen. She's played in cover bands her whole life, she said, but she got more serious about her music career and headed to Nashville when she was thirty-one. She'd self-recorded a country-pop album of her own by then and brought it with her as a calling card, of sorts. "A lot of really good stuff happened for me when I was there," she said, "but I kind of realized that if I was going to pursue my music, I would need to leave home to do that. And I just wasn't ready to leave my children at that time."

She's never gone out and toured playing her own music, but she wasn't bitter about that. Her marriage didn't last, though, and she got divorced in 2015. She said that led to a nervous breakdown. These were better days.

"Now that I'm fifty, and I'm not married anymore and my kids are grown, I'm actually getting to do all this stuff I've always wanted to do. I'm getting paid well to do what I love. And, you know, what's different about now and back then was I might go play some bars where people might clap or not. You know, they're there to have dinner. Here, people are paying tickets to see me perform."

By now it was just Fonda and I talking, as everyone else had slipped away to get ready for the show. She'd had a talk with Paul earlier in the day, she said, that she hadn't even been able to catch Billy up on—namely that, with Paul guiding the band, "within the next two years we'll be making about twenty grand a show—that's the hopes." For now, she said they could make anywhere from $4,000 to sometimes $10,000 per gig.

Fonda said she was aware of a dozen Stevie Nicks tributes in Florida, but she believed they weren't very good, since they didn't have that Stevie vibrato, and she saw this as a chance to be at the very top.

Billy came back to make sure she wasn't talking so much that she would be late taking the stage. For his part, one aspect Billy didn't have to worry about in transforming into Tom Petty was the hair—he'd cut his long black hair to approximate a Petty chin-length bob a while back, with a dye job to match.

Fonda started working her blonde tresses, training a dryer on it and working a bottle of hairspray for an optimum '80s volume. She took out a trademark Stevie black lace dress, with a black shawl on top.

Billy reached for a small case and held it in front of me. "What do you have there?" I asked. He opened it up to reveal a set of false teeth: Tom Petty's sizeable choppers.

"It forces you to talk a little more Southern," he said as he worked them in. Plus, the teeth gave Billy the Petty look he was trying to capture. He hadn't had to re-learn how to sing with them, he said, and for him it was just one more detail to help him get into character, along with the red shirt and dark sports jacket Petty wore on the cover of his *Damn the Torpedoes* album he made with the Heartbreakers.

Paul, who stepped back into the room, said, "Just be glad it wasn't Freddie Mercury," referring to the Queen singer's buck teeth. (For the record, Billy says he could front a Queen tribute act, too, and handle Mercury's operatic pipes.)

Now it was time to start the show. The Quail Creek Country Club members appeared, on the whole, about a generation younger than the group I'd seen last night. Nearly 350 of them had paid $45 for their tickets, and there was, at least by country-club standards, even something of a rock vibe in the air. More women had showed up with their female friends—one in leopard-print pants, another in leather pants, and overall the skirts were shorter.

Soon a man in a pale-blue suit came to the microphone and introduced the band, who launched into Petty's "Runnin' Down the Dream." Billy sported the Rose Morris Rickenbacker guitar Petty regularly played, and sure enough, from the opening words, that familiar laid-back draw of Petty's vocals poured over the crowd. Yes, Billy could sing like Tom Petty, too.

In what would be the established rhythm of the night, when they weren't playing a Stevie Nicks song, Fonda was a backup singer for the Tom Petty song, and vice versa. From the opening notes of the next song, "I Need to Know," Fonda's vocals made clear she could bring that authentic Stevie Nicks vocal. It was pretty well perfect, in fact, and so was her Stevie twirl. The crowd let out a raucous cheer of appreciation when the song came to an end. "I Won't Back Down" came on next, and two women danced in the bocce court next to me.

Robin's guitar tone didn't quite match Mike Campbell's of the Heartbreakers, though she was playing the right notes. But in that discrepancy it made me newly appreciate how important Campbell's guitar sound had been to Tom Petty's music.

"He's a little too tall," a guy behind me said of Billy's Petty.

What took some getting used to was that anytime Fonda sang harmony on a Tom Petty song, it altered the experience of the song. It was an exercise in imagining that Petty and Nicks had recorded it together, and just a bit distracting for that reason. Still, when Fonda covered her mic stand with her shawl and gave it that trademark look after her contribution to "Free Fallin'," it was also easy to appreciate all the things the two performers were doing right.

Billy donned a top hat, like Petty sometimes wore, for "Don't Come Around Here No More," and then came Nicks's "Talk to Me." "Refugee" brought more country-clubbers to the stage, and after a few more hits, the moment the crowd likely anticipated the most was here: "Stop Draggin' My Heart Around." Billy and Fonda's performance matched the video of the song, with the two singers locking eyes during each other's vocals. "Edge of Seventeen" and "American Girl" finished out the set, and by the end, as had been the case with the previous night's show, a new momentum had settled in with the crowd during the second half.

Was there something about the dress and look and sound of the tribute band that just took a while to warm up to, I wondered. Or did people come to these kinds of concerts needing to exude a kind of cool distance so that no one could, in the case of a spouse exhibiting too much obvious excitement or thrill, say, "It's not really *them*, you know"?

After the show, Jill Nilsen, who lived in Massachusetts but spent a lot of time in Naples, told me that this music they'd just heard "takes us back to a time in our life when we were the most happy and the most carefree. Like, I listened to 'Gold Dust Woman' when I was a freshman in college, and I still, whenever I hear the song, I'm transported back to that time. I can picture myself sitting in my dorm room."

I asked her when she stopped making the same kind of musical discoveries with such specific memories.

"I would say after I had kids," Jill said, and laughed. "You know? And then I was all about them, and I didn't really have time to listen to [new music.] But now I will say though that I've discovered music through my adult children that I never would have discovered on my own that I really enjoy."

Last year, Jill said, the country club had a Stones tribute band perform. "It was kitschy. They were, like, you know—they had wigs. They weren't quite musicians. They were trying to act the parts more than [play] the music. These guys—" in the Petty/Nicks band—"were very good musicians, I thought."

Her point was straight out of Tribute Acts 101. If you were going to play an evening of songs people had spent their whole lives listening to and loving, you better well be able to play them right.

◎ ◎ ◎

When I pulled up to the Wyndemere Country Club, in Naples, where Never Stop Believin' was performing on this Saturday night, the band, minus Gary and Billy, who were working out sound kinks, was jamming on Kansas's "Carry on Wayward Son." When I got to Gary, he let me know he was feeling much better after getting treatment for his UTI.

Mike, Steve, and Kam took on Living Colour's "Cult of Personality" next, with its main, glorious riff sailing over the nearby putting green. The band was in a rockier mode this evening, and the show hadn't even started yet, though that harder rock edge they'd been playing with softened as Gary jumped on keyboards and led them through Steely Dan's "Rikki Don't Lose That Number."

Tonight's event was a full-dinner affair, with long tables of a gleaming buffet of shrimp and salmon being prepared on the side, and on the tables were centerpieces made up of old record albums, like platters, underneath vases of flowers—Barbra Streisand's Greatest Hits Volume 2 to AC/DC's Let There Be Rock to the less than auspicious debut by the short-lived Jimmy Page-Paul Rodgers band The Firm; 45s were worked into the flowers: Marty Robbins's "It's a Sin"/"I Feel Another Heartbreak Coming On;" the Stories' "Brother Louie"/"What Comes After;" the O'Jays' "Who Am I"/"Love Train." I knew that by the early '90s most record labels had stopped producing 45s, but still, it was moments like this that felt like new music didn't even exist.

Tonight's gig, Gary said, would bring the band $3,400, and on the discussion of money, he let me know that he had earned

$85,000 the last year from his Journey shows and all his many tribute gigs he had on the side. (At the time, he was also either playing keyboards, guitar, bass, or singing background vocals in a Led Zeppelin band, a Steely Dan band, a Doobie Brothers band, a Chicago band, an Eagles band, a Beatles band, a Motown band, and acts performing Tony Bennett, Frank Sinatra, Elton John, Barry Manilow, and Neil Diamond. Had there been an area Go-Go's tribute band, I was sure Gary would have found a way to be in that, too.) All in all, he felt very good about how he was making out. He had no boss talking to him about budget cuts for the staff, no annual review that declared Gary "Meets requirements" or meetings about the new software IT was rolling out. Gary was making a living making music, and sure, he had to fight with people who didn't want to provide tents for the band and a whole host of other challenges and frustrations in addition to an endless amount of hustling to get work and get paid. And yes, Gary was always playing someone else's music, but it was also music he loved.

The band mostly stuck to the same sequence of songs as the earlier show, and when they got to "Open Arms," as if on cue, a small horde of dancers from the audience of 335 gathered by the stage and began to slow-dance. Soon after a woman named Samantha Oman approached me. She had recently taken a job as events director at Wyndemere, and in a previous job in which she was booking talent, she had hired Never Stop Believin' to do a Journey/Bon Jovi gig.

I explained yet again to someone I didn't know what I was doing here scribbling in my notebook. Samantha, who was only thirty, surprised me when she said about new music: "We don't need it." I was so surprised by her absoluteness, in fact, that I tried to clarify. Did she really mean that?

"I truly mean that," she said. "Everyone dances to *this* music. I grew up on this music." She explained that her father had played Journey's music "in the car, at home, on the TV. I mean, this is real music."

Sure, on her own she had grown up listening to Backstreet Boys and *NSYNC, she said, and she had a soft spot for groups like that, "but like, these are roots," she said of Journey's music. "I go out for live music somewhere, I want to hear this."

I can't easily say why I was determined to talk her out of this point of view, but maybe it's because she was so young and had so much new music to discover still. She hadn't, I tried to reason with her, gone through breakups or held the object of a crush's hand for the first time with Journey's music playing in the background, surely. Journey's wasn't the soundtrack to her prom. "But I would say it's emotional," she contended.

Journey's music made perfect sense for a crowd like tonight's, she offered. It was this generation's music—the country-club crowd who could afford to come here to Florida seasonally. "I mean, this is the demographic that goes to things like this. I don't know that you would fill a lawn with 300 thirty-year-olds" with a Journey band. But she also made this point: "The demographic in southwest Florida is changing a

little bit—it's getting younger, so you got to kind of play that
late '70s, early '80s [music]. For a long time, it was Motown.
It was all Motown. And it's changing."

If she ever had children, I wondered, would she play them
Journey songs?

"Oh, I would," she said.

"Because you're probably not going to play for your children *NSYNC," I ventured.

"I don't think so."

A handful of couples danced during "Send Her My Love,"
and then between songs Billy, who it was clear now tended
to get looser in his stage patter as a show went on, told
the story of Never Stop Believin' being "sued" by the real
Journey, and how Journey tried to sue the band again after the name change didn't quell their punitive ways, but
this time Billy added a new wrinkle and imagined it was
Neal Schon himself who sicced the lawyers onto Never Stop
Believin's nefarious activities. Was the audience supposed
to boo the real Journey? Were they supposed to boo Gary
and the guys for crossing Journey in the first place? In Billy's
telling, the joke was on Journey the second time around:
Journey couldn't stop Gary and the gang from copyrighting
Never Stop Believin'! (In fact, they very well could have.) At
this Billy coaxed a few hoots for . . . legal justice? Classic
rock retribution? The limits of copyright infringement? At
the very least, it was this tendency of Billy's, as Steve Perry,

to go very off-script that Gary told me earlier in the evening that he was not going to miss.

During "Be Good to Yourself," a guy named Keith Harris approached me. What was I up to, he wondered. I explained, and he told me proudly, "I listen to all the new music." Keith, who was sixty-eight and lived in Ontario, Canada, said, "I'm still a big fan of all of the old music, too. I saw the Beatles in 1964, when I was ten years old—my aunt took me." He mentioned the Eagles, James Taylor. "I mean, I'd go on and on and on, but there is great new music coming out." Some of his favorites from this century included the National, the War on Drugs, Ocean Alley.

Keith admitted that he was an exception to his friends in this way, but the way he saw it, he'd been making great musical discoveries his whole life. Why would he ever stop doing something he loved? "I still go to concerts all the time," he told me. Journey was never his band, he explained, "But, you know, I mean, they've got great songs, obviously. We're here to have fun. Dancing and chilling out." And like most parents who share music with their kids as part of their bond, he'd learned about a lot of new music through them now that they were grown up. His thirty-year-old son and he still went to concerts together. Right now, he was trying to get someone to go see Umphrey's McGee with him in nearby St. Petersburg, but so far there were no takers.

And the challenge for old rockers everywhere raged on.

Never Stop Believin' was in high gear as the second set wound down. Much of the crowd had abandoned their tables and crowded the front. "Lovin', Touchin', Squeezin'" had them waving their arms over their heads, and "Faithfully" got them all slow-dancing again. The catering staff fed off the band's energy as well, and I saw at least a couple of them disappear into the crowd by the stage.

By the time Gary played the opening chords of "Don't Stop Believin'," the crowd went into ecstatic overdrive. As I watched from the edge, it was easy to imagine their younger selves, rushing to the front of stages so many decades ago. Based on what I was seeing, new music had had them in its grips once upon a time, and it was impossible to know, of course, when that began to fade, but when the club members screamed "born and raised in South Detroit" it was as if their lives depended on it. They weren't just singing along with a song they knew and loved, but, it seemed to me, they were re-claiming part of who they were, if even for a few fleeting moments—just as Paul had described to me the previous night, and Chris Richards had during our walk.

A country club responding to a Journey tribute band with that kind of wild-eyed vigor wasn't the grandest spectacle I'd ever witnessed, but it was, oddly, one of the more inspiring.

The band, spent but energized, held the last note for a long time, for as long as it made sense, and still the crowd screamed for more in the immediate hush afterward. It wasn't quite clear yet if the band would uncork one last hit when one club member's fervent plea sailed through.

"Never stop playing!"

◎ ◎ ◎

I hadn't known that there was no south Detroit until Jonathan
Cain, from the real Journey, told me a couple of weeks later.
He had the day off from touring when we spoke by phone.

"I knew the song had something special when we first created it," he said of "Don't Stop Believin'." It was, he said,
"the permission-to-dream song, you know?" Its main theme—
and the title itself—came "from my dad's pep talk with me
one night. I was going to come home to Chicago and quit the
music business. And he said, 'Don't stop believing.' But the
amazing thing of the song is that Perry and I first came out of
the night club thing, you know? And so *we* were the singers
in the smoky room. *We* were around the smell of wine and
cheap perfume. I mean, we lived the life. And we were writing about making it in the music business—and never giving
up. So it was kind of an autobiographical look. We went,
'Well, listen, everybody has a dream, you know?' It's that city
boy and the small-town girl—they're not stuck where they
are. You know, 'cause Steve came out of Fresno, California. I
came out of a little Schiller Park suburb out of Chicago. An
accordion player in Chicago. How did he end up in Journey,
you know?

"You're not stuck where you are," he said. "South Detroit
doesn't exist. It's an imaginary city. It's the city of possibilities,
the city of dreams. It's the midnight train going anywhere. You
can dream a bigger dream. Anything is possible. I think that's
what resonates in that song. It's got hope. It's going somewhere."

As for the other Journey songs that meant so much to people, Jonathan wasn't at a loss for why that was. "We're selling out all these places because these are older folks that still have their identity in Journey. It's certain music in uncertain times. We have war looming; we have China, Russia. Ukraine. But Journey brings them back to, you know, when things were stable, when Ronnie Reagan was president, when we were in the boom. Everything was happening. Before Generation X showed up, before the flannel shirts rock showed up, the grunge rock.

"Music back in our era was designed to lift you and to melodically hook you," he went on. "In other words, make you feel something, whatever it was. So our music from the '80s and '90s—and I'd even put the '70s in there—was all intended to entertain, to romance you, to woo you, to make you feel something. We were trying to sell a feeling, weren't we? You know what I mean?"

The pride and pleasure he took in those Journey songs, though, was in clear contrast to how he saw today's music. "I'm amazed at how little craftsmanship really goes into it," he said. "There's very little melodic structure left. They're sort of just loops and beats and rhythms and forgettable music. Today, the bands produce themselves—they call themselves producers—" but they "don't have a clue, and they're terrible."

But like Nancy Wilson pinning her hopes on Taylor Swift, Jonathan had his own artist he thought represented the best of the old in today's music. "I listen to Ed Sheeran's songs," he said. "Here's a guy who still writes a melody. He is truly a gifted, gifted writer. And it's what is going to last through the generations. He'll have the evergreen catalog—he's that good. He speaks to me, you know? He does. Same way [Don] Henley, you know, back when he was writing those great songs in the Eagles."

On the subject of new music, I asked him about the 2021 *Freedom* album, which hadn't received much attention, and he said, "Yeah, well, you know, it was COVID. We were all bored, and Neal started sending me stuff, and I just started writing lyrics and melodies and finishing things, and we amassed the record long distance. We never even saw each other, so it wasn't really a sit-down, thought-through Journey record. It was kind of a cut-and-paste, if you will. We wanted to certainly retain the Journey sound and have fun with the—maybe recreating a few of the moves we had back in the '80s. And then going some new places. You know, it was just sort of an exploration record, just exploring what we could do."

"I'd venture to say that we might've made our last record," he admitted. "The cost of making an album—you don't make any money anymore. You do it for the fans. [But] we have the music we need now. We don't need to make any more. Why spend $700,000 on an album [when] you'll never see a dime? I mean, this *Freedom* album's barely limping down the road. It's not selling. You know, the fans, they want to hear what they know."

I told him I'd just spent time with Never Stop Believin' and was curious about his perspective on that whole scene. He wasn't familiar with Gary and the band, though he was familiar with the Journey tribute bands en masse.

"There's more Journey tribute bands than I think any other band in the world," he said. That didn't track with what I'd learned from David Victor, but neither was he way off the mark. I asked him why he thought there were so many.

"I don't know," he said, and laughed. "I don't know. I can't answer the question. The music, it's durable. It lasts. It's timeless music. Perry used to say, 'Timeless music takes time, John. So don't rush it.'"

His believed tribute bands were "a great way to keep the music alive, and any time a tribute band can honor the body of work that Journey represents, it's a plus for us. Songs are disappearing. If they're continuing to play our music, they're representing us—however good or bad it is. It's still important that music lasts.

"I mean, since we took our break— I think we were gone for about eight, nine years; we weren't playing at all—that's really when [the Journey tribute bands] all started. But it's an honor. I'm flattered." He said he knew about the Frontiers tribute band and Escape, and that he'd checked out three or four others.

The end of our conversation took us back to Journey in the present. "We're seeing the rock crowd show up," he said of the new tour. "Last tour was remarkable. We sold out almost every arena. Maybe there's kind of a renaissance, you know, for music. I hope it is."

Whatever was going to happen, or whatever *was* happening now, Jonathan Cain had done plenty to make people care about music in his time. Not necessarily every Journey song, or even every album, but enough to fill concerts by whatever the current incarnation of the band existed now—and also whatever version of the band Gary could keep together. New songs didn't come into that equation. The classic songs had once been new, of course, and whether they would be discovered by a generation that hadn't been born yet, who could say for sure? The hope had to be that they'd be discovering "old bands" that came along well after Journey.

Or maybe the whole future of music was South Detroit.

SIDE THREE

OK COMPUTER?

ON THE ROAD
WITH THE DEAD

I f the popularity of tribute bands only underscored our obsession with music from the past, what did the rise of music holograms say about our relationship to new music?

In the studio, on tour—there's one truth that remains about the industry itself: Where music is headed next has always been about where the new technology is taking it. Imagine the intrigue—and deep sense of relief—for early Homo sapiens after endlessly banging animal bones together for melodic stimulation when a figure we might consider to be the planet's earliest musical genius carved the first known flute out of cave-bear bones. New possibilities for the developing ensemble!

The modern recording studio was in existence by the mid-1920s, with partitions between the control room and studio; microphones to sing into versus the primitive recording horns; an intercom system so producers could communicate with musicians without running back and forth. Still, if anyone was unhappy with what got recorded, the only choice was to try another take. But in 1948, the advent of magnetic tape changed all that. As Susan Schmidt Horning writes in *Chasing Sound: Technology, Culture & the Art of Studio Recording from Edison to the LP*, "No longer were musicians required to perform flawlessly from start to finish; now mistakes could be erased, edited out, and new parts overdubbed with relative ease." Previously, recordings were made on wax or lacquer-coated disks. With magnetic tape, whole sections of music could be stitched together. And as the Beatles and producer George Martin would be exploring, tape could be run backward or at different speeds to capture fresh, strange sounds. Too, the sound quality with magnetic tape was superior and helped usher in the "high-fidelity" era of music recording.

Or consider the impact of the accidental invention, in 1965, of the wah-wah pedal by twenty-year-old engineer Brad Plunkett. Plunkett worked for Thomas Organ Company, and he'd been tasked for finding a way to make Vox amplifiers the company was going to be releasing in the U.S., via a partnership with Vox, slightly cheaper to manufacture. His boss pointed to an amplifier and explained that the rotary switch they had for changing the frequencies on the equalizer was too expensive. So Plunkett came up with a circuit that would allow him to move this midrange boost with a potentiometer rather than with the switch. And in doing so, he discovered that famous wah-wah sound.

"The real effect was when you were moving it and getting a continuous change in harmonic content," Plunkett told the webzine Universal Audio in 2005. "We turned that on in the lab and played the guitar through it—this friend that I worked with who played the guitar. I turned the potentiometer and he played a couple licks on the guitar, and we went crazy." They then grabbed an organ pedal, since the hands were too occupied with the guitar to be operating this potentiometer, and the wah-wah pedal was born.

The wah-wah got the immediate attention of Frank Zappa. From there, the pedal unleashed a boundless litany of guitar freakouts that not only changed the sound of rock guitar but also put a new emphasis on the originality of the guitar solo—more daring, more bombastic, more screaming—so that sometimes the solo would be more celebrated than the song itself. Try imagining the solos in the following songs without the wah-wah: Jimi Hendrix's "Voodoo Child (Slight Return)," Eric Clapton on Cream's "White Room," Jimmy Page on "Whole Lotta Love," Chicago's Terry Kath's marathon romp on "25 or 6 to 4" on up through the next generation of guitar heroes—Vernon Reid of Living Colour's on "Cult of Personality," or Slash's wah-wah blast on Guns N' Roses' "Sweet Child O' Mine," the wailing jam on Metallica's "Enter Sandman" by Kirk Hammett on through Pearl Jam's "Even Flow" by Mike McCready.

Sometimes profound innovations don't just change the course of music, but they change what we can imagine for music. In 1979, the Fairlight CMI synthesizer, augmented with its own computer, became one of the first commercially available samplers. Created by Australians Kim Ryrie and Peter Vogel, the Fairlight had a built-in microphone that recorded sounds digitally—or any snippets of recorded music—and then played those samples back in whatever key the musician or producer wanted. DJ Afrika Bambaataa would use the Fairlight's half-second sample—which was as long a sample the Fairlight could record at the time—of Igor Stravinsky's *Firebird Suite*, which Vogel and musician David Vorhaus had recorded, on his song "Planet Rock." That little musical dart became the most ubiquitous sound in all of hip-hop and the most used sample in the history of the genre.

As it relates to the future of music, one of the most significant advancements of late isn't exactly new, since I first encountered it when I was five. In 1972 my parents drove my brother and me to Disney World. It had only opened the year before, but even then a sojourn to Orlando was fast becoming ubiquitous as families piled into their Lincoln Continentals and Buick LeSabres to partake in the latest American Dream. There was, of course, no Epcot Center, no Toy Story Land, or Typhoon Lagoon. But you can't pine for what you can't imagine, and the Magic Kingdom seemed wholly astonishing to me and John, who was almost six years older, compared to anything else we knew. We spent three days taking in the park's mechanical wonders, such as the Jungle Cruise, the Country Bear Jamboree, and the Hall of Presidents— in which President Lincoln told a sedate, plaid-clad crowd, "Man was made for immortality."

One of the highlights of that trip was the Haunted Mansion. After stepping into the gloom of a byzantine manor and being welcomed by the narrator's fiendish baritone, my dad and I were guided into a little car that shuffled us through a series of spooky tableaus. Below us, so that we had to peer down, was a lively ballroom scene, and here the ghostly effect was breathtaking. By a long banquet table spectral diners and dancers foxtrotted in their ghoulish glory. You could see them, but you could also see through them. As the cars proceeded, the last image you encountered in the room was an organist. He was caped and transparent—blueish—and floating upward from the organ pipes were tiny skulls. The organist was in studious concentration and took no notice of the onlookers. He was there to play.

Before we left Disney and headed back to North Carolina, we stepped inside a Main Street U.S.A. gift shop, where I gravitated toward a postcard rack, and among the offerings was one of the Haunted Mansion organist. The hours of contentment I could get from a single postcard seem unimaginable to me today, but on the long drive back—and in the days and many months afterward—I kept studying that picture. I was too young to wonder how the technicians at Disney had pulled off this effect, but old enough not to believe what I had seen. I just happened to be fascinated by the notion of musician for whom death had not kept him from his beloved instrument.

Forty-seven years later, in 2019, I began to hear about artists that made me think of that organist again—tours featuring Roy Orbison, Frank Zappa, classical pianist Glenn Gould, opera singer Maria Callas, Buddy Holly, heavy-metal belter Ronnie James Dio, and Amy Winehouse. The one defining and irrefutable commonality among these acts was that they were dead, and yet they were all or about to be back on the tour circuit—or, rather, their holograms were. These holograms wouldn't look like the ghostly organist, but the stuff of Hollywood-style digital recreations. Imagine Gollum from *The Lord of the Rings* or Thanos from *The Avengers: Infinity War* not trying to steal a ring or destroy mankind but rather singing "Pretty Woman" and "Maybe Baby" and playing lead guitar.

Was this rise of music holograms just one more indicator of our ever-shaky relationship to new music? Was the future of live music, whatever that was going to be going to be, destined to be so much more about technology than the musicians themselves? And what was it like for the musicians who had once made up the backing band for some of these icons and now settled for playing alongside their computer-generated likeness? At least, those were the initial questions I had. So I went looking to talk to the people behind this new experience. What I'd learn, needless to say, was that as industry folks began to pursue what was possible, almost no one was doing it in the name of new music. And in those conversations I'd be having—some with people who had devoted their lives to the music business—it was as if the very idea of new music was some distant memory. Like doo-wop or swing or the folk-music revival. Or Stryper.

All I really knew when I headed out to Los Angeles to start my exploring was that I was about to see dead people.

The poster read "Dio Returns." It featured the face of heavy-metal singer Ronnie James Dio, who had been dead for almost ten years. His head seemed to be peeking out from neither heaven nor hell, but a cosmic hole.

I was at the Beverly Hilton, most known for hosting the Golden Globe Awards, but today it was housing 2019 Pollstar! Live—a huge, annual event focused on live music and the concert industry. In front of one room was the Dio poster, which said, "US Tour Spring 2019," and next to it, under the moniker of the company Eyellusion, was a poster for "The Bizarre World of Frank Zappa." It showed a stern Zappa, the iconoclastic singer and guitarist who died in 1993, in the middle of a sea of cartoon characters—many of them transformed into Zappa himself: Zappa as a hot dog, Zappa as a giant robot. In a few minutes Jeff Pezzuti, Eyellusion's founder, and Ahmet Zappa, son of Frank Zappa and the company's vice president of global development, found their seats in the conference room. Eyellusion's Chad Finnerty, director of creative development, was on a panel, and he was the first speaker asked to introduce what his company was up to.

"We're putting together these awesome tours with Frank Zappa and Ronnie James Dio right now," said Chad, whose chiseled handsomeness and deep voice made him seem like he should have been promoting his latest action movie. "They're full-stage productions. We're not just a hologram company. We're an experience company." He talked about the technologies involved, how the company was pushing the limits of what was possible. And then he cued a video, set to the kind of pleasant keyboard drone you hear in aquariums, that showed behind-the-scenes efforts to bring the holograms to life. Here was a prototype of Dio, bald as an egg, then with his wild nest of digital hair, then the face in the early motions of singing. Similar footage showed the Zappa hologram as Chad narrated over it. "It takes a huge army to create these kinds of effects," he said. The original debut for the Dio hologram was in 2016, in Germany, which was followed by a European tour. Now it, or he, was poised to travel across America.

The next presenter represented a company that used drones for dynamic concert lighting, then Marty Tudor, CEO of Base Hologram, moved into his presentation, and as soon as he did, Jeff, who had been occupied with his phone, turned it off and crossed his arms in a standard show of suspicion. Ahmet crossed his arms, too, and arranged his face in the same expression.

"We've been around a long time," Marty began, explaining that Base Hologram was a part of Base Entertainment. "And so we approach our shows differently. We approach them as if we are doing a show. We develop a show like a Broadway show. We produce it like a Broadway show-slash movie because there are film elements to what we do. And then we tour it like a rock show."

He went on to mention the high-powered technology that they were using—"We managed to find technology, and we literally searched the world"—and that the Epson projector employed "a military-grade laser, so if somebody managed to hack it, they could literally cut a hole through the wall. I mean, it's serious, *really* serious technology. And that gives us the ability to present our hologram shows in a very different way than most everybody else does."

Ahmet leaned over to me in disgust. "Why would you say that?" he said. The music hologram business was in its infancy, but already real-life elbows were being thrown.

Marty mentioned that many upcoming shows would be announced, and that Amy Winehouse—the hypnotic, modern soul singer who died such a public, slow-motion death in 2011—was one of the acts that would be coming back as a hologram. He mentioned their shows of Roy Orbison, the velvet-voiced crooner who died in 1988, and Maria Callas, the influential but controversial opera singer who died in 1977. He presented a video that showed the two holograms backed by live orchestras. "We believe this is the epitome of augmented reality," Marty said, "where we've taken a live group of musicians on a stage in a live environment and then added a piece of technology to make it seem as it's part of the real world."

In terms of the visuals, there wasn't a notable difference between what Marty's footage showed versus Chad's. Both clips showed their performers resembling high-end video game characters singing and moving on the stage with realistic-looking movement and singing motions. The larger differences, as I was about to learn, were in the overall visions.

As the panel was drawing to a close and each presenter was given the chance for final remarks, Chad said, "We're artists creating art, paying respects to the musicians that we love and putting on these shows for the audience."

Hearing it put that way, it was a little hard to take issue with that as an impulse, and yet I knew enough that it was certainly more complicated than that. In the weeks before I had headed to Los Angeles, I told my youngest son, Anderson, that I was going to be writing about the rise of music holograms—having to explain first what this was all about. Anderson, who at eighteen had become obsessed with '60s psychedelia artists such as Jefferson Airplane and the 13th Floor Elevators, was aghast.

"That's bullshit!" he said. Anderson had no interest in seeing new music performed in concert whatsoever, so he didn't care at all about the larger consequences holograms could have there, but he was very focused on the ethics of the whole enterprise. He said the idea of music holograms was disgusting and amoral—bringing back dead musicians—and in a hot flash he was stomping his way back to his bedroom. As an eighteen-year-old, he was not always interested in looking at every facet of a situation, and as it was for me—at eighteen and now—music was the most important thing going for him. I couldn't help but admire his principled stand. And really, my feelings on the ethical aspect weren't so different from his.

After the panel, and on the way to lunch, Jeff, with a neatly trimmed beard and who has clearly seen the inside of a tanning bed, told me, "We were the first ones to ever take something out on the road," referencing the Dio hologram tour through Europe. "One thing that I wanted to specialize in, conceptually, was, I wanted [the artist's] live vocals because I wanted the energy of the artist to come through versus the actual studio recordings." The holograms for the Orbison and Callas shows used their studio recordings for the vocals, and Jeff was counting on this distinction being significant to fans.

At lunch, the Eyellusion folks ordered drinks and felt triumphant about the day's event—and the way people had responded afterward. They were keenly aware, too, of all the work ahead of them, since both the Dio and Zappa shows would hit the road soon.

For a while we talked about some of our favorite bands, many of whom were still around—technically speaking, at least—but whose heyday harkened back to a time when the cast of *M*A*S*H* first graced the cover of *TV Guide*.

"For me, my father is kind of this cosmic force, right?" Ahmet said. "And the fact that now he can be back on stage in his prime—ageless, timeless—that's a whole other aspect of what's happening now. So when you have this snapshot in your head of all your favorite bands, are you thinking of the seventy-year-old version of them, or are you actually thinking about the first time they made an impact? And that's what we're bringing to life."

"If you look at the top touring acts year every year, right down the list, most of them are legacy acts," Jeff said. "So how are you going to continue that trend when the legacy acts are no longer even touring?" He mentioned the Who, the Rolling Stones, U2, and Bruce Springsteen as examples. And in conjuring their names, he was underscoring the stronghold acts from the '60s and '70s had had on multiple generations. As Jeff saw it, holograms were a way to not let go of those artists we loved because in so many ways, we didn't really love today's artists quite the same way.

Ronnie James Dio wasn't the most obvious choice for the world's first touring hologram. As a solo artist, Dio never had a song on the *Billboard* Hot 100 chart, and the highest any of his albums peaked on the *Billboard* 200 album chart was No. 23, though his first few albums stayed on the charts the better part of a year. Dio was a popular live act, but in terms of larger visibility, on a presidential scale we might think of him as music's Woodrow Wilson. That is, he had a tremendous impact but never rose to the highest ranks of popularity, and the average person couldn't string two sentences together about his legacy.

But heavy metal enthusiasts aren't exactly known for courting what's popular, and in metal circles Dio is more like Abraham Lincoln: easily one of the greatest and most revered singers ever. And Jeff was banking on the metal community turning out for a chance to see Dio again, despite the fact that his remains were buried at Forest Lawn Memorial-Park in Hollywood Hills, in Los Angeles, alongside jazz singer Al Jarreau, Liberace, Toto brothers Jeff and Mike Porcaro, Motörhead's Lemmy, and Jerry Buss, owner of the Lakers.

In other ways, though, it made a certain sense that Dio was the first in this hologram foray, since no genre of music had indulged in the imagery of dark fantasy more than heavy metal. Black Sabbath, whose debut album in 1970 is widely credited as the first metal album, wanted their music to play like the soundtrack to a horror movie. The album's cover features a woman so ghoulish, draped in a black cloak in front of what looks like a moat, you might conclude that the only reason she wasn't burned at the stake in the Salem witch trials is because she dispatched the town's court officials herself. Many of the bands that followed in Sabbath's dark footsteps experimented with the use of macabre simulacrum—upside down crosses, demons and ghastly creatures, the Devil himself—along with portraits of gore and savagery. So a digital resurrection of Dio seemed like a natural enough way to honor a heavy metal icon.

After Ozzy Osbourne left Sabbath, the band tapped Dio to fill in. By that point Dio, after fronting the bands Elf and Ritchie Blackmore's Rainbow, had already established his own lyrical bent, which made him like metal's stand-in for J. R. R. Tolkien. Dio sang of wizards and spells and the legend of King Arthur; and on tour he even did battle with a mechanical dragon on stage. To attend a Dio concert meant you were going to be singing along to lyrics like:

Rainbows and blue skies / Are black and white / Killed in their sleep by the queen

Dio was back, then—sort of—and it hadn't happened by way of a cauldron. I was still computing everything I'd heard and seen that day of the conference, and one element I kept thinking about was this: What was it like to *play* with a hologram on stage? Dio's longtime drummer Simon Wright happened to be at the bar of the Beverly Hilton that night. He estimated he'd played with the singer for thirteen years, all told, with some interruptions. After we talked about our favorite drummers, living and dead, I wanted to know what he thought when the idea of a Dio hologram originally came up— and whether he had any ethical issues he had to sort through to sign on.

"I was a little skeptical first," he said in his pleasing British accent. "I didn't really know what a hologram was." But Jeff had been a particularly convincing salesman of the idea, and Simon particularly appreciated Jeff's zealous enthusiasm. "He knows all about Ronnie's music and lyrics, the shows," he said. So when it came time to showing Simon an early Dio prototype, he found himself gradually getting comfortable with the idea. Which helped since, once he was on board, he encountered a harsher, more cynical response. "When it was first put in the press that that's what was going to be happening, people were really upset," he said. "They would say, 'Oh, you know, you're raising the dead.' 'It's sacrilege' and all this kind of thing, when really all it is is an image. We're not here trying to rebirth Ronnie. He passed. He's not here. It's entertainment, it's not voodoo."

Simon saw playing behind the hologram, in fact, as the ultimate tribute to his friend and his songs. In another way, he'd already been doing that in recent years in a band called Dio Disciples, which played Dio's music and featured two singers carrying on Dio's vocals, with Dio band members guitarist Craig Goldy and keyboardist Scott Warren, who were in Dio's last band, along with Bjorn Englen on bass.

Still, playing Dio's music without Dio himself hadn't prepared Simon for what happened next. "When we started to play with the hologram and Ronnie's voice, it's like the songs just came alive," he said. During the performances, Simon couldn't even really see the hologram, but "it's still a live rock band," he said. "We're still playing."

The hologram tour had been an exciting development for Simon, but he also admitted that none of it was easy. "I've gone through a lot of emotions," he told me. "I just get on with it. I think [Ronnie] would enjoy me getting on with it."

◎ ◎ ◎

A full day's talk of dead musicians had me looking for a place that had a little more life, and that's how, late that night, I ended up at the Mint. In its heyday, the Los Angeles club had been graced by the likes of Taj Mahal, Bonnie Raitt, Duane Eddy, Earth, Wind and Fire, Ray Charles, Sheryl Crow, Stevie Wonder, and Colin Hay from Men at Work. (Way to move on, Colin!) I'd arrived to catch the Mint Jazz Jam, with a group tearing it up in front of a modest crowd. That band soon finished, and the next group, led by drummer Kevin Kanner, would soon start up. After that, anyone who wanted to come up on stage and try to hold their own was welcomed.

Before he could get behind his kit, I explained to Kanner what I'd seen and heard that day and wondered how he, as a working musician, might respond. He hadn't heard anything about music holograms, but he nodded his head in some intrigue, then said, "I mean, it's cool." But he was focused on his musical idols and the style of jazz he played. He said he didn't see a way you could bring back famous jazz musicians. "It would just be an insane amount of codes and algorithms needed," he suggested. To play jazz means you have to know how to improvise, and he couldn't foresee any kind of technology that could make that kind of magic happen.

Our conversation made Kanner think of the sci-fi novel *Do Androids Dream of Electric Sheep?*, published in 1968 by Philip K. Dick. It's about a bounty hunter who takes a job to kill six androids—who look entirely human—so that he can have enough to purchase a live sheep to replace his robotic sheep. The movie adaption, of course, was 1982's *Blade Runner*, one of the most influential sci-fi movies of all time. In bringing *Androids* up, Kanner was cutting right to the very point I'd been cogitating: You can create the illusion of live music being made by a hologram, sure, but was that still real music?

But maybe this was also missing the point of holograms. Everyone knew the hologram was a hologram—no audience member was going to think by the third song, "Wait a minute, why does Ronnie look so *bright* tonight?" The people who would buy a ticket to a hologram show had already made their peace with the illusion that the dead singer was back on stage. It was like visiting one of those haunted houses you see advertised on billboards every October: Field of Screams. Blood Manor. The point is not whether it's real, but how real does it *feel*?

Soon Kanner and his fellow musicians started up their set, jumping into Duke Ellington's "Caravan." On the first solo the trumpet player let loose a series of upper-register staccato notes that kept wrapping around themselves, and each player seemed inspired to responded in kind. The entire band was locked in with each other, as the alto sax player, bassist, pianist, and Kanner drove the tune like they intended to crash it through the walls. They were playing a dead man's music, yes, but it felt visceral and overflowing.

As their set went on—all jazz standards—a bevy of musicians who didn't look old enough to drink started finding seats, their instrument cases at their feet. I figured they were students in the jazz departments at nearby UCLA or Cal State. They looked nervous and fidgety, but I admired their spunk in turning out. When Kanner's band finished its set, the young musicians eased onto the stage, sometimes stepping in for the band members looking to take a break. On stage they looked even more overwhelmed, as if they were on an airplane and the pilots had just called out "Good luck!" before exiting by parachute. But they carried along the various melodies with pretty steady assurance, and in their brief solos they revealed little parts of their developing selves: slightly stiff, uncertain, frisky, curious believers in a pulsing music no matter how old it was.

In 1862, John Pepper—who had been teaching classes on physics, science, and mathematics, among other subjects, at London's Royal Polytechnic Institution—perfected a captivating idea by Henry Dircks, an engineer who had worked out his scheme but not fully implemented it. Pepper made significant changes to Dircks's plan, and the result was used in a stage production of *The Haunted Man* by Charles Dickens. The effect in question made a ghost appear onstage.

This is how it worked: Underneath the proper stage, a smaller stage was set up on which a large sheet of glass was positioned. The actor playing the spirit would be illuminated from behind, and the reflection from that lower-stage glass would bounce upward onto the plane of glass on the main stage, positioned at a forty-five-degree angle, and produce the phantasm effect for the audience. The illusion was soon known as Pepper's Ghost—and it was the same effect that would later be reintroduced to a mass audience at Disney's Haunted Mansion.

"Hologram" is pretty much what everyone in the music-hologram industry uses to describe their shows, though they almost all acknowledge that it's not really the proper term. An actual hologram is an intersection of light and matter that produces a three-dimensional object, intended to be viewed from all angles. Today's music holograms are digital creations projected onto a screen or scrim and are more analogous to videos. And they all took their cues from a curious intersection between '90s gangsta rap and F. Scott Fitzgerald, in 2012. John Textor, the CEO of Facebank Group, a company that created and stored the digital likenesses of celebrities and consumers, told me, "There would be no Tupac [hologram] unless Dr. Dre hadn't seen *Benjamin Button* and decided he wanted to rap with his friend."

In 2012, John was co-chairman of Digital Domain, which was responsible for the special effects of such movies as *Thor*, *Transformers*, *Titanic* and, most important for the future of the hologram industry, *The Curious Case of Benjamin Button*. The 2008 movie, starring Brad Pitt and based on a Fitzgerald short story, chronicles the saga of a man born old who ages in reverse. It includes an all-digital re-creation of Pitt's face, aged decades, through a process that captured the full range of the actor's expressions.

John, whom I met at his office in Jupiter, Florida, told me that after Dr. Dre reached out about his Tupac idea, a group of about twenty artists, led by Janelle Croshaw and Steve Preeg, worked to recreate the rapper—who was killed in 1996—in digital form. The project involved filming a body double who mimicked the rapper's stage moves, then putting that footage through digital animation. The artists created a digital head for the rapper and merged that with the real body, producing an all-new performance. The company AV Concepts handled the projection technology. The project took six weeks to complete and cost $600,000, John said.

When it played at Coachella, the Tupac hologram was a revelation and a sensation—today, it has well over 70 million views on YouTube—but it never went on tour. As John saw it, a touring hologram production could, without the right creative concept, be a limited use of the technology. "Because it's boring after the third song," he said. How are you developing a connection with the character? he asked. The risk is that "you're just looking at a projection and you're sitting there thinking, 'How much did I just pay for this seat?'"

John had also been involved with a Michael Jackson hologram and early work for Elvis and ABBA shows. (An Elvis hologram was set to debut in 2024. In 2020, there was supposed to an ABBA hologram tour, but that didn't materialize then. It took until the spring of 2022 to open in London, and one of the many ways the show, titled *ABBA Voyage*, differed from the Tupac hologram was that the members of ABBA, still very much alive, had fully participated in the production, using motion-capture technology to create digital avatars. In its review, *The Guardian*, which gave the story a headline calling the production "a dazzling retro-futurist extravaganza," noted that for the show "corporate sponsors, branding, and ads are conspicuous by their absence." When I originally read that, I thought, given the immense interest in ABBA all these years later, that we were a bit further off from fully accepting holograms as a viable concert experience than Jeff and the others pursing the medium were counting on. But according to a September 2023 *Bloomberg* article, the show had grossed more than $150 million. The show's producers were also in talks to expand the production to other cities. "Its success," the article read, "has created a potential model for other aging artists who want their fans to see them forever." That was exactly the level of nostalgia Jeff was banking on.

Throughout my teens and twenties and thirties and forties—and only slightly less so in my fifties—I was going to see my favorite bands regularly—and taking the chance on someone much newer occasionally. I've seen performances that I can still remember in exceptional detail, and even though I was just a spectator, some of those moments are some of my favorite memories ever. Music has always had that grip on me, and I go into every show hopeful and heedful of something that goes beyond a strong performance but speaks to the deep and primal ways we can feel connected to the music as it's being made right in front of us. Sometimes it can be single note from the lead guitarist where you don't expect it, or a singer spontaneously changing the lyrics of the song to comment on some recent event. It can be the drummer crashing a cymbal in the wrong spot and thinking he got away with it until another musician looks back at him quizzically, and the drummer howls in delight.

In 1994 I saw the band Crowded House for the second time—they were promoting their fourth album, *Together Alone*. Crowded House had always been a terrific live band in part because they were so spontaneous. They could make up a song on the spot. They might have a false start, and rev back up again, laughing at their ineptness, or the singer, Neil Finn, might good-naturedly rib a bandmate after a song for getting lost or spacing out. I have a live recording of the band in which they plucked someone from the audience to play keyboards on a song, having no idea if the guy could play. It turned out he could, and he played beautifully.

Crowded House was always loose and jovial, but they were also exceptionally sharp players, and the music—exquisitely crafted pop songs in the studio—could, on stage, push into territory that was raucous and unpredictable and thrilling to witness. Well into two hours of the show at Boston's Orpheum Theatre, someone from the crowd threw a paper airplane, and it sailed expertly over many rows before landing right at Neil Finn's feet. Finn was charmed by such a precise delivery and opened it up. It was a song request, he announced. He told the crowd that they hadn't planned on playing that one this evening—the request was for their biggest hit, "Don't Dream It's Over"—but given the fan's impressive aim, Finn said they would certainly play it now. And so they did.

That spontaneity is what I always want from a concert experience. These days, though, a show like that is so much harder to catch as bands with big budgets put increased emphasis on the visual spectacle—the big arena tours in which the music is synced with videos and computer graphics down to the very second. Not everyone wants that kind of spontaneity from a show that I do, of course, but when I'm seeing music performed, I want it to feel like anything can happen, that the musicians can react in real time to each other, the crowd, a mood.

I was trying hard to stay open to this landscape of dead singers taking the concert stage again in digital form, but I also felt protective of something that felt sacred. But maybe that was part of the problem—that I felt sacred about the ways music used to be. Music had always been what I cared most about in life, outside of family, but now I'd ended up writing books about music, and that required a perspective that can and often should differ from the passionate fan's. I had to separate my own feelings and experiences and maintain an open-mindedness.

Plus, I knew that from the very beginning almost all major shifts in music initially brought shock or scorn. When Igor Stravinsky presented his *Rite of Spring* for the first time, in May of 1913, some members of the audience, in raw response to the dense, intense, and dissonant music, broke out into a shouting match, which gave way to slapping and punching there in theater. Today, *Rite of Spring* is widely considered not just a masterpiece, but one of the most important and greatest pieces of music of the twentieth century.

Spearheaded by Ornette Coleman, Cecil Taylor, and the evolving direction of John Coltrane, in the '60s a new and extreme strain of jazz known as free jazz was establishing itself—music free from any fixed time keeping, traditional melody, or harmonic chord changes. With its simultaneous soloing from sometimes multiple instruments, free jazz could sound to even the most devoted be-boppers like New York mired in 5:00 traffic—all horns blowing, no discernible way forward, interminable to sit through. And yet to others this atonal revolt was the sound of a spiritual awakening.

In the '70s disco proved to be the soundtrack of liberation for multitudes—a luxuriating in the bottom-heavy groove that took you out to the dance floor and let you reinvent yourself, if even for a few hours. The penetrating harmonies and siren calls to disappear into the night—whether you were gay, straight, male or female, white, Black, Latina, a misfit, loner, or divine diva—were anthems for a new movement. But many saw the music as a cultural threat. In July 1979, at Chicago's Comiskey Park, White Sox fans showed up in droves for what was dubbed Disco Demolition Night—otherwise, it was a double-header between the Sox and Detroit Tigers. Dreamed up by a rabid local DJ but in full cooperation with the team, the game pulled in the White Sox's biggest crowd of the year, around 50,000, but not because of the home team, who was mired in fifth place in its division. There were chants of "Disco sucks" throughout the game.

After the first game, a 4-1 win by the Tigers, the real marquee event provided an actual explosion. To the crowd's delight a box of disco records was detonated in centerfield. Fans rushed the field to exalt in their rage against a music that didn't rock but pranced and thrusted. Someone started a bonfire. A batting cage was damaged. The unrest previewed the ugly melee, twenty years later, of Woodstock 1999. With thousands joining the free-for-all and the field like a battle zone, the White Sox finally had to forfeit. Eventually so did disco.

With popular music always in flux, what you think of the latest shift is all about where you find yourself musically speaking as well as your connection to the current culture, your personal wants from music and the wider world. I knew all that, and yet I still worried that music holograms represented a larger change we couldn't come back from: a future clinging to the past more than ever. I understood, too, that the rise of music holograms, just like the proliferation of tribute bands, spoke to a larger malaise in today's music. And I hadn't yet attended a hologram concert and had only caught short glimpses. I needed to drop my prejudices but stay observant about the quandary they could be.

The reason Eyellusion existed stemmed directly from Jeff's excitement about new music when he was young.

"There was this compilation record I got for Christmas called *Masters of Metal*," he explained when we decamped for breakfast one morning after watching the latest Zappa hologram updates, "and I was probably nine or ten. [Dio's] 'Rainbow in the Dark' was on it, and I put that song on. And I was like, 'Fucking A, this is amazing.'" Back then he was a paper boy in Rochelle Park, New Jersey. "I made, like, thirty-five bucks a week. And literally I would take that money—every dime from it—and buy records. That would be the only thing I would buy. So I bought my first Dio record, which would have been *Holy Diver*. I couldn't get enough of Dio."

In 1985, Dio was on tour and making a nearby stop. Jeff's brother, Tim, was also into the singer. "I said to my dad, 'Listen,'" Jeff recalled. "'He's playing Sunday night, it's in April,' and I said, 'Tim and I want to go.' He goes, 'Well, how much are the tickets?' I'm like, they're twenty-four dollars or something, but I go, 'We're going to pay, and we're going to pay for your ticket to go, too. That's how bad we want to go.'"

So Jeff secured three tickets, and his father picked his sons up at their mother's house to go to the show—the parents were divorced. Jeff and his brother loved the concert, and the father, not saying much afterward, drove them home and returned to his house. When he got home, his wife asked him how the show was. "He told me this many years later," Jeff said, rising to the punchline. "So he said to his wife at the time: 'Just give me two Advil or put a gun to my head.'" Jeff, who had no doubt told this story endlessly since he'd gotten into the hologram business, erupted once more.

Ahmet, too, had fallen hard for Dio as a teenager. He said he'd been listening to pop-metal bands whose songs were always about falling in love, but "with Ronnie, the magic of his lyrics, he was singing about fantastic beasts and witches and warlocks and rainbows and unicorns. I'm like, this is some other kind of mystical metal, you know? It's so rooted in my heart now."

"I saw him every tour," Jeff said dreamily. So when a friend called him, in 2010, to tell him that Dio had died, "I was *shocked* because—there were rumors that he was sick, but it was so different. It wasn't like now," by which he meant the immediacy of social media.

Two years later, Jeff, like millions of others, watched the Tupac hologram on YouTube. But Jeff may have been the only one whose life would change so dramatically as a result.

"I don't know why it struck me; I wasn't even a fan of Tupac," he said. But his mind began churning with the possibilities he saw in the technology. "I was telling my girlfriend [Rita] at the time, I said, 'Yeah, have you seen this thing, this Tupac hologram?' And she said no, so I show it to her. And I'm like, 'How cool is that?' She goes, 'Yeah, it's cool.' I'm like, 'No, it's *so* cool! It's just *so* cool.'"

Jeff was making good money at the time. In 1999 he passed his CPA exam after graduating from the University of Central Florida. "Did my VP of finance, did some CFO work for eighteen years in New York, but I can't say I was loving what I was doing." Finally, he had a proposal for Rita—perhaps not the one she was looking for. "If you give me two years," he began, pausing to explain that in this two-year plan of his, he would quit his job as VP of finance at Bluewolf, a cloud-based software company, and spend the first year researching every aspect of the hologram business, from the technical innovations to the feasibility of his bringing holograms into the concert-touring industry. He figured he'd need that second year to try and make it happen. What he was saying to Rita was: *I want to pursue my dream.* Rita, he said, encouraged him from the beginning.

He felt a little daunted without having industry contacts, but he did his research and kept sharpening his pitch. As he began meeting with people, the response was consistent: *Go away.* But Jeff believed in his vision of using the Tupac technology but employing more storytelling opportunities. The first manager he got a meeting with was Wendy Dio, Dio's widow.

"One of the first things she told me was that she has spent the last ten years thinking of a promise she made to her dying husband," Jeff said.

When I met Wendy Dio in Los Angeles, she explained that promise to me. "I did say to [Ronnie] when he was very sick that my lot in life was to keep his music and legacy alive. Which I've done."

In their initial meeting, Jeff told her he thought he could test the idea with $350,000 as an investment, thinking he could secure another $50,000 himself. By then he and Rita were existing together on her modest Catholic-schoolteacher's salary.

Wendy was intrigued, but she needed six months or so to sort through her feelings about it. Finally she agreed.

"Ronnie would always like to go to Disneyland and watch all the holograms there," she told me. "I think he would really be one hundred percent behind this. If you go into the Haunted [Mansion], you've got all the holograms dancing and all that. Ronnie was always an innovator in music, so I thought: Why not an innovator in technology?"

Now that Wendy was on board, it was time to do the actual shoot. Jeff would utilize the same process used for the Tupac hologram, this time finding a five-foot-four actor to play the role of the spritely Dio. He organized a conference call with the principals he'd wrangled into the idea. "So we get on the phone," Jeff explained.

"'OK, who's directing this?'

"'I guess I am.'

"'Who's your DP?'

"'What's a DP?'" Jeff asked.

The technical shoot advisor said, "What do you mean what's a DP?"

"I'm like, What's a DP? Do I need that?" Director of photography.

More back and forth. "'Who's shooting the plate?'"

"What the heck's a plate?" Jeff asked.

Thinking back to that time, Jeff said, "When I say it out loud it sounds even crazier."

When he got to Los Angeles for the shoot, he was given Chad Finnerty's number, since Chad had forged a notable career in digital animation and had his own company, Digital Frontier FX. (One of Chad's first questions for Jeff was, "Who's your DP?") Two days before the shoot, Jeff rented a camera. "So now I have a whole team," Jeff said. "We show up on Monday. We do the shoot for two songs." Once Chad's team was finishing Dio off in digital form, the talk turned to where to debut the hologram. It was Wendy who suggested Wacken Open Air, a heavy metal festival in Germany, and Wendy who initially reached out to Dio's former band members to gauge their interest.

Once the band was on board to perform with the hologram

and everything was booked, Jeff prepared for the big debut—four months after that initial shoot. "I'm flying to Germany," he said, "and I'm like, I'm putting Ronnie James Dio back on the stage in front of 75,000 people."

At Wacken, the Dio hologram was kept top secret, and it also closed the festival, after a set by Dio Disciples. Until that moment, the process of creating the Dio hologram hadn't been emotional for Wendy. "It wasn't Ronnie," she said. "It was parts, and it was *created* and so on. But then when it was actually on stage with the band, that's a whole different story. I cried. We all cried. Because it was Ronnie on stage again with his band."

The fervent response from the crowd led to Jeff and Wendy plunging forward with the Dio hologram. Wendy's motivation to partner with Jeff, though, went beyond just paying tribute to her beloved husband. She saw the future of live music as revisiting the great artists and bands who started so long ago, since they were rapidly retiring or dying off. But it also went further than that. When we were sitting on a sofa at the Beverly Hilton, she leaned forward and asked me, "What [current] band, can you tell me, in thirty years is going to be remembered?" She was arguing, essentially, that people would rather have a hologram of the great musicians from an earlier era who were dead versus the current crop of bands.

"You don't have another Led Zeppelin," Wendy said. "You don't have another Beatles. You don't have another Metallica.

You're not going to have another Zappa, with his avant-garde-ness and his craziness. All these people are icons. There's no icons [now]." Of course, this all depended on your point of view. In the pop world, Beyoncé, Taylor Swift, Madonna, Adele, and Lady Gaga were icons to countless millions. Wendy was talking about rock music, but she was also talking about legacies—musicians or bands that forever *changed* the music that came after them. How many rock or pop acts that had come along this century could we say seemed to be on that path?

Wendy imagined what it would be to see the Beatles together again. "That's not going to happen," she conceded. "But in a hologram it could happen."

Once Finnerty joined the company, they had to take what had been a one-song Wacken performance and expand it into an entire show for a tour of Europe—nineteen dates that Jeff booked the majority of himself. It was an investment in the future—not just Jeff's, but possibly in music's, too.

Along the Hollywood Walk of Fame, all I could think about was musicians and their legacies. Here was Liberace, in front of a store called Hollywood Perfume. Here was Count Basie in front of Calle Tacos. Nat King Cole. The Monkees. (Wait, did I really just pass a place called the Museum of Selfies?) Here was B.B. King and, ten feet over, Ray Charles. Johnny Cash. Donna Summer. People were kneeling on Michael Jackson's star, posing for pictures. The action was decidedly quieter around the Carpenters' star. How many young people knew their music, I wondered. But I wondered this, too: When is it OK to stop honoring someone's great career? The range of musicians' influence here was staggering. Duke Ellington was one of the most important musicians of the twentieth century. Jimi Hendrix re-imagined the possibilities of the guitar. The Doors introduced darker elements to rock audiences, making a rock concert feel dangerous and theatrical. Those musicians' back catalogs were always going to sell. But if you were in charge of the estate for Louis Armstrong and it was your job to think about ways to keep the legacy of Armstrong intact—to make sure future generations weren't clueless about one of the greatest trumpeters and showmen in the history of music—would a Louis Armstrong hologram be a way to keep his name out there? The Beach Boys didn't have to worry about their legacy, but what about Fats Domino or Buck Owens? Or the Everly Brothers? Or opera singer Blanche Thebom? As I was walking over these stars, it occurred to me how few of these once-famous musicians were going to have another renaissance, new catalysts for reappraisal. The truth is, not everyone's legacy was meant to stay so bright forever.

Billie Holiday, her star at 1540 Vine Street, is one of the most important jazz singers ever. But a monumental legacy doesn't always guarantee contemporary relevance—or visibility. If she had a hologram, would that automatically attract new attention? What would it sing? It turned out that just a few minutes away, at HologramUSA, I could see for myself. Out front of the theater, one poster announced a chance to see Holiday back on stage, and another promoted the original Tupac hologram.

The theater was closed to the public when I visited, but David Nussbaum, the company's executive vice president, ushered me into a room with red curtains and vinyl sofas. While Digital Domain created the Tupac hologram, Alki David, HologramUSA CEO and whose family's fortunes came through bottling Coca-Cola in many countries across the world, had bought the patents to the technology used to project the Tupac hologram. That move wasn't just controversial—it was possibly illegal. Later that year, the Securities and Exchange Commission would file a civil enforcement action against Alki David and Hologram USA Networks in New York federal court, alleging that they engaged in a "fraudulent scheme to induce the investing public" to believe they held rights to artists they didn't hold rights to, including Tupac. ("This is an idiotic suit over paperwork that is of no real consequence," Alki David wrote me in an email. "We did everything right and never made any false claims.")

David Nussbaum, in jeans, sneakers, and a gray sports jacket, said the place was mostly a showcase these days—a way to demonstrate what they had to theater owners, producers, and movie studios. He told me that the company's future was in franchising HologramUSAs all over the world—imagine Hard Rock Cafes, only instead of guitars and fringed vests hanging on the walls, it would be filled with dead musicians.

And the reign of old music just kept sailing into the future. With a tablet-looking feature in his hand, David began swiping across as he got ready to show me some highlights. He hit a button and said, "Here's Billie Holiday," and the jazz legend materialized at the microphone. She looked vibrant and mortal, and as she began to sing her haunting classic "Strange Fruit," the hologram carried that wounded coolness that poured out of Holiday's high register. David explained that they'd licensed the music from the company that retained those rights, worked with the Holiday estate to approve the likeness and overall effect. Eventually others began to join in around her—live dancers who had been filmed traditionally and were added to fill out the scene. I asked David why the need to add the others, and he conceded that this wasn't Lady Gaga or Jennifer Lopez, for whom there would always be dancers around, but that that was how people thought of female performers in these contemporary times, and in taking Holiday from a different era, "An audience now might not be cool with just a single person standing behind a microphone."

Even if that person was Billie Holiday? If you were going to bring twenty-first-century technology into the realm of live music, it seemed, you had to deal with twenty-first-century expectations about music and entertainment.

David tried to show me the hologram of Jackie Wilson—the soul singer nicknamed Mr. Excitement—but it kept freezing. "Well, this is embarrassing," he said. We moved on.

"The thing that specifically put us on the map was when we beamed Julian Assange out of the Ecuadorian Embassy in London" so he could speak at a conference in the United States, David said. What Tupac had done for digital resurrection, "I wanted to do something that big for live telepresence because nobody had really been doing anything with that." David had had the idea of beaming O.J. Simpson out of the Las Vegas Penitentiary to do an interview for—say, *Dateline*. He'd wanted to do the same for Charles Manson. "Maybe speak on a stage and answer questions from an audience." Because who wouldn't want to be in the same room as the image of Charles Manson as he peered into a crowd and said, "OK, you in the third row—I see your hand raised."

David as much as anyone understood what the Tupac hologram had done for the hologram industry, but he underscored that it wasn't just musicians that some people wanted to see in hologram form. "We get everything from, 'I'm a pastor at a church, and I want Jesus to walk on water during an Easter Sermon' all the way to 'My dad died last year, and I want him to walk me down the aisle at my wedding.'" He said the company had also met people who knew they were dying. "They come to us. 'Film me, because I want to speak at my own funeral.'" The scenarios seemed endless. And, to me, endlessly worrisome.

He also told me about a mega pop-star hologram that hadn't worked out well. "We digitally resurrected Whitney Houston," he said. "Pending with the estate's approval. She performed on the season finale of *The Voice*, and she did a duet with Christina Aguilera. A living Christina Aguilera sang opposite Whitney Houston's hologram on the season finale of *The Voice* a couple years ago."

I'd heard about this—you couldn't talk to anyone in the

music hologram business without hearing about it. But footage of Houston's hologram was leaked before the show could broadcast. "We didn't feel like, and the estate also didn't feel like, the hologram was done," David explained. "We were rushing to get it done for the season finale, so what we wanted to do was film in a couple of weeks in advance, and then edit it in post-production." But then came the leak. "And so we weren't happy. They weren't happy. Nobody was happy because it was not what we all signed on for." The consequences didn't just impact the season finale.

"The idea was that Whitney was going to perform," David explained. "She was going to go on tour, and so we were going to announce the tour on *The Voice*." But when word got out that the hologram didn't look good enough and the Houston estate subsequently pulled the plug, it sent a chill to many who were toiling away at the next big hologram production. Sensing disaster, would people just stay away from the other tours that did take off?

(The Houston estate wouldn't comment on what David told me, but through a publicist directed me to a 2016 statement from executor Pat Houston: "Holograms are new technology that take time to perfect, and we believe with artists of this iconic caliber, it must be perfect. Whitney's legacy and her devoted fans deserve perfection. After closely viewing the performance, we decided the hologram was not ready to air.") Working with a new team of animators, the Whitney Houston hologram made its debut in 2020 in the U.K. instead, following with a tour through Europe and a residency that lasted eight months in Las Vegas before closing. The reviews weren't exactly charitable, with potshots like *Entertainment Weekly*'s "the design and production value was more befitting of a cruise ship singer than one of the greatest performers of all time" being a constant theme.)

Soon David brought on Tupac. The rapper's motion was sinuous, and his roped muscles gleamed as he strutted around. "Ah shit, you done fucked up now," the hologram said. "Ain't nothing but a gangsta party." But instead of Snoop Dog being next to him, as he had during the Coachella debut, David had climbed on stage alongside him. "You done put two of America's most wanted in the same motherfucking place at the same motherfucking time," Tupac declared. He'd said that once—the vocals were his—but it wasn't, of course, David Nussbaum whom Tupac had in mind at the time.

Then David came down, and we watched together. "I don't want to tell you what to write your story about," he said, "but that is the future."

In New York, at the famous auction house Sotheby's, the holograms were on display but not for sale. Base Hologram was holding a showcase for their creations. Behind a curtain in a dark room, a projector hummed ominously. (The one that could shoot a hole through the wall, I assumed—uneasily.) I talked to one of the men slinking around in all black, who explained that he and others had been hired as extras. They weren't musicians, but when Roy Orbison and

Maria Callas performed later, they were there to give the feeling that, well, people were on stage watching them with the proper degree of awe.

The founder of Base Entertainment, Brian Becker, and Marty Tudor, whom I'd seen in Los Angeles, came to the podium. "What we want to show you today is what we are developing as a new art form for live entertainment," Brian began. "It combines live performers on stage, actually playing or singing, combined with holographic, content, augmented reality, and even cinematic special effects. We use the original master recordings of the artists, then everything else we add and put together. We create something that we think is very compelling, very exciting, and delivers an extraordinary entertainment experience."

He explained that they'd had two tours that went out last year—Callas and Orbison, both with orchestras. This year, he said, Orbison would be paired up with a Buddy Holly hologram and a band. He referred to the earlier tours, the reactions, and that this technology could be used in a variety of settings—museums, tourist destinations, cruise ships. He then said that part of what this technology could deliver was more than dead musicians performing to audiences again—but historic pairings. "So, for example, can you imagine Whitney Houston and Aretha Franklin?" he asked. "Or can you imagine, you know, Winston Churchill and Abraham Lincoln?" Singing harmony? Who was the Art Garfunkel in that pairing, I wondered.

"The advantages to this, we think, are many," he said. "One is that we will build a library over time that will then allow us to combine different artists together or different elements together."

He said they could do product placement and left us to imagine how that might work. (Would Whitney Houston be making a pitch for Verizon between songs?) He also mentioned a desire for artists to interact with the audience, but not in the manner of Siri and artificial intelligence. "We could have plants in the audiences saying, 'I love you, Roy!' And Roy could say, 'I love you, too, baby.'" He talked for a while longer, then showed Orbison, who appeared from a mist and ran through a medley of classics for about ten minutes. There was a kind of bluish haze, I thought, a little Princess Leia "Help me, Obi-Wan Kenobi" feel to him, and in moments I could see through him. He sang hits such as "Pretty Woman" and "Only the Lonely" as the black-clad extras behind arranged themselves attentively.

Next up was Maria Callas. The tempestuous opera star was known for performing with a torrent of expression and drama, and the hologram radiated that human intensity. At one point, she had a deck of cards and hoisted them into the air, where they floated down like snowflakes. Apparently even Callas's *hologram* was a diva.

After the presentation, I talked to both executives backstage. Brian said that Base, which was primarily based in Las Vegas, got a call from Marty about three years ago, and Marty told him, "I have this idea." There was this technology, Marty told him, and he thought it could be interesting for new touring possibilities.

Marty had been a manager in the music business—Paula Abdul was one of his clients—and he had also been a consultant to a booking agency. And just as Jeff had drawn inspiration from the Tupac hologram, so had Marty. "My immediate reaction was, I can't believe they did this," he said. "It was amazing. And then they didn't follow up with it." Marty kept waiting for an announcement, but there was nothing. "I thought: That's where they missed the boat." Brian agreed, and they began to explore the possibilities, ultimately forming Base Hologram.

"We don't see ourselves as bringing people back to life," Brian said. "We're celebrating artists, and we're using their virtual image. I mean, we're not denying what we have on stage, but we're doing it with in the contexts of stage craft as well."

I could tell they sensed my resistance, and Brian asked me if I'd seen the Queen biopic *Bohemian Rhapsody*. David Nussbaum had also asked me this in trying to draw a similar comparison. When I told Brian I had, Marty jumped in and said, "So when you watched *Bohemian Rhapsody* you didn't go, 'That's a tragedy that you showed me Freddie Mercury.'" Already my face was twisting up in protest, but he elaborated on his argument. "And when you sit at home and watch TV you see, you know, *Some Like It Hot*, and you see Marilyn Monroe and Tony Curtis and Jack Lemmon, there's nothing different about watching them."

"The difference," I said, "is when you're watching Marilyn Monroe—she chose that role, worked with that director, and did those performances."

"So we're recreating their performances," Marty offered—not the actors' but the musicians'. What he wanted me to accept, in other words, was that there was no real difference in having an actor play someone famous versus re-creating that famous person digitally.

We talked more about how they brought their holograms to life, and Brian explained that they used prosthetics on the man who modeled for Roy Orbison's digital creation. "In the case of Orbison, we had our actor go on a diet, lose twenty-seven pounds," Brian said.

I asked why they didn't just find a thinner actor. But that actor also played guitar, they said. And with Maria Calas, Marty explained, they had found a true opera singer. "When you look at an opera singer sing, everyone just thinks, 'Oh, the mouth is moving.' Every muscle in their body is moving. And those little, subtle things is what sell you on the humanity of it."

I was eager to ask them about the Amy Winehouse hologram, in part, because her death, then, was still quite recent—in 2011. When I first heard about the project, I thought there was something unseemly about a digital Winehouse—who had a series of drug arrests and gave increasingly erratic performances or canceled shows altogether toward the end, —whose biggest hit centered around a refusal to go to rehab.

"The reason we are holding back on moving forward with Amy is because she died [eight] years ago," Brian said, "and she died in a tragic way."

But, I pointed out, that was true when they first announced the tour.

"I think there is a sensitivity there," Marty said. "With Amy particularly, there were a lot of people who said to us, 'Oh my God, I can't wait. I never got to see her in concert. She never really toured and seeing her perform would be wonderful.' And then we had other people that said, you know: 'Wow, it's only been a few years, and she died tragically. And she had a lot of people pulling on her, that took advantage of her. And doesn't this, you know, fit into that?'"

"It just wasn't the right time," Brian said. "We learned a lesson with Amy. We actually had done a lot of work and a lot of homework, but we didn't do enough." But the very reason they had focused on an artist like Amy Winehouse, Brian quickly added, was the desire to bring back to audiences people "that really made an impact on the world."

"There's an enormous demand for nostalgia," Marty said.

Of course, that barely got at it. Who were we if we weren't longing for what had already happened, for what we'd heard or seen in the distant past? But that demand can make you do a lot of things. That was one of the dangers I saw in all this. Brian acknowledged that but said, "We wouldn't put, you know, we wouldn't have Winston Churchill talk about Donald Trump." Too bad! Who wouldn't want to read the Trump social media screed that came out of that? "The FAKE Winston Churchill is a total disaster for England! A real Emberrasment!"

"There is a line," Marty said. "I believe there is a line, you know, and if you cross that line, then you're really taking advantage of that person." But who was the arbiter? The estates had the final say when it came to creative decisions, but that didn't mean an estate couldn't cross a line, especially when so much money was potentially at stake. And who was it that was defining what that line even was?

It was all polite enough conversation the three of us were having, and yet I couldn't help but think that arguing the larger ideas was a bit pointless. Or maybe I was just arguing with myself. We were at this place in time, and all of this was happening. I was just a reporter with a notepad and a digital recorder in my hand who had opinions.

Buddy Holly was twenty-two when he died, along with Richie Valens and DJ J. P. Richardson, known as the Big Bopper, in a chartered plane near Clear Lake, Iowa on a snowy evening in February 1959 —a day famously referred to as "The Day the Music Died" and immortalized by Don McLean in his song "American Pie." On the tenth anniversary of the accident, Greil Marcus revisited the tragedy for *Rolling Stone*. About Holly he noted that Coral Records had released half a dozen albums of Holly's music after the crash, and some of these recordings Holly had made at home—demos—with tape-recorders in his high-school years, which had been re-recorded with studio musicians. "The feeling one gets from listening to these cuts, an uneven collection of various Number One records," Marcus wrote, "is that of visiting a funeral parlor to watch an embalmer touch up the face of a body mangled in an accident. The guy does a great job but you still don't recognize the face."

I didn't get to see the Buddy hologram that day at Sotheby's—presumably it was still being worked on. But that disconnect Marcus was pointing to—how we honor the dead, or don't, whatever good intentions we have—sure resonated with me.

◎ ◎ ◎

In Collingswood, New Jersey, it was already a little disorienting attending a rock concert by an artist known for albums such as *Burnt Weeny Sandwich* and *Uncle Meat*, but then nothing was straightforward about a show featuring Frank Zappa twenty-six years after his death. At the Scottish Rite Auditorium, in a room off the grand ballroom, I caught up with Jeff as he was into their second week of the *Bizarre World of Frank Zappa* tour. He was still in the glow of an enthusiastic article/review from *Rolling Stone*, which had declared "The Tupac hologram is still surreal . . . One artist whom the practice makes complete sense for, though, is Frank Zappa . . . More than a quarter century after Zappa's death, his dream is a reality—and a success."

Already Jeff felt like the music industry was waking up to the possibilities he'd seen years earlier, since his phone was "blowing up" after the initial reviews started pouring in. "Interesting requests, new requests," he said. "People are—some big things that we would love to work with are interested." He couldn't tell me what those were—outside of classical pianist Glenn Gould, which was already in the works—but one of the feelings he was clearly expressing was just relief that his gamble was paying off. "I put in my whole life savings," he reminded me.

Soon Ahmet Zappa, who, as one of Zappa's four children was a co-trustee of the Zappa estate, strolled into the room, and he was in the same haze Jeff was.

"It's been this self-discovery process because I feel more connected to Frank," he said of the early shows. In Los Angeles, Ahmet had mentioned how in his father's *The Real Frank Zappa Book*, published in 1989, he details his attempts to explore the technology. "He wanted to have this hologram business so that he could send that out on tour and stay home and work on more music, you know?" Ahmet told me then. "So that's why I feel like I'm finishing something that he started."

Now that the tour was underway, the new connections he felt to his dad were coming through felt profound. "You get exposed every night to a whole community of people who spent their whole lives listening to your dad in ways that wouldn't have been possible all these years," he said. For Ahmet, and despite all the incredible technical aspects of the show, its fundamental purpose was clear. "The goal for me of this show is music first, right? Like, this is the only way someone's going to hear Frank's vocals, his guitar, with his band. That really is at the core of why we do any of the shows. It's because we're fans first." As far as he was concerned, the visuals that he had dreamed up for the show were simply "the icing on the cake."

Mike Keneally, on lead guitar, played with Zappa on what would prove to be Zappa's final tour, in 1988—and Mike's first tour of any kind—and he echoed that point when I met him. With his square glasses, gray beard and sparse gray hair, he looked more like a cool high school computer-programming teacher than a musician who'd toured with monster guitar icons Steve Vai and Joe Satriani. Mike said the first time he heard about the opportunity of playing with a hologram, "I remember thinking, this might be spooky. And then I saw the footage of it, and I, you know, found it strangely moving."

Mike got his first big break with Zappa, in fact. He was twenty-five. "It was an ecstatic thing for me because that was all I ever wanted when I was a kid was to play with Frank."

Just as I had asked Simon Wright of Dio, I asked Mike if he had to go through any moral calculations before he signed on.

"No, because I knew that—to me, it's all bound to how would Frank have felt about it. And he wouldn't have one moment of moral compunction. I think he would be fascinated by what's possible technologically."

When I asked him if he felt like he was, in some way, playing with his old mentor again, he said, "Yeah, during the guitar solos there are definitely moments where—because we're responding. The guitar solos are the moment where we can respond improvisationally to what we're hearing, as opposed to playing an arrangement that's been worked out." As with the vocals, Zappa's guitar had been isolated from live recordings that had gone largely unheard.

The whole experience was a lot to go through, Mike explained—the past mingled with the present. "There's definitely a through-line, and so there's a part of me that feels very young," he said. "But at the same time, I'm feeling: Here I am. I'm fifty-seven. I've gained whatever skills I've gained in the intervening years. There's a part of me that is like, Man if I could just take what I know now, my awareness of the world, plus my facility, my technique, bring that back thirty-one years and be able to serve this up to Frank because I feel like I can serve his music better now than I was able to back then. So that's for me, personally, a very important part of the tour."

For Mike, a digital creation had given him an opportunity to take a decidedly personal inventory.

When I got to my seat, I took in the whole set up on stage: All the musical equipment—the drums, the guitars and keyboards, the electric vibraphone—were to the left or right of center stage, and in the middle was the screen in which the hologram would be. Around that space, framing it, were big LED screens that also ran below the stage. The hologram space was like a stage within a stage.

The majority of the crowd was sixty and older, though quite a few were parents—decked out in faded Zappa concert T-shirts that might have, all these years later, still have a whiff of Mother Earth baked into them—who'd brought their adult children. The near-capacity crowd of 1,050 was casually milling around when the lights went out and musicians found their spots to start up the opening number, "Cosmik

Debris." On the screens flashed a constellation of lights that began to gather as the song went on, finally merging into the human form of Zappa, in a striped short-sleeve shirt and jeans, his hair cascading over his shoulders, and positioned behind the other musicians slightly. Zappa cranked out his first guitar solo to rapturous applause. The Zappa hologram, in this form, appeared a little less natural to me than compared to what I'd seen of Dio. Zappa looked like a character from an R-rated cartoon of the 1970s, but then, that was how Zappa, with his trademark moustache and soul patch, had always looked to me. What was remarkably lifelike, though, were the human details Chad Finnerty and his group had worked in and made so subtle—the occasional head nod to something he'd played on guitar that pleased him, the casual pacing around as he jammed coupled with an intense appearance of listening to the musicians, who seemed energized to be spurred on by their leader again.

In Zappa's guitar playing, the fingering was convincing and exact. But the next number made clear that "regular" Frank would appear only every once in a while, and that's because the show was about the bizarre world of Frank Zappa—all the strange imagery he'd created through his lyrics and album and song titles, as re-imagined by Ahmet. Zappa now appeared in the form of dental floss for "Montana," a song about, um, the dream of owning a dental floss farm. Where the human Zappa had been, there was a strip of floss bouncing around, sometimes forming a map of Zappa's face, sometimes responding to the music, and snapping to an outline of him playing the guitar solo, complete with working the wah-wah pedal with his foot. It was funny and dazzling, hitting that generally untapped spot where a jazz-rock acid trip and Hollywood computer animation meet. For the next song, "Trouble Every Day," inspired by the Watts riot, we were plunged into the world of newspapers' coverage of late '60s race riots, and here Zappa showed up as the narrator in a newspaper picture, hovering above images of police brutality. Next, for that family favorite "Penguin in Bondage," Zappa took the form of a naughty penguin with a penchant for doling out punishment. Over the course of the show, Zappa would also show up as a Claymation Frank, a superhero, a poodle, a dirty plate in his kitchen, a disco doll, a giant robot, and a hot dog. He'd also appear on the toilet.

At the end, Zappa, back in his human form, told the crowd in that game-show announcer voice of his, "You've been a great audience," unplugged his guitar, and walked off before vanishing.

I felt awestricken and had a sudden conviction that I suddenly understood the '70s much better. Somehow the show made me confront the *idea* of dead musicians and their holograms much less than I'd imagined. Instead, I was awed by the *possibilities* of a hologram show, its range of storytelling possibilities. That's what Jeff had been trying to explain to me in Los Angeles. Now I better understood when Ahmet had earlier taken issue with the production being called a "hologram show" at all, when we first began talking. At times the visuals made it difficult to focus on the music, but there were also times when the visuals receded and the music was front and center. Still, Zappa's spirit conducted everything—in fact, at one point the hologram dons a conductor's long tails, his baton waving over his head.

One of Zappa's last interviews was for a 1993 *Today* show segment, and Jamie Gangel was talking to him about his penchant for such complex music and bizarre content rolled into one. "I don't know if it's even fair to ask: How much of it is for the sound and how much of it was for the humor?"

"Both," answers Zappa, nonplussed. "The goal here is entertainment." I was entertained, certainly, but was it that simple? I wasn't nearly ready to say I'd been overthinking everything. I was staying focused on what was good—or what *I* thought was good—for music's future. I'd really enjoyed the concert, but it hadn't tempered my larger worries.

But maybe David Nussbaum, at HologramUSA, was right: Maybe this *was* the future. If I couldn't embrace that, maybe I was stuck in the past, too.

In Glenside, Pennsylvania, inside the Keswick Theatre, Jeff, looking every bit the rock impresario with his shirt unbuttoned halfway down his chest, was at the front of the stage, concerned that the screen holding Dio's image was a little crooked. He directed a tour member to straighten it, then asked for the Dio hologram to come on, the way a singer would do sound check. The hologram looked sharper than when I'd seen it four months earlier, and the soaring vocals poured through the hall like an aural tsunami.

Jeff was assuaged and previewed some of the effects I'd be seeing tonight, but he was quick to add, "But the idea is, I don't want people to think they're watching a fucking hologram. I want people to think they're at a real rock show."

He mentioned that his brother was coming up from Washington, D.C., for the concert and that his father would be catching a show later in the tour, too. That was its own closing of a circle—the teenage Jeff seeing a healthy, vibrant Dio with his father, his father, all these years later, seeing the hologram of Dio that Jeff had made a reality. *Heavy* metal.

After a while, Jeff, took me to the tour bus. Inside he rustled up Scott Warren, who emerged from the back in black pants and a T-shirt, with a tangle of blond hair. Scott, the keyboardist, was the longest-serving band member from Dio, having played with him for seventeen years. Before we talked about playing with the hologram, I asked him about Dio's passing.

"In so many ways it was, obviously, very difficult," Scott said in a quiet voice. "We were getting ready to go on tour when we learned of his cancer. When he got diagnosed, we had rehearsal to go on a major world tour in Europe—all our equipment had been shipped off—and suddenly, he didn't come to rehearsal one day. And I instinctively kind of thought something was wrong."

After Dio's death, was it hard to move on to the next musical situation, I asked him.

"Well, I said to myself, 'I'm never going to play another Dio song again. This is it.' 'Cause, I thought, you know, this is his name, his band, his music.'"

Only it didn't quite turn out that way, once the Dio Disciples formed. True, they were playing much smaller audiences—imagine the E Street Band playing Bruce Springsteen's music without him. (Then imagine them all dressed in black. And scowling.) Scott, like Mike Keneally in Zappa's band, didn't go through much soul-searching when he heard about the hologram. "I thought it would be cool," he said, "if it was possible, you know?" It was more than possible, but there were still mental adjustments he had to make. When I asked him how much the hologram captured the singer he knew so well, he said, "It's not going to be him. I have to—it's hard to accept, you know. I know all his mannerisms and everything like that. And how he was, and sometimes the glares." He laughed thinking about those glares. "'You didn't do it right,' or whatever. I know all about that, but you do have to sort of step back from that and sort of accept what it is because it's not a human being, you know?" He laughed with a sense of resignation. "So there is that."

He remembered, then, a moment between him and Dio before a new tour started up. "I said to him, 'You know, I just want you to know as long as you're rocking, I'll be there.' You know, 'I'm into doing this.' And that really meant something to him." Scott had kept his promise in a way both men could have never imagined.

Once inside the venue, I saw that the crowd was younger on average than Zappa's—old enough to get direct mail for AARP membership, young enough to be ticked off by it. Jim Pezzillo, who'd driven down from Parsippany, New Jersey, had no qualms about seeing a hologram show. "I'm all for it," he said. "If it keeps the music and the spirit alive, and, you know, gets to keep it for future generations, I don't find it weird like some people find it weird."

His friend Russ Ciffo, from Columbia, New Jersey, wasn't quite as confident about what they might be in store for. "Truthfully speaking, from my heart, it might be weird," he said. But Russ was a devout Dio fan, and while he knew there were fans who weren't open to this, he was willing to take the chance. "This is what I really mean: They're dead. Either you come see them or you don't come see them. That's the choice you need to make. I want to see him."

Seeing how Dio had performed at venues like the Meadowlands, and now his hologram and the band were in front of fewer than 1,000 people, it was clear that a lot of people didn't want to see him—not like this.

The lights soon went down, and the opening band kicked the evening off. The singer, Jizzy Pearl, navigated mostly a sliver of available stage, since the front was designed for the screen. The band used to be called Love/Hate, but maybe because Jizzy Pearl was the only original member left, it was now called Jizzy Pearl's Love/Hate. That felt like something I should hate.

Between songs Pearl said that they were honored to be on this tour and that Dio "was the greatest rock singer ever." The crowd roared their approval.

The venue was at about two-thirds capacity when the Dio set began. On the LED screens a forest came into focus, then bats. And then a dragon. An explosion of digital flames, and now here was Dio belting out "King of Rock and Roll" in his signature, operatic frequency. There was no hushed puzzlement from the audience, no collective riposte that said, "*That's* supposed to be Dio?" The crowd ate it up instantly, thrusting into the air the ubiquitous devil horns—fist balled, with the pinky and thumb jutted out. (A debate as to whether Dio was the first to introduce devil horns into the metal world still plays out in metal circles. His grandmother was Italian, and she would flash the sign at people as "protection from the evil eye" Dio said in an interview on VH1's *That Metal Show.*) Even from this distance there was still a faint CGI glow to the hologram, but that might have been compounded by the fact that Dio, with his white blouse, long hair, and leather pants, already looked like a character in "Lord of the Rings." But the audience was clearly relishing hearing these Dio songs they loved, and there was a convincing fluidity coming through the hologram's movements. Presumably Dio did a lot of gesturing with his left hand, a lot of leaning to that side of his body, since the hologram kept doing that. A lot of devil horns flashing. The hologram covered a small area when he paced, which I understood for technical reasons, but it was akin to watching a big cat at a zoo pacing back and forth due to captive stress syndrome.

With that first number complete, the rotation of singers for the evening began. The singer "Ripper" Owens took the stage—everyone knew him as the singer in a Judas Priest tribute band Priest who became the replacement for longtime singer Rob Halford. (That story, which in many ways was just like Arnel Pineda's for Journey, inspired not a documentary but a predictably mediocre feature movie treatment starring Mark Wahlberg called *Rock Star.*) Once Owens finished, the singer Oni Logan took over, and then it was back to Dio, carrying on in that rotation. Jeff had told me earlier that he didn't think a crowd was ready to sit through a whole show focused on a traditional hologram—which the Zappa show avoided, thanks to Ahmet's dizzying kaleidoscope of ideas. Now that point seemed prescient to me. Every time Dio reappeared, there was a little jolt of alertness in the crowd.

Jeff had found a seat in the row behind me, and throughout the show, despite how many times he'd sat in on rehearsals and every performance since the show had begun touring, he was smiling like a jack o' lantern, singing every lyric, thrusting his hands out in time with a guitar riff or cymbal crash. I thought about his leap of faith, the ways a financial guy from New Jersey had believed in his vision to bring Dio back to the stage so deeply, and all the ways that that could affect the concert industry. I thought about what it had meant to him to discover Dio in the first place and what he must have felt like having done with that connection what he'd done.

Throughout the show, the visuals around the hologram, impressively animated, took the form of trees or gears, oceans, skies, misty forests, time pieces, sparks, fire. Sometimes it was just scary eyes. Often the hologram disappeared during guitar solos, which made sense; watching a hologram that isn't playing an instrument or singing is as engrossing as watching a

Pac Man machine after you've run out of quarters. Sometimes the Dio hologram morphed into flames, or just mist. At one point it turned into ice particles.

Later in the show the dexterous bassist, Bjorn Englen, walked over and appeared to be just inches away. Up until that point, the hologram mostly seemed to exist outside of the band, since the musicians rarely looked the hologram's way, so this gesture brought a real-life concert feel to it. The problem was that Bjorn stayed in that position for several minutes, and after a while I became aware that the hologram never looked his way, so I was knocked out of that authentic-feeling moment all over again.

For the finale, "We Rock," both Owens and Logan came out to sing with the hologram, at one point flanking him. This was when the whole effect seemed the most real to me, since each of the three singers would take a chorus, and when one of the living singers took over, Dio just exalted in the music. And maybe it had done this before, but at one point the hologram, encouraging the audience to sing along, cupped his ear, turning the mic outward to the crowd, and said, "I can't hear you." As illusions went, that went a long way in conjuring authenticity.

In the seconds after, the song winding to a close, the Dio hologram disappeared for the last time. The band gathered at the front of the stage, their arms around each other, and acknowledged the cheers of the crowd. I thought it would have been cool to somehow have the hologram in the middle of that group, waving to the crowd. The fact that I even thought that—*Why isn't the hologram bowing with the others?*—was pretty telling about the show's overall sense of authenticity. But I continued to think what was at stake in all this went beyond a sense of realism.

Just as it did with pretty much every musician in the world—alive or created—COVID shut down Eyellusion's shows for the better part of two years. Jeff and I kept in touch, comparing notes about what was going on with some of our favorite bands—though not much was—and talking about the touring industry's long dig out of the nightmare pandemic.

For a long stretch during that time Jeff hosted Friday night Zoom talks with his passionate, music-loving friends spread out all over the country and other people he knew in the industry, and he'd graciously included me. Jeff picked the topics beforehand and asked everyone to prepare; the talks revolved around what we thought were the best albums from a particular year he'd chosen—generally from the 1970s or 1980s—though sometimes we'd talk about overrated albums, underrated albums, or best albums out of Canada. Other times the discussion would turn into long discourses on Kiss's best albums.

After we'd caught up, I asked Jeff a question I'd never put directly to him before: "What's your relationship to new music like these days?"

"I mean, it's like I have my arms out waiting to be punched in the mouth," he said and laughed. "That's how I feel. I want something to really knock me out." In fact, he'd made a recent discovery—a band called Nothing But Thieves that he loved. He had tickets to see them next month in New York.

Otherwise, every Friday morning he had a routine of Googling "New music released today." "I just go through the list, and I say, 'Oh, wow, this band put a record out.' And I mark it. And then I go into my Apple Music, and I pull it up. And then I put it in my library if I know the band already or listen to it first. And then what I'll do is, I'll make a playlist of new music released for the week."

I asked him when he made a new discovery like Nothing But Thieves, did that connection feel different from when we were younger? "Is it still as exciting?" I wanted to know.

"It's still exciting, but it's just not the same," Jeff said. "You know, what I do miss is going to the store, getting the physical copy, looking at the liner notes, reading about the band. You know, that whole part of the journey." He rarely bought musical in a physical format anymore. It was just too inconvenient.

When I asked him if he thought he was able to let new music carry new memories, happy memories, he said, "Yeah. I hope it happens. The way I feel is, there's never enough room, right? It's not like my brain is totally full it can't take anymore [or] my heart is totally full it can't take anymore. I always want more."

Given that, I was trying to reconcile his own feelings about the importance of new music versus the whole essence of the hologram business—the contradiction in that, as I saw it. Did he feel that contradiction himself?

"No, a lot of the artists that we're working with probably are either not active anymore or have retired, or whatever. So, you know, obviously if they're not doing new music, that's fine because the opportunity to [do a hologram show], for me, is to pass the music that I love down to the next generation so that generation can feel what I felt. Because the radio's a dinosaur. You're not going to have a fifteen-year-old kid scrolling through the radio. It's just not happening. The only way they're going to experience new music is [through] something with a technology aspect to it. You put on a show that's featuring, you know, the Grateful Dead and they've never heard of that, but they heard it's a cool show to go see because of the visuals or the effects or whatever. Well, then you've got a hook for them to hear it. And then maybe that sends them down the rabbit hole that we got sent down when you hear something for the first time, and next thing you know you're discovering, 'Oh, what else have they done? What else have they put out?' Everyone has their own take on it, but for me, it's always been about exploration."

Through Eyelussion, Jeff had created a touring holograms business, but what he really had done, I understood now—and for better or worse—was re-define how old music could be new again.

◎ ◎ ◎

Kiss's farewell tour lasted almost exactly four years. True, most of the 2020 dates were postponed due to COVID, but we could reasonably conclude the tour may well have lasted this long even without the pandemic. Among the many things Kiss is known for, a minimalist touch is not one of them. Long gone were original guitarist Ace Frehley and drummer Peter Criss, but Kiss had been carrying on with their replacements, Tommy Thayer and Eric Singer, for many years. Lead singer Paul Stanley's voice had turned ragged, and throughout the tour there were charges that he was singing to recorded tracks. Eventually the band's manager, Doc McGhee, acknowledged that Stanley was both singing live but singing along with recorded vocals. But for Kiss fans, in their chance to say goodbye after fifty years, that was like complaining that the blood bassist and founding member Gene Simmons spit out on stage wasn't real. From the beginning, the very essence of a Kiss concert, with all the pyrotechnics, the risers, Simmons breathing fire, the costumes and makeup, the personas on stage (Frehley as a spaceman, Criss as a catman and Simmons as demon) had been about not the performance itself but producing a spectacle.

The final two shows were in Madison Square Garden—the band had started in New York and thought it only fitting to end there. "End." On the last night, after the band finished its main set, they came back for a few encore tunes, closing with, naturally, "Rock and Roll All Nite." Stanley smashed his guitar as the remaining members sustained the long wash of the final note.

"You know something?" Stanley then cried out. "The end of this road is the beginning of another road. We're not going anywhere! You'll see us in all different things! All the time!

Even in your dreams! We love you! Good-night!" The band let loose one final crunch, and then, on the screens framing the stage, before they'd even gotten off the stage, Kiss made clear that there would be future Kiss concerts, but now Kiss would be represented by digital avatars, just like ABBA was. A two-minute film previewed the creations, created by George Lucas–founded Industrial Light and Magic company. The avatars had superpowers—they were shooting rays out of their eyes; Simmons had giant wings and could fly; the Peter Criss/Eric Singer avatar was playing drums that were light beams, or something like that.

The video showed a few behind-the-scenes clips of the process—the current members (Frehley and Criss aren't involved in the production) performing in special suits that held all those little motion-capture cameras, a flash of folks at a bank of computers. Simmons made some nebulous comment about the future, and Paul Stanley said, "We can live on eternally."

When the video ended, there was one last explosion, and the screens cut to a still of the four members' avatars. Underneath it read, "A new era begins now."

Kiss had done a good job of keeping the avatar plan a secret, but the new era, of course, was anything but new. And that road Stanley had mentioned was one we'd *all* ended up on. It wasn't a road taking us forward, though. It was only circling back to where'd already been.

ENCORE

WHILE YOU
SEE A CHANCE

I n all these years of thinking about our relationship to old music, new music, I was aware I could be something of a drag when the subject came up around friends or family. As with movies, TV, food, and pretty much anything else in life, people seek out what they want, and they don't generally want or need your approval—and certainly not your disapproval. Listening to music is supposed to be fun, and besides, haranguing individuals doesn't get you very far. After all, even if we have the will, very few of us have the power to bring about real change.

We've always been prone to nostalgia, and that truth plays out in an endless loop. The highest-grossing film of 2023 was *Barbie*, which was a new take on . . . Barbie. At Woodstock, do you know the act that came on right before Jimi Hendrix's, career-changing, generation-defining set? It wasn't the Who,

Sly and the Family Stone, or Janis Joplin, but Sha Na Na, a band that performed '50s doo-wop music and was decked out as greasers. When I was growing up, in the '70s, one of the most popular TV shows was *The Waltons*, about a family living in the mountains of Virginia during the Great Depression on through World War II; the first season's episodes revolved around such plot devices as a typewriter, moonshine, and polio. And my family loved it.

But the biggest difference in how people experienced nostalgia then vs. now—and the reason why nostalgia today is so immutable—is that so much of the Internet serves to remind us of life as it once was. Whether it's a Facebook post of Jimmie Walker as JJ saying "Dyn-o-mite!" that gets 700 "likes" or yet another clip someone has put on his Instagram page of the Macarena, the Internet can lull us into a perpetual state of looking back and believing that what the culture offered us through the decades was more gratifying, more fun, and that life in the past was inherently a richer time.

Consumer capitalism is well aware of the hold of nostalgia, of course, and so as long we cling to the past, it's going to continue to be exploited. This doesn't keep new albums from coming out, of course. But what we don't know about this still-new century is how those albums will endure in the decades to come—or if they will at all.

One seismic change in music today is who the decision makers have become. For much of its existence, the history of music, and to a large extent the business side of the music industry as it once stood, was populated by people who loved music and saw the making of it as miraculous work: the musicians, the managers, the engineers, the A&R folks at the labels, the producers, the studio owners, the arrangers. And no matter how flawed the judgement at hand could be at times, no matter how drugged-out individuals were, no matter how egotistical someone—or the whole band—had become, no matter the pressures, the music was what mattered most. Not annualized returns or market value.

If the musicians had gone to school, it tended to be art school, or the Berklee School of Music, or Juilliard. But mostly their training, their school was the music clubs, the cafés when cafés were still smoky and featured a musician who had made it or seemed destined to make it sitting on a stool and playing new songs on the guitar or piano.

What the musicians didn't do was get their MBAs. They didn't study mathematics or statistics or finance or analytics. They wanted to make money, sure—piles of it! And so many did. But they were going to make it by being true to their music. They might have traveled Highway 61 or cased the promised land on Thunder Road, but Wall Street was never supposed to be the final destination.

And whatever weird names existed in music (Toad the Wet Sprocket, Captain Beefheart, the String Cheese Incident, Hoobastank), none felt as uncomfortable as CatchPoint Rights Partners, Kobalt Capital Ltd, or Harbourview Equity—some of the equity firms who are becoming big players in the music rights business and acquiring back catalogs of artists. In an opinion piece in *The New York Times*, writer Marc Hogan lamented that development, which he referred to as a "Wall Street takeover" of the music industry and argued that "This creative destruction is only further weakening an industry that already offers little economic incentive to make something new."

I'd been talking to a close friend—an editor and a former boss of mine at *The Washington Post*—about the central ideas in this book as soon as I was developing them. Lynn Medford, sixty-nine, is also a fellow music lover, and soon after she read an early version of this book, she emailed me this note:

> Dang it, Rowell. I went to a friend's band's happy-hour performance in Rockville Wednesday night, and the whole time I was rocking out a little devil in the back of my mind was saying: "You just like this music because it's covers of your 20s era. You're addicted to nostalgia and closed to new music!!!!" I had to do a lot of soul-searching on the drive home. Yes, I think your book makes a strong point. I am just not sure what to do about it. I hear today's new music and try to stay open-minded about it—but I would say I loathe 98 percent of it. It is such a great time for women vocalists, but they all sound the same to me. And rap is and has been for decades THE dominant cultural force, but I can't stand any of it except Flo-Rida and Pitbull. And I am really trying to be open!

Lynn's dilemma stayed with me for a long time. It haunted me, in fact, because I could feel her genuine anguish, and I'd been wrestling with what the answers should be for years. And all this time later I wasn't prescribing any novel remedy for what we could do about this precarious state we found ourselves in. In writing this book, I'd seen myself as sounding the alarm bell, but now I worried that that wasn't enough. Not being able to appreciate new music anymore clearly concerned Lynn, but what about all the scores of people who couldn't care less that they weren't listening to any new music. If they didn't see that as a problem, why did I care so much? It's a free country, however subscription-based it's become.

Besides, Lynn was at least *trying* to listen to new music. Wasn't that all we could do, or should do? The point wasn't that the new songs or artists were necessarily supposed to supplant any of your lifetime's other profound finds. The point was to simply open yourself up to new possibilities.

Maybe I should have written a ten-step book instead. But what were the other nine steps besides, say, setting up your Spotify feed to play only new music, or, for the old-timers in their cars who still instinctively turned to a radio station, keeping it on a station that played new music, letting it stay there for a while before tuning it back to NPR or the podcast about *The Office*? Trying one new song a day? One new album a month? Regardless of your age—and forgetting for a moment what genres you like or don't like—if just listening to new music with some regularity could secure its future, didn't we all owe music that much, after all it had been and done for us?

Remember, none of us ever woke up one morning and just decided that instead of trying any new foods again, we'd spend whatever time we had left on this planet eating Smurf Berry Crunch, Big League Chew, Lunchables, Pop Rocks, Ho Hos, and drinking cases of Mr. Pibb because we once loved them. Music is no different.

Or is it? My editor for this book, Mike, believes that capitalism is approaching a cannibalistic end-point, since it's easier to pipe in music that is already made (and purchased!) than it is to make investments in new music. Over the course of my reporting and writing, Mike and I had lots of discussions about what we're supposed to do about the ubiquity of old music and the threat to new music. Sometimes his idea for action felt akin to forming a mob, carrying torches, and running out into the streets. But there is no Frankenstein's monster to hunt down for all this mayhem. Besides, aren't we all made up of some parts that probably should have stayed buried?

As AI continues to evolve, though, our allegiances—and musical morals, really—are going to be tested like never before. If that audio clip you can find on the Internet with the created voice of prime Frank Sinatra taking on Lil Jon's "Get Low," with the Chairman crooning "'Til the sweat drop down my balls" against the swinging horns from his orchestra doesn't give you a strong sense of where music and technology are headed, then you are still listening to "Camptown Races" back on Walton Mountain.

If anything, maybe this book will at least help us get conversations started about what we value, what we want (and don't want), and how we can shape our musical culture for the present and for the future. In the meantime, I'll keep listening to the music I grew up with, and I'll keep listening to the newer music I'm growing older with. There's so much worthwhile awaiting me—and you. The history of music doesn't just promise that. It's already shown us that.

NOW I'M GOING TO INTRODUCE THE BAND

I thank my editor, Mike Lindgren, for his belief in this book from beginning to end and for his passionate vision and guidance for what it could and should be.

I thank Steve Levingston for helping me get it into Mike's hands in the first place.

Lynn Medford and Carlo Rotella continue to be the readers to whom I turn with my music books. They are both my producers and mastering engineers, and I am forever grateful for their generosity and their friendship.

I'm indebted to Dan O'Connor for his inscrutable eye and meticulous handling of the text and to Sofia Demopolos for diligently handling changes throughout.

More musicians, music writers, industry professionals, and devoted fans spoke to me for this book than I can thank here, but I want to acknowledge the following for sharing their stories and observations with me: Steve Howe, Nancy Wilson, Jonathan Cain, Matt Reid, Ben Ratliff, Bob Funck, Jason Hanley, Mike Edison, Chris Richards, Gary Bivona, Billy Lindley, Kam Falk, Fonda Cash, David Victor, Jeff Pezzuti, Ahmet Zappa, David Nussbaum, and John Textor.

Having friends who are also writers has been a great solace for me, and I'm particularly appreciative to the following colleagues who were routinely checking in with me and asking, "So how's the book going?"—and remained interested listeners for whatever report I might offer. Sandra Beasley, Beth Castrodale, Bill Donahue, Tom Dunkel, Howard Fishman, Glenn Frankel, Caitlin Gibson, Leigh Ann Henion, David Montgomery, and Tom Shroder.

I'm grateful to Fergus Shiel and Krissah Thompson for their support and to Jimmy Harney at Luminate for all the helpful data.

I thank my sons Griffin and Anderson for continually exposing me to new music.

My wife, Kim Menzel, was there for me when I was still trying to figure this book out, there to celebrate with me when I did, and showed boundless patience with all the late nights that went into it. I'm fiercely grateful to her and for our life of high harmonies.

ABOUT THE AUTHOR

David Rowell worked as an editor and writer at *The Washington Post* for nearly 25 years. He has taught literary journalism at American University and is currently a senior editor at the International Consortium of Investigative Journalists. He lives just outside of Chapel Hill, North Carolina. *The Endless Refrain* is his third book.